DEADLY
OBSESSION

D0027967

MAGGIE SHAYNE

DEADLY
OBSESSION

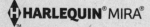

Recycling programs
for this product may
not exist in your area.

ISBN-13: 978-0-7783-1680-0

Deadly Obsession

For questions and comments about the quality of this book, please contact us at
CustomerService@Harlequin.com.

Printed in U.S.A.

Prologue

Flames were like pets. Hungry, devoted little pets that would do pretty much whatever you wanted them to do, as long as you treated them right. You had to show them, of course. Sort of steer them in the right direction. You had to give them plenty to eat, too. Like a dog that would do a trick in exchange for a tasty treat, tongues of fire would go just where you wanted them to with the help of strategically placed snacks. They were insatiable, the little demons. They would devour everything and everyone in their path, growing bigger and bigger with every morsel, until they became giant ravenous dragons. Until they ate everything available. And then they died, their life over, their purpose served. Their master satisfied.

The master, in this case, had spent two decades learning about the care and feeding of fire. It was easy to give birth to it. So many ways, so many clever, creative, concealed ways to do it. It had become a challenge to invent new methods over the years. *Genius* wasn't too big a word to describe her.

This particular baby was about to be born from the basement up. It was a simple method, but a very effective one. A little hacksaw action on the natural gas pipeline, just inside the basement. A tiny transformer box with two bare wires touching, so it would spark as soon as the wireless signal was sent.

The timing, of course, was crucial. Turning that switch too soon, before the gas had time to build to the right concentration, would result in nothing. Or worse, a survivable fire. She couldn't wait too long, either, or her targets might smell the gas and have the brains to get out of the house without investigating.

Fortunately, timing was something else she had perfected over years of practice. She'd gotten it wrong at her former lover Anthony's house. She'd thrown the switch too soon. The concentration had been too low. The sparks had amounted to nothing. She'd had to wait until the gas had overcome him and his wife before slipping back inside to retrieve the device. Dangerous, that. But she'd done it, and no one had been the wiser. They'd both died in their beds. A gas leak had been blamed. She hadn't used a hacksaw on their pipes but had loosened a joint. It had looked accidental. No one knew, and Anthony had paid for choosing his wife over her.

But it hadn't been anything like a fire. It had been anticlimactic. She'd almost wanted to place an anonymous 911 call and save them, so she could do the job right later on.

But she hadn't. She knew when to cut her losses and move on.

She had to do it often, with men. Cut her losses and move on. So often that she took precautions now in new relationships. She used a false name and a disposable prepaid phone, and never told the truth about what she did or where she lived.

Someday she would find the man who would recognize her for the prize she was. Someday she would find one worthy of her. A heroic, handsome, selfless man who would fall head over heels in love, and put her ahead of everything and everyone else in his life.

She would find him.

Peter Rouse had not been the one. Like Anthony and so many since—like her own parents, so long ago— Peter had chosen others over her. His wife. And his kids. They'd already left him by then, to move into the two-story house half a block from where she now sat in a borrowed car. But he was determined to get them back.

She got out of the car, walked to the house in the darkness. It was a quiet neighborhood. No one noticed her. She angled into the backyard and moved to the casement window, crouching low.

Through binoculars, she'd watched as Rebecca had tucked her two kids—Jeffrey, who was eight years old and had his father's eyes, and Rose, who was three— into their beds and walked back downstairs for a little quiet time. The whole neighborhood was in that quiet-before-bed phase of the evening. Watching their TV shows, reading their novels. No one paid attention to her. Not even a dog barked.

She picked up her small digital meter and pulled the dangling sensor out through a tiny hole she'd cut in the windowpane, then quickly smoothed a piece of duct tape over the opening. Then she checked the readout. The gas-to-air ratio in the basement had reached a beautiful 8:1. Oh, this was going to be something.

Dropping the device into a pocket, she walked quickly back to the car. Then she started the engine and put the car into Drive but kept her foot on the brake as she pressed the button on the remote.

There was a delicious moment between cause and

effect, a moment lush with anticipation of the delight to come. The release. The birth. The precipice of a full-body orgasm.

And then it came, a newborn spark followed by the instant ignition of all that lovely gas. The baby gobbled it all up and grew so fast it exploded into a fireball. The roar reverberated way down deep in her belly, and the glow of it burned in the night like the flaming sword of an avenging angel.

And that's what it was, in truth.

Shuddering in gut-deep pleasure, she released the brake and drove away.

1

So if the bullshit I wrote was true, then why the hell didn't I practice what I made so much money preaching? You know, that whole "live in the moment" and "milk the joy out of every second of your life" bit.

I should. I knew I should. It was just a hell of a lot easier to tell other people what to do than to do it myself. Because, seriously, if I were giving advice to me—and I was, because my inner bitch never shuts the hell up—the conversation would go something like this:

Inner Bitch: "Say it back."

Me: "I *can't* say it back."

IB: "Why the hell can't you? *He* said it. He laid it right out there for you. He said, *I love you.* And what did you say back to him?"

Me, flooded with shame: "I said, 'You're shitting me.'"

IB: "Yeah. Real romantic."

Me: "I was fucking surprised. Shocked. I wasn't ready."

IB: "No one's *ever* ready, dumb-ass. You still have to say it back."

Me: "It's too late now. I let the moment pass."

IB: "He's waiting for you to say it back."

Me: "Or maybe he's changed his mind. He hasn't said it again, after all."

IB: "Why would he say it again? That would be like sticking his finger into a socket for the second time, hoping for a different result. Say it. Or you're gonna lose him."

Me: "I'm not gonna lose him."

I glanced across the car at my favorite cop and silenced the imaginary conversation in my head. Actually, it wasn't all that imaginary. My inner bitch and I had been having it over and over again since that night by the campfire a couple of weeks ago when I'd absolutely blown the chance to move this relationship up to the next level.

And I was sure there was no getting that moment back.

I was also sure that things had been a little awkward between Mason and me since then. My fault, I knew. I hadn't responded the way I wished I had. But dammit, I was scared shitless to think of changing anything about this thing between the two of us. It was good. It was more than good. It was freakin' amazing. It was bliss. Why fix what isn't broken? Why move things to another place when the place they're in is so damned wonderful? Why risk screwing it up? Why?

He looked at me, caught me staring. "What? Have I got fettuccine on my face?"

"No. You have gorgeous on your face. It's all over you, in fact. Damn irritating."

He smiled, flashing the dimple of doom. "Thanks."

"De nada."

Say it. Tell him. Just tell him. You can't leave him hanging another minute.

I hated to admit it, but Inner Bitch was kinda right.

"So," I said, as we rounded a corner, "Mason, um, I've been meaning to, uh, you know talk to you about—"

"Holy shit!" He hit the brakes so hard that my seat belt hurt me. Then he jerked the wheel, gunned the car to get us out of the road and hit the brakes again. I saw the flames, then the people standing around outside— one filming everything on his damn smartphone—and then Mason was getting out of the car and shouting at me to call 911 as he ran toward the chaos.

"Mason, wait, where the hell are you—" I jumped out of the car, too, phone to my ear, running after him. "Mason!"

"Nine-one-one, what's your emergency?"

"Um, house fire. Big one. Right off State Route 26 near Glenn Aubry."

"Yes, help is on the way, ma'am."

I clicked off and shoved the phone into my pocket, running now, despite my killer heels, because Mason hadn't slowed down. Someone was screaming that there were kids trapped inside, and I wanted to punch them in the face, because there would be no stopping him now. Mason and kids was like me and…bulldogs.

Somehow I caught up to him and grabbed his arm from behind. Smoke stung my eyes and throat, and the heat was like a living thing. There was roaring and smoke, that acrid smell of burning stuff that wasn't like any other smell. House fires didn't smell like wood fires or campfires. They smelled like destruction.

He glanced back at me, removed my hand firmly, looked me right in the eyes and said, "I have to."

"I know you do." *Dammit, dammit, dammit.*

And then he was gone again, pulling his shirt up over his face and charging right through the front door, into the jaws of hell.

I swore it got hotter and wondered if that was because he'd just provided additional fuel.

You really should've told him.

"I know, Inner Bitch. I know."

I stood there for what felt like a hundred and ten minutes but in truth was really only two. Fire trucks came screaming up. I ran over to the first one that stopped, jumped up on the running board and yanked the door open, startling the firefighters inside. "Hurry. My detective is in there!"

"Your—"

"Someone said there were kids inside. Detective Mason Brown went charging in to save them. Go get them out. Now."

"We've got a cop inside!" the driver shouted to his fellows as he jumped out. By then more men were jumping out of the other trucks. Hoses had been unrolled and water was cranked on. They all started beating the hell out of the flames with their hoses. A couple of them, wearing so much gear I didn't know how they could walk upright, ran inside.

I'd never seen anything like this fire. No matter how much water they put onto it, it kept burning, kept coming back to life, like one of those trick birthday candles you can't blow out. The crowd had backed up into the street now. Neighbors in their bathrobes and slippers, some of them even barefoot, shaking their heads and muttering to each other, and hugging their kids close to them. I glimpsed them in my peripheral vision but couldn't take my eyes off the front door. Flames were shooting from the roof and licking out from every window. I was way too close. My face felt like it was getting an extreme sunburn. Someone grabbed my arm and said I should move back, but I just jerked away from his touch and stared at that door.

"Universe, if you take him from me, I swear I'll never write another word. Don't you dare even think about—"

Then I saw him. Mason came stumbling out the front door with a limp, unmoving child in each arm, their heads bouncing against his shoulders. They were both bundled in blankets. He wasn't. His whole face was black with soot and he dropped to his knees before he even got clear of the flaming wreck of a house, just at the bottom of the front steps. Firefighters surged around him. The first two took the kids, unmoving in their blankets, and the next two picked Mason up by either arm and carried him across the lawn. Someone shoved a gurney under him, and his bearers dropped him onto it as it trundled toward a waiting ambulance.

The crowd closed between us, but I fought my way through it to get to his side, elbowed myself up close, grabbed hold of his hand, and saw that the skin was peeling off it and sticking to mine. I sort of yelped and yanked my hand away, and swore and cried all at once. The EMTs were working quickly, putting an oxygen mask on him and then cutting away his shirt to reveal that his left arm was badly burned, and the flesh underneath was trying to come away with the ravaged fabric.

Oh, God, it looked awful! They draped a clean white cloth over his arm and started soaking it in bottles of sterile water. I'd lost track of the kids. I think they'd been put into the back of another ambulance, and I knew they were as surrounded by EMTs as Mason was. But I couldn't take my eyes off him. His eyes were closed. He wasn't moving.

When one of the guys adjusted the oxygen mask,

he smeared the black away from Mason's cheek, and I realized it was soot, not charred skin, and almost sank to the ground in relief.

Someone grabbed me by the shoulders. "Easy, ma'am. Easy. Are you family?"

"Yeah." I blinked. "No. Is he… God, is he…?"

"He's alive. His vitals are good. Not great, but good. We've gotta get him into a burn unit. We're gonna airlift him to Saint Joe's. It's the closest one. All right?"

"Airlift him?" Oh, God, it was bad. It was bad.

"Can you let his family know?"

Oh, God, the boys! And his mother. I nodded, mutely. "But I have to go with him."

"You can't, ma'am. We need room to work on him. If he has family, they're gonna need your help more than he does. I promise, he's in good hands."

Already they were moving the stretcher into the back of the ambulance. I jerked free of the EMT and lunged toward Mason and leaned in close to his face, "I love you, too, Mason. I love you, too."

But he couldn't hear me. I'd waited too long. Dammit, I'd waited too long!

Then they peeled me off him and put him into the ambulance. It sped away screaming. I turned in a slow circle, not knowing what the hell to do next. I saw the ambulance with the children inside just as they closed the doors, but I had time enough to see them working on the kids. They must be alive, too, then.

Not so the body on the front lawn. The firemen who'd gone inside must have brought it out after Mason had emerged. It had a blanket over it. Too big to be a child. I hoped.

They were finally making progress beating down the flames. One of the firemen said something about gas, but I didn't have time to listen. I had to go. I had to get to the boys, Mason's nephews, who were at my place with Myrtle and my nieces.

Oh, Lord, how was I going to handle this?

I got into Mason's oversize black Monte Carlo, his pride and joy. I had tears streaming from my eyes. I couldn't let the kids see me like this. I didn't know what to do. So I pulled my phone out of my pocket, stared at it for a long moment, and then I did the best thing I could think of.

I called my sister.

"Snap the *fuck* out of it!"

I'd been in midrant, complete with hiccuping sobs, when my big sister, who never even said *damn*, brought my runaway emotions to a sudden halt.

"Do I have your attention?" Sandra asked.

"You do."

"Okay, first. Set the phone on your lap and put me on speaker so you don't get killed, okay?"

Apparently she'd discerned from my initial projectile word vomit that I was driving while having a complete breakdown and talking on the phone. I did what she said and paid attention to the road. If I wrecked Mason's ride he'd never forgive me. If he lived.

God, let him live.

"I'm going to meet you at your place, Rachel. But before you get there, I want you to pull yourself together. Right now."

"But I don't know how bad it is. I don't even know if he's going to—"

"Yeah, and you know what? Neither do those boys."

Cold water in the face might have been as effective. But I doubted it.

"They're kids. Their father is dead, and their mother is in a maximum-security nuthatch. At this moment, you are all they have, Rachel. You need to step up for this. It's important."

That brought me to full attention. I sat up straighter, and my tears dried up like they'd never been there. "I don't know what to do for them, sis."

"You go in there and you tell them the truth in the most positive manner possible. Live your books for once. Tell them you've got no reason to think he won't be just fine, and make sure you sound confident when you do. If you look scared or uncertain, they're gonna be terrified. They need a mother figure. So talk to them. Reassure them, and most of all, make sure they know that you're there for them, no matter what happens to their uncle."

I blinked hard, because those words hit me deep. I did not want to be a mother figure to those kids. I'd said it over and over.

"You would, wouldn't you, Rache?"

"What?"

"Be there for the boys if anything happened to Ma—"

"Yeah. I would." And it was the truth, even if I had only just realized it. I was shocked, to be honest. I'd become way more attached to the dynamic duo than I'd been aware of. Josh was like Myrtle's freakin' littermate, and Jeremy was Mason's mini-me, with a fair amount of teenage angst (most of it hard-earned) thrown in.

"Then you have to let them know that."

"Okay."

"I'll be there by the time you arrive."

"Okay."

"Now hang up and call his mother."

"Aw, jeez, Sandra—"

"Tell her not to drive. I'll send Jim to pick her up and drive her in. Tell her he'll be there soon. Just as fast as he can."

"Okay."

"Hang in there, sis."

I nodded hard, disconnected, thanked my lucky stars for a big sister who knew how to talk to me and called Mason's mother. She took it pretty well, I thought, and I did a great job holding it together as I tried to reassure her, and told her my brother-in-law was on his way to pick her up.

And then I was home, rolling slowly through the wrought-iron gates I'd left open and along the driveway up to the my house. My haven. I shut off the engine, got out, then stood there a second looking at my front door like I was looking at my own grave. I did not want to walk in there and blow those kids' lives to hell and gone. How much more could they take?

Then Sandra's minivan pulled in behind me. The headlights shut off, and she was out and hugging me hard before I even took another breath.

It made me choke up when she hugged me, so I pushed her away, wiped at my eyes, looked into hers. "How's my face?"

She took a tissue out of her purse and dabbed some smudged makeup away. "You're good. You can do this."

Nodding, I marched up the front steps, opened the door and stepped inside.

Joshua, Jeremy, and Sandra's daughter Misty were playing video games on the sofa. Jere and Misty sat close enough so their elbows were bumping. Ah, young love. My other niece, Christy, who I think was trying out for the role of the bad twin lately, sat in a chair off to one side, her nose glued to her smartphone.

Myrtle was the only one who noticed we'd come in, and she came barreling across the living room unerringly and bashed me in the shins with her forehead, which was her typical greeting. I yelped, because bulldogs have skulls made of lead, and the kids finally noticed us there, paused their game and turned our way.

Jeremy met my eyes and went a shade paler. "What happened? Where's Uncle Mason?"

I drew a breath. "Your uncle was hurt a little while ago. He's going to be okay, though. They're taking him to the hospital. We're all going to meet him there, okay?"

Joshua blinked slowly and didn't say a word. He looked terrified. They both got off the sofa, moving toward us.

Jeremy said, "Hurt how?"

I swallowed my fear and tried to feel confident. "There was a fire." Be straight with them, said my sister's voice, echoing in my head. "There were kids inside, and you know your uncle. He ran in to get them out. And he did. But it looked like he got burned a little, and he probably took a few whiffs of smoke in the process."

Jeremy nodded, joining us near the front door. "Let's go, then. Josh, c'mon."

Josh moved slower, like he was sleepwalking. He had this shell-shocked look, and his eyes were wide and unblinking, and kind of vacant.

I crossed to him, put my hands on his shoulders. "Josh, you don't have to be afraid. He's gonna be okay."

His lips trembled. His tears welled. "Wh-what if he's not?"

"I refuse to even consider that," I told him. Myrt

was at his feet now, affectionately butting his hands where they hung at his sides and getting no response. "I'll tell you this much, though," I said. "I'm not going anywhere. I'm sticking with you two. The both of you. No matter what."

Josh wrapped his arms around me. If I got all tight in the throat, it was just because I wasn't used to such blatant displays of affection from a twelve-year-old kid. But I tightened my arms around him and hugged him to me and stroked his hair and tried to blink back the flood of tears. I loved the kid. I loved Mason, and I loved his boys. What cave had I been living in that I hadn't realized it sooner?

"Did someone call Gram?" Jeremy asked. He was at the door, itching to go. Misty stood in the background with tears welling, and Christy had stopped texting.

"Jim's picking her up," Sandra said. Then, to me, "You okay to drive?"

"I am."

"All right, the girls and I will take care of things here, then we'll be along."

I hugged my sister. I didn't hug often, but it was called for. "Thanks, Sandra." When we pulled apart, I saw Misty all wrapped up in Jeremy, whispering that she wouldn't be far behind him.

Then the three of us headed out, jumping into Mason's car without even thinking about it, because it was closest. As soon as we got to the end of my almost-private dirt road and took a right to head for the I-81 north ramp, instead of left toward I-81 south, Jeremy said, "Why are we going this way? The hospital's—"

"They took him to Saint Joseph's in Syracuse, Jere. It's apparently the standard place to go for burns."

He was looking at me like I'd just kicked him in

the shins, and he opened his mouth to say something else, then glanced at his kid bro and bit his lip. He was growing up. Graduating high school in a few weeks. He swallowed what I told him and knew what it might mean. I could see that. "Just a precaution, I think. I mean, if you have burns, you want a burn unit, and that's the closest one."

"Yeah. Okay."

But he was scared. Terrified.

And so was I.

Mason was hurting like hell and resenting the fact that they'd dragged his ass all the way to Syracuse when there were three perfectly great hospitals within a half hour of his home. And while they'd cleaned (excruciating) and dressed the burns on his left arm and shoulder, and doped him up with enough morphine to slow down a rhino, he was still in pain. Not just the arm, either. His chest hurt like hell. Every breath was torture. It felt like he had shredded glass lining his lungs.

And then he saw Rachel, behind Jeremy and Joshua, with an arm around each of them, and the pain took a backseat. She was all smudged with soot but still in that sexy red clingy dress she'd worn for their weekly date night. He'd been admiring it all night long. She was wearing a big phony mask of confidence and ease, but he could see the fear behind her baby-blue eyes.

Damn, he loved her eyes. Even when they'd been blind, they'd been beautiful.

"Uncle Mace!" Joshua broke into a run. Mason managed to lift his left arm out of the way before impact, wincing because it hurt to move the arm at all. He tousled the kids' hair with his good hand. "I'm fine, Josh. Don't worry, I'm fine."

"I was so scared," Josh said.

"I know. I'm sorry."

"You've gotta be more careful, Uncle Mace. We need you."

The kid meant every word. Mason looked over Josh's head at Jeremy. "C'mere, you."

Jeremy smiled and went to hug him, as well. "The nurses in the waiting room said you saved those two kids' lives. Said you were a hero."

"Yeah," Rachel said, still standing back, giving them room. "She was all cow-eyed when she said it, too. If she didn't have your life in her hands, I'd have to kick her ass just to establish my dominance."

"I can't help it if I'm irresistible to women," Mason told her. "It runs in the family. Be forewarned, Jere."

Jeremy grinned. "Yeah, I'm fighting them off all the time myself."

"I'll be sure to let Misty know," Rachel said.

I leaned against the doorjamb and forcibly held back tears—relieved ones—while Mason continued to talk and tease and joke. Bit by bit the terror left the boys' faces. God, he was good at that. How did he get to be such a pro? Was it because he was a cop, or because he was their uncle? I was damned if I knew. I had a ways to go to catch up, though. His mind-easing, reassuring abilities were damn near supernatural. Even with me.

Eventually I could tell the emotions were coming out whether I liked it or not, and I didn't want to lose it in front of the boys, so I said, "I'm going to get food. We really need some junk food. I'll be right back." I started to leave, but when I reached for the door to open it, Mason's partner, Rosie, was standing on the other side.

"Hey, buddy," he said, eyeing Mason hard, assuring

himself that he was all right. "I can't leave you alone for a minute, can I?"

"Apparently not. Boys, I need a minute. Would you go out and see if your grandmother got here yet? She's probably out in the waiting room giving the staff a hard time."

"Yeah. But we're coming right back," Jeremy said. He took Josh by the arm. "C'mon. We'll scope out the cafeteria while we're at it." He sent Rachel a very grown-up look. "We'll get the junk food, Rache. You can hang here."

The boys left. I didn't. I was eyeing Rosie, then Mason, then Rosie again, and my NFP (for Not Fucking Psychic, because whatever I had, it wasn't that simple) was heating up to a slow simmer. "What?" I asked. "What's going on? I can see something is."

Rosie gave himself a shake. "I'll never get over that shit. Yes, something's goin' on. That fire is goin' on. You saved the kids, Mason, but their mother didn't make it. And it was arson."

Peter's wife was dead, according to the TV news. Police were investigating the fire, which had been ruled arson only hours after the flames were doused. Then again, hiding that fact hadn't been her goal.

The kids had survived, which defeated part of her purpose, but she supposed the lesson had been delivered all the same. Peter would think twice before he treated her like garbage again. Like some disposable toy he could use and then throw away. He would make her his top priority or else. And he had to know that now.

She'd warned him. She'd *warned* him. But he was just like the rest.

She picked up the remote to turn her little 27-inch

flat-screen television off, but then they flashed a picture that brought her to a stop. It was a man, on his knees on the front steps of the burning house, one of her lover's kids in each arm. His clothes were charred, and so was he. The caption read Hero Cop Saves Children. The reporter was running her mouth. Gretchen Young turned up the volume and sank onto the love seat—her apartment didn't have room for a full-sized couch.

"This tragic arson, resulting in the death of thirty-six-year-old mother of two Rebecca Rouse could have been an even bigger tragedy had it not been for the actions of off-duty homicide detective Mason Brown. Brown, a decorated member of the Binghamton Police Department, was off duty when he saw the fire and rushed inside to rescue Rouse's children, ages three and eight. Detective Brown has been in the news before, most notably for solving our city's first-ever serial killings last year and, more recently, for arresting his own mentally ill sister-in-law for another spate of bizarre murders. The hero cop is listed in satisfactory condition at Saint Joseph's Hospital. Police aren't commenting on the arson investigation, though newly minted Police Chief Vanessa Cantone will hold a press conference tomorrow afternoon."

Gretchen hit the rewind button, then paused the TV on the shot of that hero cop. He was the kind of man she deserved. The kind of man who would know exactly how to love a woman like her. How to make her feel important. Special. Treasured.

Peter Rouse wasn't worth her time after all, was he?

She looked at her bag of tools on the kitchen counter, where she'd dropped it after coming home from her night's work. The bag, a little black leather satchel like an old-school doctor might carry, had been her gift to herself way back when she'd graduated and received her pin.

She wouldn't part with the bag. But she *could* afford to get rid of a few of the tools it held. Since they knew it was arson, they were going to need an arsonist. Peter Rouse's punishment wasn't quite complete. Yet.

2

"Two freaking weeks," Mason said. It was his routine now. The first thing he said every morning when I walked into his hospital room was an exaggeration of how long he'd been imprisoned there. I showed up at my usual time. Eight o'clock with a Box O' Joe, a pair of breakfast sandwiches and a couple of doughnuts.

"Ten days," I corrected. "You'll survive, I promise." I pulled the bedside tray around and adjusted the height, cleared it of books, magazines and an empty plastic Jell-O container from the night before, and set the feast for him. I even poured his coffee. I was spoiling the man rotten. And I still hadn't told him I loved him, because there were bigger things going on. Okay, and because I was a fucking chicken. I'd managed to decide that I'd say it back if he said it to me again. I'd do it immediately. So all he had to do was say it again and make it easy on me.

What if he'd changed his mind?

"Earth to Rachel," he said,

I blinked out of my own head and said, "I brought you a great big present today."

"My discharge papers?"

"Better." I slid my bag off my shoulder, took out my laptop and set it on the nearby easy chair, my new workstation. I worked on my book-in-progress right here in his hospital room, every day until noon. Then I headed home for a few hours of quality time with my dog, and then I came back with the boys in tow as soon as school let out for the day. I didn't mind it a bit. The four of us usually had dinner together, cafeteria food or takeout, depending on what I had time to grab, and then I took the kids back to my place for the night.

Amy, my personal assistant, was handling everything else. Copy edits, Facebook and Twitter posts, newsletter mailings, and fan letter replies. I needed to come up with a new title for Amy, because personal assistant didn't begin to cover it. Maybe something like "She Whose Quitting Would Result in My Complete and Utter Annihilation." Yeah, that would do it. Goth chick had made herself indispensable to me. Probably all part of her evil plan for the ultimate in job security. As long as I stayed flush, she'd stay flush. And I was staying flush.

I pulled a manila envelope out of my bag and slapped it onto the tray in front of "my detective." I'd been calling him that inside my head ever since the night of the fire, when I'd screamed it at the Binghamton FD.

Mason was in mid-coffee-sip, but he stopped when he looked at the file. "What's this?"

"The full case file. Everything to do with it, from the arson investigator's report to Rebecca Rouse's autopsy report. It also has Rosie's notes from the interrogation of Peter Rouse, the victim's estranged husband." He knew that Rouse was our most likely suspect, being that his wife had taken the kids and moved out only a few weeks prior to the fire.

"Finally!" He set the coffee down and tore open the envelope. "You didn't even peek?" he asked.

"I did not. I promised Chief Sexy-pants that it would get into your hands unopened, and you can now verify that I lived up to my word." I moved up beside him so I could read while he did. And I grabbed my doughnut out of the paper bag because, you know, I'd already resisted it all the way here, and I was only human. He was lucky I hadn't eaten them both *and* read the file.

He was skimming, though, flipping pages so fast I couldn't keep up. Police speak required slow, careful reading for me. It was not my native tongue. "Whathitthay?" I asked around my delicious cream-filled, chocolate-frosted bliss.

Mason correctly interpreted my question, which proved he was my perfect mate, and said, "Gas line was tampered with. Marks that appear to have come from a hacksaw were found on the pipe. The killer let the basement fill with gas, then remotely activated a simple detonator to create a spark."

"A spark?" I asked. "A single spark?"

He nodded. "That's all it took." He was still skimming. "They found the detonator in the rubble, but what was left wasn't much to go on." He read some more, nodded. "Search warrant was executed on Peter Rouse's place. They found a hacksaw in the back of his pickup. Forensics matched the shards in its teeth to the gas line that was sawed through. Teeth marks matched, too."

"Not the brightest murderer on the block, is he? Keeping that stuff in his pickup." Mason frowned at me. I shrugged. "Not saying I don't think he's guilty, just saying he's also effing stupid." Then I lifted my brows. "Notice how I abbreviated the cuss word there?"

"I did notice. Nice job. The boys must be having a good influence on you."

"I'm turning into Carol fucking Brady." I clapped a hand over my mouth, but he just kept grinning at me. I sighed at my own difficulty with habit breaking and tried to steer us both back on topic. "So the almost-ex is not only guilty but stupid," I said.

"Not too stupid to figure out how to remotely ignite the fire," he said softly. "Arson investigator says it's tricky to know how long to wait to spark one up with a gas leak."

I shook my head. "Those poor kids down the hall don't have a mother anymore, and now they've got to deal with the fact that their father killed her."

"They're not down the hall anymore. They were moved to the pediatric hospital last night," Mason said.

"That's good news, isn't it?" I hoped to God it was.

"Yeah. Not even in ICU. They put them in a regular room, my nurse said. They're out of danger. Probably going home—or somewhere—in a day or two."

"Have you seen them yet?"

"No. I haven't tried."

"But you saved their lives, Mason."

He shrugged. "And I'm not going to go present myself to them in hopes of receiving their undying gratitude. They've got enough to deal with right now." He sighed and closed the file. "Speaking of kids, how are the boys?"

"They miss you. I mean, visiting you for a couple of hours every day isn't the same, you know? They miss their stuff, too, or so they keep saying, though I don't see how they could. We've hauled most of it to my house by now."

His face turned serious. I hadn't meant to wipe his

smile away. "They've taken over your place. I'm sorry, Rache. I know how much you love your home and value your space. Any damage so far?"

"Don't be a dumb-ass. They keep most of the mess to their assigned bedrooms." *And the kitchen and the living room and the dock out by the lake and the bathrooms. Good God, the bathrooms. Still, it's odd how much I honestly don't mind. Really odd.* I shook the baffling state of my contentment away, because I wasn't yet ready to talk about it. "Myrtle is happier than a carnivore at a meat market. She's already figured out their routine. She waddles right over and plunks her ass in front of the door at a quarter to three every weekday and waits for them to get back from school."

He smiled at that, because he loved my dog almost as much as I did. "She is one boy-loving bulldog." Then he opened the file again.

"Rouse said the hacksaw in the back of his pickup wasn't his." He flipped a few pages. "No fingerprints on it. Looked like it had been wiped."

I nodded. "They searched his house, too, though, right?"

"Yeah."

"They find anything related to the detonator?"

His eyes raced over pages, his lips tightening. "Nope."

"So all we've got is the hacksaw?"

"His fingerprints were found inside the wife's house," he pointed out.

"Yeah, but his kids lived there. I'm sure he was in and out a lot."

"There was a silver Chevy Cruze seen parked a couple of blocks away at the time of the fire. The neighbors say it didn't belong there," Mason said. "Another neighbor said Rouse's truck was seen in the area that night." Then he shrugged. "But Rosie says it was there every weeknight. He drove the kids home from school. And this neighbor's sighting was several hours before the fire." He looked at me—waiting, I knew, for my feedback. He counted on me for it. And since I was an official police consultant now, I was happy to give it.

"Sounds like they must've been getting along, then. She'd have picked up the kids herself if she thought he was dangerous, right?"

"Women seldom think their spouses are dangerous until it's too late. But when a woman is murdered, it's almost always the spouse," he pointed out.

"Says a lot for the state of marriage, doesn't it?"

He peered up at me, but when I looked back he turned back to the report and flipped a page. "He admitted during questioning that he didn't want the divorce. He didn't want to lose custody of his kids."

"So why try to burn the place with them inside?"

He met my eyes again, and his were brighter than they'd been since the fire. He loved his work, and this was the first chance he'd had to really sink his teeth into a case since nearly getting his gorgeous ass killed.

"Lots of men would rather see the kids dead than lose custody."

"I refuse to believe it's 'lots of men.' Granted, we see it in the news, but it has to be rare or it wouldn't *be* news."

"That sounded dangerously positive, Rache."

"I know, right? Having the boys around, I just can't imagine how a parent could hurt their own kid." I heaved a sigh. "I suppose it's possible he did it. But still, all we really have is the hacksaw." I finished my doughnut, sipped my coffee, leaned back in my chair.

"You have an idea, don't you?" he asked.

"How can you tell?"

"If I look deep into your eyes I can see a bunch of gears turning in your brain."

I nodded. "Get me in to see him. I mean, he's still in custody, isn't he?"

"No. He made bail. Probably because our evidence is so freaking weak."

I shrugged. "Even better. I can talk to him more easily that way."

"Uh-uh. No way. That's a very bad idea."

"Oh, come on, Mason." He hadn't touched his breakfast sandwich, so I picked it up and took a bite, then put it back. After some yummy caffeine, I went on. "You know I can tell if he's the guy with a single conversation."

"He could be dangerous."

"So am I."

"This guy probably killed his own wife, almost killed his two kids and damn near took me out with them. I don't want you anywhere near him."

"You're worried he'll turn his focus to me?"

"That too. Mainly I was thinking about your temper."

I smiled sweetly and batted my eyes. "What temper?" But he was right. If this man *was* guilty, he had almost killed my detective. It might not be safe for me to be in the same room with him surrounded by armed guards, much less all alone.

Mason sent me a look that spoke louder than words, but it changed to one of worry when he returned to the file. "We need more or this guy's gonna walk. A decent defense attorney could find a dozen experts who'd testify that pipe shavings aren't unique. It's not like DNA.

And his pickup was parked outside in the open. Anyone could've thrown the saw into it."

"That would be a hell of a coincidence, wouldn't it?"

"Not if they knew who he was. Besides, it only takes reasonable doubt to get him off."

I shrugged. "All the more reason I should talk to him."

Mason said, "Your ESP isn't admissible in court, Rache."

"NFP. And it should be."

"Whether it should be is irrelevant."

"But if I talk to him, maybe I can get more. A clue that will lead us to better evidence or—"

"Rachel, stay away from this guy."

He pointed at me with a forefinger, something I didn't remember him ever doing before. Like he was telling Josh to eat his vegetables. I did not like it. I sent him a look, my eyebrows arching, my gaze on that finger, and he lowered it and shook his head.

"He's dangerous, Rache."

The door opened, and Dr. Earl came in. I thought his photo was probably next to the word *stately* in the dictionary. Tall, lean, silver-white hair so neat it looked plastic, and the face of an aging *GQ* model. He looked up from the chart in his hands and flashed us a cheerful white smile. "Good morning, you two. You beat me here again, Rachel. I must be slowing down in my old age."

"Well, you know, I couldn't have a doughnut until I got here, so I was highly motivated."

He laughed softly, turned his attention to Mason. "How are you feeling?"

"Like I don't need to be here. Like I need to be home and back on the job, building a case against the guy who put me here."

"Well, we just might be able to make that happen today. The home part, not the back on the job part."

"Today?" Mason's brows rose, and he looked at me, then back at the doctor. "Where the hell are my clothes?"

"Ah, not so fast now," said the AARP poster boy. "There are going to be some conditions."

"Anything, Doc. Anything you say, I promise. Tell me, and I'll do it. To the letter."

"You are such a liar," I muttered, but under my breath, so Dr. Earl could pretend not to hear.

He winked at me, though, so I knew he'd heard just fine. Then he started ticking off conditions on his immaculately manicured fingers. "You need to hire a nurse to come in and change your dressing twice a day to prevent infection. You need to come back if there's any sign of any problem whatsoever. Any trouble breathing, or if that cough comes back. And you need to take another week at home before returning to work. And then only after I've examined and cleared you."

"Yes. Yes, I agree to all of it. Anything just to get out of here. Rache, my clothes?"

Dr. Earl shook his head. "You know better, Detective. Let's proceed with your morning exam, and then I'll get started on the paperwork as soon as I finish my rounds. You should be out of here by—" he looked at the clock "—midday, if all goes well."

Mason shot me a bug-eyed "my head's gonna explode" expression, and I had to clap a hand over my mouth to keep the laugh from busting out. I refilled my coffee cup from the box. "I'll get out of here to give you some privacy, then. Help yourself to coffee, Dr. Earl."

Then I left the room, shaking my head. Thank God

he was okay and heading home today. Thank God. I think it was the first time I really allowed the full brunt of the danger to hit me, and it made my knees a little weak. It was a constant battle to keep my mind from going to what could've happened.

And, oh man, was I ever going to have a talk with probable arsonist Mr. Rouse the Louse, whether my detective liked it or not. I just wouldn't tell him. Not until after the fact, anyway.

For now, though, my main challenge was how I was going to convince him to come *home* to my house instead of to his own. I paced the hallway, tried to stay out of the way of the rush-hour nurse traffic and wished I knew how Mason was going to react to my suggestion.

Marie Rivette Brown's life wasn't pleasant. The doctors at Riverside Maximum Security Psychiatric Hospital kept her medicated. Heavily medicated. She didn't hear her husband's voice anymore. Once in a while he came through, but it was rare and usually only if she was stressed out about something else.

They even let her use the community room. They hadn't for the first few months, but now they did. It was a big room, with small round tables and plenty of chairs, lots of games like checkers and Trouble, and several decks of cards. A TV set was always playing some happy family movie with no violence or death or ghosts or voices. Nothing that might upset the inmates.

She knew what she'd done. She'd tried to retrieve her dead husband's donated organs. Eric had been a serial killer. Finding that out had been like a mortar round hitting her world. No one else knew. No one ever would. But *she* knew. She'd known for more than a year and had done nothing about it, unable to destroy her sons by letting it come out. Then, after his suicide, she'd lost the little baby girl she'd been carrying, and that seemed to make the walls of her sanity come crumbling down completely.

She didn't feel remorse. She figured the drugs kept her from feeling much of anything, so she couldn't feel sorry for what she'd done, the lives she'd taken. Without the drugs, though, she knew she wouldn't feel it, either. Without the drugs, she was convinced that what she had done was completely rational.

She missed her boys, though. That was the one thing she seemed capable of feeling, on her meds or off, completely insane or doped into a state of zombie-like calm. She missed her sons. Jeremy would be graduating from high school soon. A couple of weeks, if that. She so wished she could be there for him.

"Hi, sweetie. How are you doing today?"

Blinking out of her thoughts, Marie looked up from the table where she sat alone, an untouched meal in front of her, at the nurse. She'd seen her around before, a stunningly beautiful blue-eyed blonde with a figure her tight-fitting white dress did nothing to hide. But she wasn't anyone Marie interacted with very often.

"Fine." That was always her answer.

"You should let me take you outside. It's such a beautiful day. Lots of people are out enjoying the yard today."

Marie shrugged. "Okay."

The nurse smiled and took her arm, helped her up and held on to her gently as they walked together toward the doors, then she used her keycard to unlock them. Marie didn't think it made any sense keeping them locked, because they only led out to a fenced-in lawn, with several patches of flowers and quite a few big shade trees. Marie scuffed across the soft grass in her foam slippers toward a pair of lawn chairs underneath a pretty red maple. The nurse was right. The fresh air was nice. It smelled like summer and sunshine, and reminded Marie of picnics at the lake house up north and the kids playing on the tire swing and jumping into the water. Skinny and shirtless in baggy shorts she used to say would fall right off in the lake one of these days.

She sank into a chair, closing her eyes and breathing the air, and trying to grab hold of the joy of the memory. But there wasn't any. It was just a picture. It elicited no emotion.

Marie wasn't aware that the nurse had sat down in the other chair until she spoke, breaking into the memory and bringing her back to the miserable present.

"I wanted to show you something. I'm not really allowed, but sometimes I think the rules here are over the top."

Marie frowned as the nurse pulled a folded newspaper clipping out of her pocket, opened it and held it by two corners as the breeze made it ripple. It was a photo of a man carrying two blankets out of a fire. She looked closer, frowning. "That's Mason."

"Your brother-in-law, right?"

Marie nodded, her eyes eagerly skimming the words under the photo. Those weren't blankets, they were children. Mason had saved them from a terrible fire that had killed their mother. Nodding slowly, she understood. "He's a good man. He's always been."

"I can see that. I was so surprised when I saw this on the news and realized he was part of your family. You must be so proud of him."

Marie *wasn't* proud of him. Not really. After all, she'd had no hand in making him the great person he was. "His mother probably is."

"Oh? His mother's still living?"

Marie nodded.

"Close to him, I hope? He lives in…Binghamton, right?"

"Castle Creek," Marie said, remembering the farmhouse and wondering if her boys were happy there. Probably. They loved their uncle so much. Maybe more than they loved her. Especially after what she'd done. "His mother's in Whitney Point. Near Rachel."

"Rachel? Who's she?"

"His girlfriend, I guess. She's a writer." Something buzzed deep in Marie's mind, a little trill of awareness that told her it was odd for a nurse to be asking about her family. "Why do you want to know?"

The nurse smiled, shrugged, lowered her head, blushed a little. "I don't know. I guess I'm just impressed with him. To think we have a hero like that around. They don't make men like that anymore, you know?"

"Oh."

"What's he like?"

She's up to something. Look at her eyes.

Marie blinked. It had been so long since she'd heard her dead husband's voice in her head. Oh, she knew the doctors kept telling her it wasn't really his voice. It was her own subconscious, speaking to her in his voice in order to get her attention. And because she had a mental illness, she must not trust the things her subconscious said to her in the voice of her dead husband.

But she furrowed her brows and stared deep into the nurse's eyes anyway. There was a fire in there. It was deep, but it was there, swirling and sparking, but hidden very well behind a facade that was blank. False. Empty. She'd seen that look before. She'd seen it in Eric's eyes. It was the plastic mask of a killer.

"He's nice," she said softly, cautiously.

"He has your kids, doesn't he?"

"How do you know that?" Marie asked.

Dangerous. She's dangerous.

"I looked at your file."

Marie's eyes widened. "You stay away from him. You stay away from him and my boys."

"Me?" The nurse got up from her chair, one hand fluttering to her chest, her eyes pretending to be offended and surprised. But she didn't feel those things. Marie could tell. She was mimicking real emotions, the way Marie herself tried to do during every session with her shrink, in hopes of someday convincing him that she was well and could go home.

"My goodness, Marie, what are you talking about?"

"Stay away from them," Marie said again.

The nurse smiled. And for just a moment she let the mask slip. There was evil in that smile. Evil. She was a demon, and the fire in her eyes was a window directly into hell.

Marie reached out and snatched the name tag from the nurse's chest, tearing her dress in the process. She stared at the name, saying it aloud, over and over and over as the nurse jumped back with a squeak of alarm and then pressed a button in her pocket.

Orderlies came running out the door, crossing the yard toward them.

Marie was up on her feet. "You're evil. What do you want with my family? You stay away from them. You stay away!"

Then the strong young men in white took her arms, and another nurse, a regular, jabbed her in the ass with a needle. Marie went out with the demon nurse's name on her lips.

Gretchen Young.

3

"So when are you going to tell me what's wrong?"

Mason sat in the passenger side of Rachel's hot little yellow T-Bird while she drove him home from his endless stay in the hospital. The top was down, and her hair was whipping like a flag in a hurricane. She drove way above the speed limit, despite the fact that her passenger was a cop. Driving usually had her smiling from ear to ear. Not so today. Today she was all nervous and jerky.

She glanced sideways at him. "You're almost as good at it as I am, you know."

"What? Reading people?" He shook his head. "Only criminals and you, babe."

She crooked one brow at him but kept her focus on the road as she zigged into the fast lane to pass a jacked-out Mustang, then zagged back in front of it again. She didn't even taunt the driver with a wink or flip him off or give him a cutesy little wave. Something was definitely wrong with her, he thought.

"So what is it?"

"Nothing. I just… Okay, there's something." She drew a deep breath, and her shoulders rose with it. He knew that look. She was preparing to blurt it out, whatever it was. He braced himself.

"Why don't you stay at my place for a while?"

And there it was. He watched her face closely. She didn't have the same opportunity to watch his, but he didn't figure she needed to. The stuff she "got" didn't come from anything she could see with her eyes. In fact, most of the time when she was trying to read people she had to close those gorgeous baby blues.

"You want me to stay with you," he repeated without inflection.

"Yeah. I mean, why not? The boys are already there, and it really hasn't been as bad as I expected it to be." She bit her lip on one side, glanced sideways at him. "I mean, it's been great."

"You mean not as bad as you expected."

"Which is great."

"I think you need to look up the word *great* in the dictionary. Aren't you supposed to be a writer or something?"

She shrugged. "Look, you need to take it easy, and you can't run a houseful of boys and take it easy at the same time. Come to my place. Just for a couple of weeks, until you get your strength back."

He tried to weigh his words before speaking them. He did not want to screw things up with her, but her invitation was weak. Or maybe he was just still stinging from that unrequited "I love you" he'd dropped on her a few weeks ago. She hadn't said it back. And he hadn't said it again. If she wasn't ready for serious feelings, she sure as hell wasn't ready for cohabitation.

"Well?" she asked. "What do you think?"

"I think," he said, slowly and carefully, "that if we ever decide to…live together, I'd just as soon it not be because I'm too weak to be on my own."

She looked disappointed. "Oh."

"Jeremy and Josh will be a ton of help. My mother will probably want to move in. And there will be a home care nurse."

She nodded. "Yeah. Sure, okay."

"And you. You'll be in and out all the time, too."

"Sure," she said again.

He was quiet for a long moment. She was upset. Dammit, she'd asked him in a way that was a lot like a person pulling off a Band-Aid. Grit your teeth, close your eyes and get it over with. He didn't think she'd really been hoping he would say yes.

"I just don't want to risk messing up—"

"It's fine, okay? It's fine."

It wasn't though. Crap.

"You hungry?" she asked at length. "We didn't have lunch before we left, and there's a Nice N Easy off the next exit. They make the best wraps."

"There's a Mickey D's, too," he said, having seen the same road sign that she had.

"Yeah, but you need to heal. Junk food isn't gonna cut it right now. And I'm sure your mother and the nurse would agree with me."

He nodded. "Okay. Wraps sound good. And a Coke."

"Or water."

"Or Coke."

She heaved a sigh, but nodded as she exited the highway and pulled in at the gas station slash convenience store.

So he didn't want to stay with me. Fine, he could fucking stay by himself and take twice as long to heal if that was what he wanted.

I was sitting on my living room floor, working on my second vodka and Diet Coke, my poor blind bulldog lying with her head on my lap. "It's actually kinda nice to have the house to ourselves again, isn't it, Myrt?"

Myrt's reply was a great big sigh. She'd been heaving them every few minutes, in between pacing the house looking for Joshua. Her buddy. She couldn't stand that he wasn't here. It was mean, that's what it was. Mason shouldn't be mean to a poor defenseless bulldog. Myrtle had gotten used to having the kids around. Every afternoon we'd make cookies or brownies or something, so when they got off the bus and came in the door they'd have a snack. I mean, I remember always being hungry after school when I was a kid, so why would they be any different, right?

Myrt would hear that school bus coming a mile away and jump to the door and stand there wiggling from her nose to her stump of a tail, waiting for the boys to come through.

It was heartbreaking to see her so dejected.

Poor dog.

I hadn't packed up the boys' stuff yet. I figured I'd tell them they had to do it themselves. That way they'd have to come back and spend some time, and Myrtle could get her groove back. I'd phoned the school from my car to let them know the boys would be taking the bus back to their old place from now on, and to drop them off there starting today.

When I drove Mason home I'd gone in for a few minutes to make sure he had everything he needed. He asked me to stay for dinner, but I said no, that he'd want to get acclimated and stuff. His mother had already filled his freezer with meals. I'd seen her several times while the boys had been my roomies, because of course she had to come by a couple of nights a week to try to talk them into staying with her instead.

Poor Angela. She was kind of stiff as grandmothers went, kind of cold, but she loved the kids in her way. I hope I'd managed to convince her that they liked my place better simply because of the lake out front, the dog they adored and the super short ride to school. They could've taken their bikes, if they'd wanted to. (They hadn't.)

Anyway, I knew Angela had stocked Mason's freezer with casseroles, lasagnas, meatballs, mac and cheese, and God only knew what else. So I got him home and kissed him goodbye, then made my excuses and headed home.

I'd pretty much been moping ever since. He'd really hurt my feelings by not wanting to stay with me, and I was really good and pissed at myself for being such a fucking whiny ass.

Sighing, I got up and poured myself another drink. Myrtle followed me, then left my side to wander from one room to the next again. She paused at the stairs, sniffing, but didn't go up. Not only was it not in her nature to exert herself unnecessarily, but she probably knew the boys weren't up there without climbing the stairs to find out. Her other senses were as sharp as mine. She sighed again, plodded back to our spot, and together we sat down. I grabbed the remote, flipped on the TV.

A news crew was ambushing some guy who was trying to get out of his pickup and into his front door, and the female reporter and her camera guy were apparently doing their best to keep him from getting there.

"If you didn't set that fire, then who did?" said the reporter, who then thrust her microphone into his face and I was pretty sure bonked him on the nose with it.

Wait a minute. Fire?

"No comment." He pushed the mike away with one hand and sidestepped the camera. He was an average-looking guy, beer belly that overhung his belt, typical blue work pants, plaid shirt tucked in nice and neat. He had a ruddy complexion, like he was outside a lot in rough weather, and a thick shock of black hair that looked as if he was wearing an animal pelt on his head.

"*That* guy? *That* is the guy who damn near killed my detective?" I turned up the volume.

"What evidence do the police have against you, Mr. Rouse?"

Yep, that was him all right. Rouse the Louse.

The man lowered his head, shook it slowly. I narrowed my eyes on him, but I couldn't *feel* him. I wasn't close enough. "No comment."

"Mr. Rouse, again, if you didn't set the fire that killed your wife, do you have any idea who did?"

His head came up fast and he opened his mouth, clearly about to blurt something. But then he clamped it closed again, and I could see he really regretted his almost-slip. "My lawyer says I can't talk to you. I'm sorry. You'll just have to wait for the trial."

"But you want to tell your side of the story, don't you, Mr. Rouse? I can see you do."

He stopped walking, and I thought he was going to do it. Spill his guts. She was good, this reporter. What the hell was her name? I knew it. I'd seen her on the local news often enough. Trisha Knight. That was it.

She was holding her breath, and so was I. And then he pressed his lips tight, shook his head. "No comment. Now please let me go into my house."

He pushed past her, not giving her much choice about "letting" him.

I located the remote, hit the back button and watched

the entire story again, pausing it every few seconds to try to read the man visually. But visuals were not my strong point. I had to be near someone. I had to *feel* them.

Or, you know, dream about them. At least, it had happened that way a few times. I always tended to think that gift of dreaming about things was just going to vanish and never come back, but it hadn't, not really. It had morphed instead, turning into some kind of a sixth sense that I didn't like admitting I had.

Still, I had a feeling about that guy. I backed up the action and watched again, paying attention to the surroundings this time around. I noticed the house number: 117. Now if I could just get a glimpse of a street sign…

I probably watched that clip until my eyes bled, until Inner Bitch cuffed me upside the head (you know, figuratively) and said, *You about ready to look the guy up online yet or what?*

I rolled my eyes. It was another classic "duh, Rachel" moment. But at least no one was there to witness it.

Why the hell did I catch myself wishing that someone was? Three someones, to be exact.

I searched Peter Rouse, found his address, jotted it down, took my bulldog upstairs and went to bed. It was way too late at night to be paying impromptu visits to murder suspects. Besides, I had to figure out how to approach him. He was being hounded by reporters. He wasn't going to just open the door and let me in. And also, I had to figure out how to keep myself from kneeing him in the balls the second I got within reach. There are pills to make you happy when you're sad, pills to make you chill when you're stressed. Why the hell hadn't anyone invented a pill to make you less likely to assault a person who sorely deserved it?

Myrt followed me upstairs, but not into my bedroom. She went to Josh's room instead. Sighing, I followed her, stood in the doorway and watched her sniff around the entire perimeter. The bed was still unmade. His pajamas and a used T-shirt lay on the floor, even though I'd bought each kid a big plastic hamper to put their laundry in. Myrtle found that pile of clothes, smelled them, pawed them into a perfect little bulldog nest, and then, sighing, collapsed on top of it. As always, she was snoring before she even hit the floor.

Broke my damn heart.

I tugged the blanket and pillow off Josh's bed, tossed them down beside Myrt and curled up next to her. She snuggled a little closer. And that was where the two of us spent the night. She was missing her guy as much as I was missing mine.

You're fucking doomed, you know that, right?

Yes, Inner Bitch. I know it. I hadn't intended for it to happen. I'd tried real hard to keep this—God, I hated the word—*relationship* in perspective. Don't get too close. Don't use the L word. Don't *need* him, because if you do, then when you don't have him anymore, it'll hurt.

Too late. Too late for all of the above. Except for the use of the L word, of course, but that was on my to-do list. I just needed the right moment. And it probably ought to be one when I wasn't as pissed off at him as I was right now. Damn him for not being here with me.

Damn him for taking the boys back.

Wow. If you'd told me a year ago that *those* words would whisper through *this* brain, I'd have called you a dirty liar.

* * *

Saturday morning dawned bright and beautiful, and Mason was up, showered, dressed and halfway down the stairs before he smelled the coffee. His heart took a little leap in his chest. Was Rachel here? Had she come over bright and early to make them breakfast and assure herself that he wasn't overdoing it?

By the time he entered the kitchen, his grin was a mile wide. But Rachel wasn't there. Just the boys. Joshua was setting the table, and Jeremy was making French toast and a lot of smoke. The coffeepot was full and calling to him, though, so he grabbed a cup off the table.

"Morning, boys."

They were so focused on their work they hadn't seen him. "Morning, Uncle Mace! We're making breakfast," Joshua said.

"I see that." He moseyed to the coffeepot and gave the burner a sneaky downward turn underneath Jeremy's pan before filling his mug. "Mmm. Looks great."

Jere shrugged. "You're supposed to take it easy. We figured we'd help out." He turned the burner back up, but not as high as it had been.

Josh ran behind his uncle to pull out a chair, and Mason sat down. "Don't feel like you have to do this every morning, guys. I'm fine. I really am."

He wasn't. His lungs still felt as if they'd been scrubbed on the inside with steel wool. And his arm still hurt like hell. It was healing, but he was pretty sure there were going to be lasting scars.

Jeremy brought a plateful of charred bread to the table. Mason helped himself to a couple of slices, and applied liberal amounts of syrup to help it go down. "Nice job, Jere. Thank you."

Jere shrugged. "It was no big deal." He stabbed a slice for himself.

Josh looked at the stack. "Is it s'posed to be so black?"

"It's fine, Josh. Try it—you'll see," Mason told him.

"Oooookay." Josh speared a slice with his fork, looked at it doubtfully, then dropped it on his plate. Before he did anything else, he broke off a corner of the crust with his fingers, and looked down at the floor. And then he sighed. "I forgot. Myrt's not here."

"You miss her already, huh?"

"Yeah."

Mason nodded slowly. "Well, maybe it's about time we talk about getting you a dog of your own, Josh. We have the room here, and you're old enough to handle the responsibility now."

Josh nodded slowly. "I guess. It won't be the same, though. I want Myrtle." He looked up. "You think Rachel will bring her over today?"

"I'll call her and ask."

Josh's answering smile was as bright as the June sunshine.

June. Gosh, it was June, Mason realized. "Jeremy, about your graduation…"

"Don't worry about it. Misty and I have it all planned."

"You mean Rachel and Misty's mom, don't you?" Joshua asked him.

Jere made a face. "All of us. It's gonna be at Rachel's. We're renting a party barge, and a big tent for shade."

"Or in case it rains," Josh said.

"Rachel ordered a cake, and Misty's mom is taking care of decorations. And I'm making a playlist for the DJ."

"There's going to be a DJ?"

"Rache asked if I wanted a DJ or a band. I said DJ." He wiggled his eyebrows and grinned. "Saves more money for the present."

Oh, God, Mason thought. He needed to do something about a present. "What about the rest of the food?"

Jeremy shrugged. "Rache said something about catering. I don't know." Then his smile faded. "Don't be mad at her, Uncle Mace. You were in the hospital, and graduation is only a week away."

"Mad at her? I think I'll buy *her* a present." A week. Hell.

There was a knock at the door, and Mason started to get up, but Jeremy sent him a "don't you dare" look that reminded him of himself, so he sat back down and let his all-grown-up nephew open the door.

"Hello. I'm looking for Detective Mason Brown."

It was a woman's voice, and not one he knew.

"He's here. Come on in."

Mason did get up then, as Jeremy opened the door wider to admit a blonde who was within a year, one way or the other, of thirty. She had rivers of hair, all wavy, flowing halfway down her back, pretty blue eyes and an infectious smile.

"I'm Mason Brown," he said, offering a hand. "You are…?"

"Your new nurse, I hope," she replied, taking his hand. She clasped it firmly, still smiling, smoothing her white and sunshine-yellow floral-print sundress with her other hand.

"I…" He drew out the syllable. "I haven't even posted the ad yet. How did you know?"

"I have friends who work at Saint Joe's," she said. "I just left my job to move into a home care position in

Binghamton. But it's going to be a few weeks before I start." She lowered her head, shook it slowly. "I misunderstood, thought I would be starting immediately. My own fault, but the gap leaves me in a little bit of a lurch. I have rent and a car payment and...well..." Her head came up again, and she replaced her bright smile. She was like little Mary Sunshine, he thought. "You don't need to hear my woes. The thing is, when my friend told me about the hero cop who was being discharged and would be needing home care, I figured I could be the first one to apply for the job."

"I was going to go through an agency."

"This is my résumé, work history, et cetera," she said, thrusting a folder at him "I'm really good at what I do, if that's not too immodest a thing to say." Then she blinked. "Maybe it was. It was, wasn't it?"

"Not at all," Mason said. He was getting a kick out of her, revising his estimate of her age back three or four years. She had a very young, bubbly personality. Twenty-six, maybe twenty-seven. "I just wasn't expecting..." He shook himself, looked back at the boys, shrugged. "Why don't you come in and have a seat? I'll pour you some coffee and—"

"Oh, no!" She pressed a hand to her chest. "No, I can't possibly stay. If I don't find something soon, I'm *doomed*. Besides, I'm clearly interrupting your breakfast." She waved at the boys and shrugged her shoulders. "Sorry, guys."

"That's okay," Jeremy said, beaming.

She looked at Mason again. "Just take a look through my credentials and give me a call if you like what you see," she said brightly.

"All right, I'll do that. I just want to be clear with you, though, that I'm not going to need a lot."

"Oh, I've worked with burn victims plenty of times. You need a daily dressing change. Twice daily, maybe. And a thorough listen to those lungs of yours. It's as much the heat as the smoke that affects them, you know."

"That's what the doctor said." He was impressed. "Okay, I'll give your paperwork a look and let you know what I decide."

"Thank you, Detective Brown."

"You're welcome, Miss…" He looked at her business card.

"Gretchen," she said. "Gretchen Young."

"Myrtle!" I said, using my "this is exciting, so listen up" tone of voice. She jumped up from her circular Memory Foam doggy bed, where she'd collapsed right after our morning walk, and cocked her head to one side, ears perked. "Wanna go for a *ride*? In the *car*?"

She said "snarf!" but I knew what she meant was, "Do you really need to ask? Do you not yet know that rides in the car are my freaking raison d'être?"

What? She's a smart bulldog.

I grabbed her leopard-print goggles and matching silk scarf from the peg on the wall, along with my keys, and we went out the front door. We could've gone straight from the kitchen into the attached garage, but the steps were a bit steep for her. This was easier. I pointed at the garage and clicked one of the buttons on the key fob. The door rose slowly, and Myrt, recognizing the sound, danced around my feet, snuffing and snarfing. "Come on, then." We walked together into the garage. She went directly to the passenger-side door and then stood as straight as a pointer, smiling a mile wide. Yes, dogs smile. Don't question it. It's fact.

I opened her door, and she did what she always does. Put one forepaw on the floor, just inside the door, to accurately gauge her position relative to the car. Then she placed it on the seat instead, put the other paw beside it and waited.

I, her devoted servant, scooped her backside up for her and helped her get situated. I put her special harness on her while she panted for joy. Then I closed her door and went around to get behind the wheel. It was a gorgeous morning. Not quite warm enough yet to put the top down—I was leaving early and hoping to beat the press to my destination—so I lowered her window. She loved the wind in her face. Sitting on her ass, like a little person, leaning back slightly against the seat, she didn't need to put any weight on her front paws. They were up. Think kangaroo pose. And her round, pink Buddha belly was fully exposed for all to see. She had no shame.

We drove to the end of our narrow dirt road, which was edged by the giant lake-like Whitney Point Reservoir. Myrt couldn't see the way the sunlight was dancing on the water's surface like liquid gold, but I knew she could smell the water. She loved the water. Mainly because, now that it was summer, she'd discovered that froggies lived there, and she loved few things more than trying to catch froggies. Even hearing the word *froggy* sent her into paroxysms of pleasure.

At the end of the road we took a left, putting us onto Whitney Point's main drag. We did not pull in at the McDonald's, because Myrtle needed to watch her waistline, and we'd already had a healthy breakfast. (Chicken breast for her, oatmeal for me.) Instead, we kept going all the way to the other end of the village, hung a right, followed by a left onto the on-ramp, and sailed onto I-81 south with the wind blowing in my hair and flapping Myrtle's jowls. We got looks, waves, smiles and a few beeps from at least half the cars we passed. A bulldog wearing leopard-print goggles and a scarf, sitting up in the seat of a classic Inspiration Yellow T-Bird, was an attention grabber.

My pleasure faded just a little when we passed the Castle Creek exit, just a few miles down. I couldn't see Mason's little farmhouse from the highway, but I knew it was there, almost within shouting distance, and my heart clenched a little. I missed him. And I missed his rug rats, too.

But he was not my morning's mission. Peter Rouse, the man who'd damn near killed him, was. And he was down in Endwell, not far from where Amy lived.

Amy. I hadn't told her I was going to be out when she arrived at the house for work this morning. Not that it mattered. She knew her job. She'd busy herself answering fan mail, updating my fan page and reading over the latest set of galley proofs until I returned.

How would I ever get by without her?

I wouldn't, that was how. I'd curl up and die.

Before long we were pulling into Rouse the Louse's driveway. It was still only 8:00 a.m. No reporters were camped out. Yet.

I put up the windows, left the AC on and took the extra key with me so I could lock the running car with Myrt inside, leaving her safe, secure, and nice and cool. Then I went up to the house. It was a cream-colored ranch, with a matching one-car garage beside it. The driveway was paved, like most of the houses nearby. He had brown shutters, a white front door and a two-step concrete stoop with a tiny roof over it, supported by black iron filigree posts. There was an attached mailbox with the digits 117 on it in fake gold. And a door-bell right next to that.

My finger moved toward the doorbell, then stopped there as another car pulled into the little driveway be-hind mine. A loud (in a good way, the owner had re-peatedly assured me) boat-sized, black '72 Monte Carlo that Mason called classic and I called old.

Folding my arms over my chest, I leaned against one of the filigree pillars and watched Mason defy his doc-tor's orders on his first full day out of the hospital. He got out of the Beast, closed the door and looked at me like *I* was the one doing something wrong.

"Don't give me that look, Detective. *You're* the one who's not allowed to work yet."

"I'm not working," he said, palms up as he walked toward me.

"No? What do you call it, then?"

"Visiting?"

"Right."

"And you?" he asked. "What are *you* doing here, Rache? I thought I told you to stay away from this guy."

"Maybe you should have asked me instead." Not that it would have made a difference. "Besides, I'm an offi-cial police consultant." I know it was lame. It was the best I could come up with on short notice.

"And they've hired you to work on the arson case?"

I lowered my eyes. "Not exactly."

"Then what—exactly?"

He was right in front of me now, though, so when I lifted my head, there he was. Close enough to kiss. I was sorely tempted, too, but the door suddenly opened behind me, and I spun around like a guilty teenager at Make-Out Point, caught in a flashlight's beam.

Peter Rouse stood there, pajama bottoms, white

T-shirt, coffee mug in one hand, hair looking as though he'd combed it with an egg beater, bleary eyes. "No press. Come on, my kids are sleeping."

Liar. Or so my NFP told me.

"We're not press," Mason said, flipping his badge at the guy.

Yeah, *sure* he wasn't working. I'm pretty sure flashing your badge at a suspect is the definition of working. You know, for a cop.

Rouse the Louse met Mason's eyes, and then recognition hit. He gaped a little, then said, "Shit. Yeah, I guess you would want to talk to me." Then he looked up. "That's it, right? Just talk. 'Cause like I said, my kids are in bed. So if you want anything else…"

My lie detector was blinking like a beacon.

"Like what?" Mason asked.

"He thinks you're here to kick his ass. Or worse," I clarified. "He's not like that, Rouse." I don't know why I called him by his last name, but it's just what came out. Frankly, I'm glad I didn't slip and call him Louse. "*I'm* like that, but since he's here to stay my angry hand, chances are you're pretty safe."

Rouse thinned his lips, nodded heavily, opened the door farther and stood aside. "Come on in. Just keep it down. The kids—"

"Are still in the hospital," Mason said.

So that was what he'd been lying about. The kids weren't even home. The Louse looked alarmed, but Mason just went on.

"They moved them over to Golisano yesterday before I was discharged. I checked on their condition just this morning. I'm glad to hear they're doing better, by the way."

Guiltily, the vermin sighed and lowered his head. "Thanks to you," he said.

He moved aside to let us walk in, then pushed the door closed and didn't say a word as we followed him through the living room with its beige carpet, tan sofa, and matching love seat and chair. Cheap coffee table that probably came from Walmart, and a modest 32-inch TV mounted to the wall. The dining room was stark. Dinette, chairs, a few photos of the kids on the walls. His wife must have stripped the place *down* when she left him. Didn't seem like the act of a woman who thought there was a snowball's chance in hell she was ever coming back.

He led the way into the kitchen, a cluttered little room that looked as if it got a lot of use.

"Coffee?" he asked.

"Sure." That was Mason. I didn't want to socialize; I wanted to kick the guy in the balls. But not until I was positive he was the one who'd set the fire that had hurt Mason. I had that much of a hold on my temper, and to tell you the truth, I was fucking impressed with myself. I sat down in a kitchen chair. The table was metal with red Formica. The chairs were the same metal, with red vinyl cushions and backs. Very retro. I liked it.

Mason stayed standing, but Rouse the Louse filled two more cups and sat at the table. "I wanted to come to visit you, Detective Brown, in the hospital, but between my lawyer and your colleagues…" He lowered his head, letting the gesture finish the sentence for him.

"What did you want to do that for?" Mason asked.

Rouse lifted his head slowly, met Mason's eyes. I closed mine and tried to open my brain. To *feel* him. He said, "To thank you. You saved my kids' lives. Damn near got yourself killed doing it, the way they're telling it." His gaze drifted to Mason's arm as he said it. Some of the bandages showed from under his shirt sleeve.

Mason turned away. He wasn't good at accepting praise. "I just wish I could've gotten your wife out, too."

"So do I." Rouse's voice thickened on those words, and I shivered a little. I picked up heartbreak. Grief. Anger. Regret. Huge regret. Waves of it that made it hard for him to breathe. "I didn't set that fire, Detective."

Mason shot me a look. I felt it, but I couldn't let myself be distracted just then. I sipped my coffee. Let them think what they would about my closed eyes. Did I fucking care what an asshole who'd probably killed his wife and tried to kill his own kids thought about me? What do you think?

"I read your statement." Mason was scary when he was in cop mode. If I didn't know better, I'd have thought he knew everything and could prove it already.

"I didn't tell them everything in that statement," Rouse said. "I didn't want to make myself look more guilty. But then they found that hacksaw in my truck and arrested me. My lawyer's telling me to keep quiet, but I can't. I just can't anymore. She'll kill me, too, before she's done. And the kids. God, the kids…"

"Who are you talking about?" My eyes popped open as I asked the question. His tone, his fear, completely pulled me out of my focus. But not before I got that his fear was genuine. That didn't mean it was based on anything real. But it did mean that *he* believed what he was saying.

"I had an affair. That's why Becky took the kids and moved into that freaking dump."

I shot Mason a wide-eyed look. This was the first I

was hearing about an affair, and from the look on his face, it was news to him, too.

Mason nodded, taking a notepad from a pocket. "So you had an affair. What does that have to do with the fire?"

"It was her—don't you get it? I told her it was over, that I wanted my family back. The fire was her revenge."

I felt my spinal fluid turning to ice.

"This woman have a name?" Mason asked.

"The one she gave me was Noelle Baker."

"What do you mean, the one she gave you?"

"I don't think it was real."

"Why not, Peter?" Mason was so good at this, I thought. Using his first name. Being his pal.

"I've been trying to contact her ever since that night." He shook his head. "Everything she told me was a lie. She said she had an apartment in Johnson City, on Bleeker. But I've been to every building on the street, and no one's ever heard of her. She said she worked at Zales, you know the jewelry store at the mall?"

"Oakdale Mall?" Mason asked.

"Yeah. I called them, too. But no one there ever heard the name, either. And her cell's no longer in service."

My head was spinning as I tried to sort out what he was saying from the emotions he was emitting. It wasn't easy. It was better when I could keep quiet, close my eyes and just feel, but I'd let myself get sucked into his story.

"Okay, so you had an affair with this woman. Noelle Baker. Your wife found out and—"

"She didn't just find out, Noelle fucking told her. Called her at home and ruined my life with a single sentence." He shook his head, his mouth pulling into a tight grimace, tears welling up and spilling over. "I'd tried to end it with her. I knew it was a mistake. I loved my wife. Noelle was furious. She said she'd make me pay. And that night she called Becky and told her about us."

I wanted to say it wasn't the other woman who'd destroyed his marriage but his own idiotic inability to keep his junk in his pants. But I didn't because I could feel his suffering, and it was already plenty. I couldn't make the guy feel worse than he already did, and I found I didn't particularly want to.

Maybe I was going soft.

"She thought I'd come back to her once Becky left me," he went on. "She came over here, pawing all over me. I told her there was no way in hell." He closed his eyes. The lashes were wet. "She was like a crazy person. Screaming at me, tearing up the house."

"So you think she started the fire out of vengeance?" I asked before Mason could get a word in.

"I don't *think* it. I *know* it. No one else had any reason." He looked from me to Mason and back again. "And then she put that hacksaw into my truck. It's not mine. I never saw it before."

"Do you *have* a hacksaw?" Mason asked.

"Yeah. It's out in the garage. You want to see it?"

Mason nodded, and we headed out together.

4

"Did you notice what I noticed out in the garage?" Mason asked an hour later.

We were sitting at our favorite spot in the park, eating takeout we'd grabbed from the Spiedie and Rib Pit on Front Street and watching the Susquehanna River roll by. It was hot already, pushing up toward ninety, and I was glad I'd dressed in layers earlier because that meant I could remove them as needed. I was down to my tank top and sitting on the shady side of the picnic table because I hadn't brought any sunblock.

Mason sat in the shade, too, but he kept his sunglasses on. He looked hot in those solid black shades.

"What did you notice?" I asked, once I reminded myself of the question.

"His tools. All the same brand. Snap-on. Expensive."

I didn't know Snap-on tools from strap-on tools, which is why I was just a classic-car buff and not a true motorhead. "So?"

"So guys are the same way with tools that they are with cars. They have their brands. That's what they buy. You'll never catch a Chevy guy driving a Ford."

"You're a Chevy guy. But you've driven my Ford."

"Owning. I should've said owning, not driving."

"So your point is?"

"The hacksaw we found in the back of Rouse's truck was made by Craftsman."

I blinked at him. "Do you know that you're a fucking genius?"

He smiled. "Yes, I was aware of it, but thanks for recognizing it, too."

I rolled my eyes at him and handed another bite of my lunch down to Myrtle, who was lying on the cool grass, in full shade, and panting anyway.

"What did you sense from Peter Rouse?" Mason asked.

I nodded slowly as I chewed, took a swig of Diet Coke to wash it down. "He's a bundle of emotions, all of them intense, but I didn't get the liar alarm going off, other than when he kept insisting the kids were there so you'd be less inclined to kick his ass."

He nodded. "So you think he was telling the truth? About this...Noelle Baker?"

I reviewed my mental data. Inconclusive. "Maybe. But there was so much guilt coming out of him I can't be sure. Seems like a stretch that his mistress would kill his wife just to have him all to herself, doesn't it? I mean, he's not the kind of guy who seems likely to inspire that kind of devotion."

"Obsession. Not devotion. Very different things."

"If you say so."

"So we're looking for a Caucasian female of about five foot two with curly brown hair and blue eyes."

"Or a bottle of hair dye and a pair of tinted contacts," I said. "We women...we're like chameleons." I sucked on my Diet Coke, even though it was all gone and I was just draining the ice cubes of their life's blood.

"Is that so? Then how is it you never change?"

My brows arched up like hissing cats. I leaned back and set my empty cup down, eyeing him. "Is that a *complaint*?"

"No," he denied too emphatically.

My jaw dropped. "It *was*. It was a complaint. You're getting bored with me."

"Don't be ridiculous, Rachel. I am *not* getting bored with you."

"I've only had my eyesight back for less than a year, you know. Jesus, I've only recently mastered the art of hair and makeup at all. If I go switching it up, I'm gonna have to start all over again."

"Rachel, I'm *not* complaining."

"Fuck you, Mason. Why don't you go do something wildly different with your appearance, huh? You don't hear me bitching that you never change it up."

"Rache..."

"Don't give me that warning tone you use on the boys, either." I got up. "Come on, Myrtle. We're going home."

I was overreacting. I knew that while I was doing it, and I knew why, too. He'd told me about the new nurse who'd shown up at his door that morning, and that he'd gone ahead and hired her already without even asking what I thought. He'd called her on the way here, he said. Liked her initiative, he said. She was cheerful and sunny, and the boys thought she was great, too, he said.

It was my goddamn place to take care of him while he healed, and I was still stinging from him not wanting to move into my place to let me do that. I was starting to feel like this thing between us was getting a little shaky, and I knew it might be my own fault for not saying the

L word back to him when he'd said it to me. And *that* pissed me off even more.

Of course, I wasn't going to admit any of that to him. I tossed my soda cup into a nearby trash can, took my dog by her ludicrous leash (she didn't need it, but it was the law) and stomped down the sidewalk toward my car.

Worst of all…he didn't even try to stop me.

Well, shit.

He wanted a change, then I'd give him a change. I took Myrtle with me and headed out of town, going south, not north toward home, to the high-end salon where my sister liked to take me for mani-pedis.

They knew me there, though I didn't frequent the place very often. I mean, you know, my hair is long and, aside from the odd trim, it doesn't need much fussing. Still, they knew me, and I'd brought Myrtle along before. Never a problem.

So we sailed in through the front door, and everyone stopped what they were doing and looked our way. I swept the room, but wasn't really looking at anyone. Instead I was using my inner radar to give each individual a brief read before I settled on the cute male stylist with the gel-stiff Mohawk and the to-die-for eyelashes, and said, "I need a change."

"Oh, baby, you've come to the right place," he said, and he patted his chair.

Mason didn't know what to make of Rachel stomping off, so he let her go. Then he put in a call to Rosie, left a message on his voice mail and headed back to the house, along with a big container of spiedie chicken (aka chicken breast in bite-size pieces, marinated in Binghamton's famous spiedie sauce) for the boys for lunch. He was a little bit pissed at Rachel. He'd wanted to talk to her about the boys and Josh missing Myrtle so much, and the puppy idea, and Jeremy's impending graduation and…well, he'd just wanted to talk to her.

But she was in a snit, and he figured he'd done something, though he wasn't sure what. He hoped to hell this wasn't the beginning of the end. Hell, he'd better fix this. He didn't want to lose her. But he was damned if he knew what to do because he wasn't sure where he'd gone wrong.

Rosie called him back before he made it home. "Hey, partner. How's the rest and relaxation goin'?"

Mason said, "Right. Listen, I talked to Peter Rouse this morning, and—"

"You did *what*?"

"You heard me, Rosie. Now listen, he says he was sleeping with a woman who went all *Fatal Attraction* on him when he tried to dump her. He says he thinks she's the one who set the fire, then planted the hacksaw in his truck to frame him."

"Mason, you're supposed to be staying *away* from this case."

"Will you quit changing the subject? The forensics report on the hacksaw said 'incomplete' when I read it before. Have they found anything else since?"

Rosie sighed. "I'm gonna call Rachel on your white ass."

"Rachel's pissed at my white ass right now, so it wouldn't help. Now, will you tell me what Forensics says about the hacksaw?"

"Cantone will have my ass if—"

"Rosie, how long have we been partners?"

Silence stretched out, and then Rosie finally sighed into the phone. "A few metal fibers not inconsistent with the pipe that was cut at the crime scene, but you already knew that. There was also a human hair on the handle. No DNA. It broke off too far from the root, but it was long, curly and brunette. Rebecca Rouse was a redhead."

"That fits. Rouse said the other woman was a brunette," Mason said.

"That story sounds like something a guy caught red-handed would make up to cover his ass, Mace."

"I know. I know it does. But listen, all the guy's other tools are Snap-on, Rosie. The hacksaw was a Craftsman."

"That's not exactly proof of innocence, but…you're sayin' you believe him?"

Mason sighed. Rosie didn't even change his own oil. He wouldn't get it any more than Rachel had at first. But he had something his partner *would* understand. "Rachel thinks he was telling the truth."

"She was with you, huh?"

"Yeah."

"But she's not there now?"

"Nope."

"So what did you do to piss her off?"

"Damned if I know, bro."

"You thank her?"

"For…?"

"Shit, Mason, you really have to ask? She came to that hospital every day. Brought her work with her. Took in your boys. You telling me you haven't thanked her?"

"Well, of course I *thanked* her."

"You buy her a present? Flowers? Anything?"

"Jeez, Rosie, I've only been home a day."

"Gwen says you oughtta pin a medal on her. But flowers would be just as good. Or somethin' sweet.

Maybe take her out. She's been workin' hard for you and those boys, partner."

"Yeah. Okay. I'll try that."

"Not today, though. Your first day home, you better damn well be getting some rest so you can get back to work. Just let her know it's coming. You read me?"

"Loud and clear, partner. Loud and clear."

I stared in the mirror at my brand-new bangs for a solid half hour. Myrtle kept bumping me in the calves with her head. She wanted her dinner. She wanted a walk. She wanted my attention. But instead of attending to her needs as I normally would, many and endless though they were, I was standing still, and she probably couldn't fathom why.

She bumped me again, harder.

"All right, all right. Let me just—" I tweaked the bangs with my fingers, trying to decide if I loved them or hated them, and still couldn't make up my mind. They changed my entire face, that was for sure.

Bump!

"Okay, Myrt." I turned away from my apparently hypnotic reflection, bent low and rubbed her face with both hands. "I'm sorry I was ignoring you. You only just lost your best friend, and I should be showering you with affection, not primping in the mirror. If I were you, I'd bite me."

But she was too busy closing her eyes tight and letting me rub her wrinkly face.

"Come on, dinnertime."

She raced down the stairs at the word *dinner*, stopping at the bottom to turn and bark up at me in a high-pitched yip that was more suited to a toy poodle than an overweight bulldog.

I hurried to catch up and get her meal in front of her. Then I stood staring into the fridge the same way I'd been staring into the mirror. Myrt was wolfing her meal. But nothing looked good to me.

The phone rang. Sighing, I closed the fridge and picked up the call. "Yeah?"

"Well, that sounds morose," Mason said. "Somebody kick your dog?"

"Had a fight with my guy," I said. "It was mostly my fault."

"Mostly?"

"Watch yourself, Detective."

I felt his smile right through the phone lines. "Come over tonight. I have a surprise for the boys, and I want you and Myrt to be here when I spring it."

I looked down at Myrt. She'd inhaled her food in about 2.3 seconds and was looking up at me as if asking "where's the rest?"

"Okay," I said. "Myrt's missing the hell outta Josh."

"He's missing her right back. But I have a solution. See you in a little while, okay?"

He sounded excited. "Okay," I said, and he hung up before I could ask any questions.

So what was I supposed to think? What solution had he come up with for the problem of Joshua and Myrtle missing each other? Had he decided to stay at my place after all? I decided it was fine with me either way. I was done being hurt by his saying no. And I was done being mad at him, too. He hadn't meant to hurt me. When had the guy ever deliberately done something like that? Never. It wasn't in him, and I knew it.

He was just male and, therefore, needed extra patience and understanding. Along with very clear instructions.

Shrugging, I said, "Myrt, you want to go see Josh?"

She spun around in a circle, then jumped at me, her front feet landing about knee high on my legs, claws digging right in.

"I'll take that as a yes." I grabbed my bag, my keys and Myrt's goggles on the way to the door, while she danced, barking, beside me. I put her in her seat and buckled her harness, then got into my own, glanced up at the mirror and startled myself.

Oh, shit. I had bangs now. What was Mason going to make of that?

Wow, Rache. You've fallen a long way, girl. A long way.

I know, Inner Bitch. But it's been a helluva ride.

"You're here!"

I wasn't ready for Mason to fling the door open and greet me as if he hadn't seen me in a month. I was distracted by my dog, who was acting oddly. Sniffing the air and then growling a little.

He hugged me hard, and I hugged him back, and then he let me go and I said, "Something's wrong with Myrt."

And he said, "Wow!"

I realized he was staring at my new bangs. I automatically ruffled them with my fingers. "I decided I needed a change. I'm still not sure if I like it."

"I like it," he said. "I like it *a lot*."

I punched him in the shoulder. "Kiss up, much?"

"I was not kissing up." He stepped aside, and I walked in, Myrt beside me, sniffing all the way. The hair along her backbone was all bristly.

"Has someone new been here?" I asked. "She's really tensing up."

"She'll be okay as soon as she sees Josh," Mason said.

"Well, where the hell is the little runt? She's been waiting for like *ever*."

"I sent him out with Jere to pick up our pizza."

I wondered if we ate way too much pizza, then decided that was ridiculous, because there was no such thing as too much pizza.

"They'll be back any minute. Come on, I've got to show you first." He headed into the living room, and I was on his heels. Myrt followed along, but slowly, cautiously, like she was expecting something to jump out of the shadows and attack her at any second. I couldn't make heads or tails of her tonight.

Mason walked around behind the sofa, crouched down out of sight and then bounced upright again with the culprit in his hands. It was a tiny, wrinkly faced, pink-snouted, fat little puppy. A brown-and-white bulldog puppy, to be specific, and probably the cutest living creature I had ever set eyes on in my entire life.

Myrtle growled deep in her throat.

I hunkered down and hugged her. "It's okay, Myrt. It's a…it's a puppy. It *is* a puppy, right? Not a piglet?"

"Of course it's a puppy. I figured it was high time Josh had a dog of his own."

Ouch. That really hurt.

"And he's been missing Myrt so much, I thought a puppy would help him get over it." He carried the little creature around the sofa, then knelt down and set it on the floor in front of Myrtle.

Myrt puffed out her great big bulldog chest and growled. She was shaking. I grabbed her around the neck and held her back. "Jeez, are you nuts? She's gonna *eat* it!"

"She's not gonna eat it. Go on, let her check him out."

"Him?"

"The breeder said Myrtle would be more receptive to a male pup than a female."

Made perfect sense to me, and I felt a little bit soothed that he'd at least considered Myrtle in this decision. "She's going to kill him," I said, but I let her go.

Myrtle leaned forward and put her nose directly on the little guy, sniffing him all over. The pup whined like he was being whipped. "Yeah, I'd be scared, too. Shit, Mason, what were you thinking?"

The pup started to back away. Myrtle plopped a paw on top of him, flattening him to the floor so she could continue her inspection. I quickly lifted said paw and checked to be sure the pup hadn't popped open. He hadn't. Myrtle growled at him, and I think she was saying, "You don't fucking move until I tell you to fucking move. Runt."

"I think it'll make Josh happy to have a dog."

"He already *has* a dog," I said. "Jeez, where have you been, Mason? Myrtle has been more his dog than mine since she set eyes on the kid."

"Well, yeah, but you know, I mean *here*. Where we live."

Yeah. And just like the boys, Mason didn't live with me. Nor, apparently, did he want to. He didn't have to beat me over the head with it. I got it already. I sighed heavily but didn't take my eyes off the dogs. Myrt finished her inspection of the pup, heaved a huge sigh and walked away, crossing the room to plop down on a blanket one of the boys had left on the floor.

The pup stood where he was, staring at her and shaking. Then we heard Mason's winter rat, a Jeep, pull into the driveway out front. The boys were home. Mason scooped the puppy up again. "You really don't like him?" he asked.

"Of course I like him. Fucking Attila the Hun would *like* him."

"But—"

"No buts." There were a lot of buts, in fact. I could have listed them. But *I thought we'd move in together eventually.* But *I thought Myrtle would be our dog when we did.* But *doesn't having one dog for each household sort of mean there have to continue to be two households?* But *this isn't the solution I was expecting you to come up with.*

I grabbed hold of myself and gave myself a shake. You know, inwardly. What the hell was wrong with me?

And then it dawned, slow and dramatic. The problem, I realized, was that I had, at some point during his recovery, become ready for more of a commitment in this relationship. Or maybe *not* during his recovery. Maybe it had been during those moments when he'd been inside that burning house and I'd been sure I would never see him alive again. I got it. I got why he'd finally blurted that he loved me after seeing me nearly get shot, thinking I *had been* shot for a horrifying moment. He'd been feeling then the way I was feeling now. And he'd told me so, said he loved me. But I hadn't reciprocated. And now that I was ready to, he might have already moved on.

I mean, he'd bought his own damn dog. Wasn't that a pretty big message?

The front door opened, and the boys surged inside carrying pizza boxes and containers of hot wings and bottles of soda in bags.

Josh dropped his burdens on the table, smiling ear to ear. "Hey, Rache! Did you bring Myrtle?"

Before I could answer, Myrt came trotting into the kitchen, right to her favorite human. Josh dropped onto all fours, and the two of them rolled around on the floor together.

Jeremy, watching them, smiled. "Hey, Rache," he said. Then he blinked. "Wow, you look so much younger."

I lifted my brows, though my bangs probably hid it. "You bucking for a really huge graduation present or what?"

He grinned. "Yes, but it's still true." Then he frowned. "What the heck…?"

He was looking past me at the whining, trembling little piglet that had snuffled and shuffled its way into the kitchen and now stood in the doorway, looking longingly at Myrtle.

"Don't worry," I said to Jere. "That's not what I got you for graduation."

He was gone, though, blown away by a pair of giant brown eyes in a smooshed-up little white face. He floated across the room, picked up the little puppy and tucked it under his chin, rubbing it softly. "Where the heck did you come from? Huh?"

The pup made little snuffles and whines that sounded as if he was trying to reply. Joshua got up and came closer. "Is it a baby Myrtle?"

"Yep," Mason said. "Except he's a boy."

"Aw. He's cute. You're cute, aren't you, little puppy?" Josh petted the pup's little head as Jeremy continued to hold it.

"I thought you should have a dog of your own," Mason said. Then with another look at the sheer rapture on the older boy's face, he quickly added, "Both of you. You know, 'cause you've been missing Myrtle so much."

Josh turned to Myrtle, who was standing there watching his every move. Then he bent to pet her again.

"You got a baby brother, didn't you, Myrt? Huh? A baby brother."

Myrtle turned around, putting her back to the boys and their furry little interloper, and sat down hard. I could've sworn she said "harrumph." It certainly sounded like it.

"I think Myrt's gonna be a tough sell," I said.

"She'll come around," Mason said. "Josh, how you act is going to be the key. You can't make Myrtle feel threatened by this new guy or she'll hate him. You have to let her know she's your number-one girl. And when she's around, put the little guy second."

"Okay."

"I think he's cold. He's shaking," Jeremy said.

"I'll go get you something to wrap him up in," Mason said, and he headed up the stairs. I went up with him, because I wanted to talk to him privately about Jeremy's graduation gift. It was something we'd been planning to discuss and hadn't quite gotten around to yet.

He headed into Jeremy's room, not his own. "If I remember right, there's a little blanket Jere had when he was a kid in here." He opened Jeremy's closet door, and a stack of letters fell right out at his feet. I think they must've been stacked on the shelf. Mason looked down, and so did I, and then we looked up and straight at each other. There were six of them, all from Jeremy's mother, Marie Rivette Brown, in care of the Riverside Maximum Security Psychiatric Hospital.

"Marie's been writing to Jeremy?" I asked, my voice a squeaky whisper.

"Apparently so." Mason swallowed hard, but he didn't pick the letters up. Instead he cleared his throat. "Jere," he called. "Can you come up here for a sec?"

There was barely a pause before the teenager's size-eleven feet came pounding up the stairs. He stepped into his own bedroom and stopped in the doorway, looking at the letters, then at his uncle.

"I wasn't snooping, Jere. I was just gonna grab that blanket you had when you were kid. You know, the Teenage Mutant Ninja Turtles one."

"Yeah, I know the one." He moved closer, reached into the closet and pulled out the blanket. "Mom got it for me when I was two."

"And you carried it around until you were almost seven."

Jere smiled and bent to gather up the letters. "I wasn't hiding these from you. I mean, I was gonna tell you about them, but you got hurt."

Mason nodded. "Okay."

"Did you read them?"

"Of course I didn't read them, Jere. You're practically a grown man, I'm not gonna read your mail without asking you first."

Jeremy sighed, then went quiet for a moment. Finally he nodded. "You probably oughtta read 'em."

"If you want me to."

Jeremy nodded again. "Yeah. I want you to. Like I said, I was gonna tell you. Most of them have come since you've been in the hospital. She heard what happened, and she's all wound up about it. And about my graduation and wanting to come to it and…just read 'em." He handed the stack of letters to Mason.

"Okay," Mason said, taking the stack.

"Have you written back to her, Jere?" I asked.

"Not yet. I'm working on it, though. I mean, it's cruel not to. I just… I don't know what to say to her, you know?" He lowered his head. "Especially after what she did. And what she tried to do to you, Rachel."

I looked him right in the eyes and said, "It wasn't her fault. She was out of her mind, Jere. You know that. If she'd been herself, your mom never would've done any of that. She just lost it. Everything that happened was…it was too much for her to handle. She snapped. Some people just do."

"Yeah. I guess."

Mason put an arm around Jeremy's shoulders. "It's gonna be okay, Jere."

"I hope so," he said.

"It will. Come on, let's go get some of that pizza before Josh and the dogs eat it all."

Jeremy nodded, but he hesitated, standing still when Mason would've pulled him out of the room.

"What?" Mason asked.

Jeremy looked his uncle in the eye. They were the same height. It was weird seeing Jeremy so grown-up. "Mom…she's got some crazy idea that someone is after us. You, Josh and me. She thinks we're in danger."

Mason nodded slowly. "Like Rachel said, she's sick, Jere. She can't help it. Still, I'll look 'em over. I'll make sure there's nothing to worry about, okay?"

"Yeah. And…make sure she doesn't show up at graduation. Okay, Uncle Mace? I don't…I don't want her there."

"I'll make sure."

Jeremy seemed very relieved. "Thanks, Uncle Mace."

"It's what I'm here for, kid."

5

So we had pizza, we played video games, and then we streamed a movie that bored the kids into going to bed. Joshua was afraid Myrtle's feelings were hurt over the puppy, who hadn't yet been named, so he took her to bed with him. Jeremy surprised us both by muttering something about the pup probably being unused to sleeping alone, then scooping it up to take to bed with him.

I looked at Mason as the closing credits scrolled and asked myself why I'd been so wrought up earlier. So he didn't want to move in with me. A couple of weeks ago I hadn't wanted that, either. Why was I getting so damned weird about us?

Because you almost lost him, Rache. That sort of close call has a way of putting things into perspective, don't you think?

Yeah, Inner Bitch, I think you might be right.

He let the credits keep rolling across the TV screen, got up and brought the handful of letters from the kitchen, then dropped them on the coffee table. He picked up the top envelope, handed it to me. It was addressed to Jeremy, and the return address was stamped in the top left corner: Riverside Maximum Security

Psychiatric Hospital. "You sure Jeremy's really okay with us reading them?" I asked, looking up into Mason's eyes.

He nodded.

"Including me?"

"Yeah. Funny how they started coming just before my…accident."

His brave, child-saving, medal-worthy, selfless act of heroism, he meant.

"I totally understand why he wanted to wait till I was home and recovering to bring them up." He looked at me, waiting for me to agree with him. He did that a lot, I realized. Had his own opinion about what was going on in the boys' heads but also asked me, without really asking me, for my two cents. I guess because I had a lot of experience with my twin nieces. And maybe because I'd had a much more typical childhood than he apparently had, even though I'd been blind and he hadn't. That was bizarre, wasn't it?

I nodded. "Jeremy's a good kid, and I absolutely believe him about all that. He wasn't hiding the letters. Didn't even seem upset that you'd found them." And he knew what his mother had done, too, which was a hell of a thing for a teenager to have to live with. Josh…well, it was tough to tell how much Joshua knew. It was a small town. His mother had committed three extremely gruesome murders. We hadn't given him any of the details, and we'd tried to shield him from newspapers and the TV when the killings were being covered nonstop. Of course he heard things. That was inevitable. Mason told him that his mother had become very sick in the brain and had hurt some people but that she couldn't help herself. And that was why she had to stay in the hospital, because it might happen again.

He reached for the envelope, winced a little and lowered his wounded arm. "Why don't you read them to me while I try to put a fresh bandage on this?"

"Where's your nurse, anyway?"

"At home, probably. She hasn't started yet."

This, I thought, should make me happy. Except I sucked at first aid. Always had. Still, I had to try. I'd been wishing he would lean on me a little more, after all. "Why don't *you* read them to *me* instead? Let me play Florence Nightingale tonight."

"Deal." The way he said it, I knew he'd been hoping I would offer. He laid his arm across a pair of sofa pillows. The bandages looked as if they'd been applied by Joshua. Or maybe Myrtle. Then again, I wasn't sure I could do much better.

I got up and went into the kitchen, where the supply of bandages, ointments, tiny scissors and tape was still right on the counter, where he'd dropped everything on returning home from the hospital. He'd clearly used some of them since, but he hadn't bothered putting them away. Men. I looked around the room, spotted a cute little wicker basket that had probably arrived bearing fruit at some point, and grabbed it. Then I lined it in plastic wrap and scooped all the supplies into it. I added a gallon-size zipper bag and headed back to the living room. Then I sat down next to him and carefully began unwrapping the gauze from his arm.

Mason held the letter in his good hand and started reading. "'Dear Jeremy,'" he began. "'I miss you so much that it's hard to breathe. I'm sorry for everything I did. My mind…it's not right. Even now, with all the pills they make me take every day, it's not right. Not all the way. Not to where it should be. I hope someday you can forgive me.'"

It was sad. Heartbreaking, really. And, yeah, I ought to hate the crazy bitch for trying to gouge out my eyes, but she had been completely out of her mind. I remember thinking how much she'd been through and wondering how she'd stayed sane, right before I found out that she hadn't.

The gauze came to an end, revealing soft pads on the arm itself. I started to lift one, but it pulled at his burns. I winced, he winced. I stopped pulling. "Maybe we should soak them off."

He nodded. "Good idea."

I back went to the kitchen with a handful of sterile gauze pads, soaked them in warm water, and brought them back to lay across his arm. "Keep going."

He nodded, folded Letter One, replaced it in the envelope and took out Letter Two. "'Dear Jeremy. I only just realized how close your graduation is getting. I would give anything to be able to be there. To watch you walk up on the stage and get your diploma. I'm so proud of you. Maybe they'll let me out, just for that day. They do that sort of thing, don't they? Even with hopeless cases like me? Ask your Uncle Mason. If anyone can get them to give me a day pass, it would be him. I love you always, Mom.'"

The wet pads had soaked through the ones on his arm, so I tried again to peel them away. This time it worked with minimal pulling. Oh, but the arm just looked mean. I think meaner now that it was healing. The edges of the worst burns were covered now in a thin layer of bright pink newborn skin, but the centers were still raw and sore-looking. I dropped the old pads faceup on the coffee table and looked at his arm, turning it slightly to one side and then the other. "It looks good, I think." Then I wondered how the hell I would know.

"It's gonna scar," he said. "Badly. I'll look like I've been in a gang fight."

"You'll look like you've been in a fire."

He smiled at me. "Okay, you're right."

"If you were a woman I'd feel sorry for you. But scars are sexy on men."

"Yeah?" He lifted his brows, then wiggled them suggestively. Reminding me that it had been a while since we'd rolled around in the sheets together. I was aching to play catch-up.

"Yeah. Especially scars you got saving babies. They're the sexiest kind. Go on, read the next letter."

He nodded, and moved on to Letter Three. "'They won't let me out for your graduation, son. I've asked everyone in this place. I even wrote to the Governor. I said they could send guards with me. I said they could stand on either side of me, holding my arms. Anything. Anything, I told them. Did you ask Mason? Why isn't he helping me? Jeremy, I can't miss your graduation. I'm your mother. I have a right to be there. What happened wasn't my fault. I'm sick. But why I should be punished like this just for being sick?'

"'They're probably reading these letters before you get them. They're probably not even sending them to you. I'm probably writing you for nothing. They're probably laughing at me. They hate me here. Everyone does. Maybe you hate me, too. Do you, Jeremy? Do you hate me, too?'" I'd been squeezing ointment out of a tube onto a fresh set of gauze pads—we were clearly going to need more of them—but I stopped about halfway through that letter, because it sent chills down my spine. "Sounds like she was losing it again when she wrote that one."

He nodded. "Yeah. It's definitely getting weirder as

we go along." He frowned. "Do you think she's been writing to Josh, too?"

"I don't know," I said. "Who's been picking up the mail since you've been sick? I mean, the boys have been with me."

"Mother picked it up and left it on the counter for us while I was away, but she must not have looked at it closely or she'd have told me about this."

I nodded, remembering. "A couple of times when I brought the boys home to get more of their things, Jeremy sorted through the stack. He must have been taking these out of the pile and stashing them."

Mason unfolded the next letter. "Remind me to ask him if there were any addressed to Josh. I can't believe he wouldn't have said so if there were, though." Then he skimmed the page and sighed. "It gets worse. Listen to this. 'Jeremy, you're in danger. She's been asking me questions about you, about Mason, mostly, but about you, too. I didn't realize at first. She's crazier than I am.'"

"Who?" I asked.

He shrugged. "Don't know. That's it—that's the entire thing." He set it down and reached for another one as I settled the pads into place and started unrolling new gauze around his forearm to hold them there. Not too tight. I didn't want to hurt him.

"'I have to protect my family. No one believes you're in danger. No one believes me about her. But I know. When I looked into her eyes, I saw it. The same sickness I've seen before. But she hides it. And no one else can see. There's a demon inside her. A dragon. She's hungry. She feeds on misery. I know, I know, I know. Your father had a dragon inside him, too. I saw it there, I knew. Oh, I knew, I knew—'"

Mason stopped reading, lifting his eyes to mine. "It's still hard for me to believe she really knew what Eric was."

"She couldn't have known for very long. I mean, if she did and she didn't say anything…"

"Then she's as guilty as he was."

"Maybe not *as* guilty." I lowered my head, continued wrapping. "Maybe she only just found out toward the end. Maybe she was still wrestling with what to do about it when he took his own life, then decided, like you did, that it wouldn't help anyone to make it public knowledge."

"Maybe."

"Finish the letter, Mason. What else does it say? God forbid she told Jeremy about his father."

He looked down, shook his head, kept reading "'I won't let the demons get you, baby. I promise. They got me. It's too late for me. I've gone to hell for my sins and I'm not even dead yet. That's how it works sometimes, the death angel just puts the guilty into hell right on earth, to show us what it will be like after. There are slavering dogs that roam the halls at night. You can't see them. But you can hear their panting and feel their cold breath on your face. They poison the food here, too. To keep you crazy. They don't want any of us ever to leave, ever. Because we might tell, if we get out. We might tell that they're as crazy as we are. But I won't let them get to you, Jeremy. I promise, I won't.'"

I sighed, finishing off the gauze with a healthy portion of tape. "She's still completely insane, isn't she?"

"Yeah."

"There's no way anyone would even consider letting her come to Jeremy's graduation, is there?"

He shook his head firmly. "No. No way. And if I get

any inkling that anyone *is* considering it, all I have to do is show them these letters. It's clear she's still a mess."

"If she's still this bad, even on meds, think how bad she'd be without them."

"Yeah." He sighed and looked over his new dressing. "Nice job."

"No it's not. It's probably going to fall off before morning, but thanks for lying. And I wouldn't know the early warning signs of an infection any more than you would. You need to get that nurse in here. In fact, that was one of the doc's conditions for letting you come home, remember?"

"Yeah. I know." He moved the arm up and down a little, like he was testing it. The gauze hung a little too loosely here and there. "I guess I'd better call her in the morning. Tell her she can start."

"Good." I don't think it sounded very sincere, since it was my ineptitude at first aid that seemed to have convinced him to take the step. He was folding the letters and putting them back into their envelopes, stacking them on the coffee table.

"Has Jeremy seemed okay to you these past two weeks?" he asked.

"He really has. No moodiness. No more than typical teenage stuff, at least."

"I wonder what he made of that bit about Eric?"

"The same thing he made of the demons and dragons and the invisible dogs, I imagine," I said. "Don't borrow trouble, Mason. The boys don't know what their father was. They'll never know."

"Not if I can help it," he said. He sighed. "You're good for them, you know that? You really came through for them while I was laid up. I hope you know how grateful I am."

I nodded, lowered my head.

"And you've got the graduation party all planned, according to Jeremy. You just jumped in and took care of everything."

"Not everything," I said, blushing a little. "There's still his present."

Mason smiled slowly. "I've got that covered." He leaned forward, tugging the laptop closer to him, hitting a few keys and glancing over his shoulder toward the stairs as a page loaded. When it did, my eyebrows went up at the hot-looking green car on the screen. "Whoa. Is that a Camaro?"

"Yep. An '89 IROC-Z," he said. "The mileage is low, for its age. I had Rosie check it out for me. He says it's mechanically solid, almost no rust, decent tires."

"So you bought it for him?"

"The price was right," he said, smiling.

"My God, Mason, that boy is gonna dance on the ceiling when he sees this."

"You think?"

"Yeah, I think." I moved the pillows that had been between us and sat down close to him, leaning against his shoulder and admiring his purchase. "I should get him something car related to go with it." I bit my lip, thinking out loud. "Snow tires?"

"No way he's driving it in the winter. Not the first year, anyway."

"Mmm. Well then, seat covers? A tune-up? A year's worth of car washes?" Then I snapped my fingers. "I've got it. I'll pay his first insurance premium."

"That's perfect. I'll have Mother get him a prepaid gas card, and he'll be good to go." He set the laptop back on the coffee table and turned to me, sliding one arm around me and leaning in close. "Don't go home tonight, Rache. Stay with me and the boys. And the puppy."

I smiled, slow and sappy. "I was so afraid you wouldn't ask."

"Why wouldn't I ask? You think I burned my brain in that fire?"

He could've said "heart" and made it all emotional and awkward. That he didn't told me just how well he knew me. But his eyes told me how he felt anyway. And I tried to let mine say it back, even if my vocal chords had frozen up on me at the thought of telling him I felt the same way he did.

And then he kissed me, and all my misgivings and stupid insecurities melted away. And since when was Rachel de Luca insecure about anything, anyway?

Gretchen was watching, the way she always watched her men. She had a perfect spot, comfortable even, on a tiny rise in a wildflower-dotted field adjacent to his house. It was dark outside, so he wouldn't see her there with her tripod and telescope. She had it pointed straight through the living room window, and she could see everything.

And what she was seeing right then was the man she wanted in the arms of another woman. Rachel, Marie had called her. She'd learned a lot more about her since.

She wasn't going to make the same mistakes she'd made in the past. She wasn't going to charm the man away from another woman, only to have him go back to her later on. This time she would remove every single obstacle between herself and Mason Brown first. And then, when he was grieving and had no one else, he would turn to her for comfort. There would be no second thoughts, no changing his mind, no need for her to punish him for hurting her. Ever. He would be hers. This time she'd found the right man. Her soul mate. This time it was going to be forever.

It was the kind of night I'd been missing. *Missing* being a mild term. I'd been going through some kind of Mason Brown withdrawal. Restless, cranky, pissed off at everyone, especially myself, for not being so great at even admitting I *had* sappy-ass emotions, much less figuring out what they were and how to express them. I was slower than him to catch on to what I was feeling. So I'd frozen when it had hit me between the eyes. Jeez, when he'd said he loved me, it had sent me into shock. Not because of what he'd said, but because the sudden rush of that unfamiliar emotional shit was trying to drown me. I'd been overwhelmed. And, frankly, convinced that couldn't possibly be what love felt like.

I'm not a hearts-and-flowers type, if you haven't figured that out by now. I'm practical. I'm self-sufficient.

I'm fucking in love.

God *dam*mit. I'm in love.

I managed to make love to the man I loved, for several hours, as gently as I possibly could, which wasn't easy, 'cause my man was *eager.* And I managed to do that all without once saying the words I had decided to say to him. Why was I having such a hard time blurting out three simple words?

As I lay there all curled up in his arms while he slept and I didn't, with the kids and the dogs safe and sound down the hall, I kept thinking that this was a life I could embrace. That I was happier here, in this run-down farmhouse than in my own *Home Beautiful* centerfold. That I liked noisy, overly rambunctious kids and a new puppy better than I liked living with nobody but

Myrtle. And she wouldn't be insulted by that because she liked it better, too. (Except for the puppy part. She hated the cute little interloper's guts.)

Wow. Who'd have thought that getting my eyesight back would turn out to have been the *smallest* change in my life over the past year?

We were cooking breakfast for the kids, the picture of domestic bliss, except that my nerves were tighter than piano wire and my mind was apparently on strike. I walked into things, tripped over things. You'd have thought I'd gone blind again, except that I'd never done that blind. This was something else. Something different.

Mason had phoned the new nurse first thing, to tell her she could start today, and now he had sausages and bacon sizzling away, and blueberry waffles steaming in the biggest waffle iron I'd ever seen. I was in charge of coffee, but all I'd managed so far was to bang my elbow on the edge of the fridge and scatter ground roast all over the counter. I laughed self-consciously and scraped the mess into one hand with the other, then brushed it into the trash. "I'm clumsy today."

He grinned, flashing that dimple that made my belly ache, had a quick, conspiratorial look around the room and whispered, "I was too much for you last night, huh?"

I smiled back at him and glanced into the living room, making sure the boys were nowhere in sight, just like he had. It was automatic once you got used to having them around. "You had a lot of stamina," I admitted. "But I was trying to go easy on you, you know."

He slid his good arm around my waist from behind

and nuzzled the back of my neck. "Come on. I was amazing and you know it."

"Jeez. Vanity, thy name is Mason Brown."

He nibbled my earlobe. I closed my eyes and said, "Okay, okay, you're Super Stud. Now stop it before I make you burn your bacon."

"Never heard it put quite like that before," he said. "But okay. As long as you call me Super Stud."

A throat cleared. We jumped apart like guilty teenagers. Jeremy was leaning in the doorway, grinning like an orangutan, the puppy cradled in his arms. "So, Super Stud, I thought you were supposed to be taking it easy. Why are you, uh…cooking?"

My eyes got huge, and I think my face turned three shades of red. Kids. I couldn't even come up with a smart-ass comeback.

"I'm never gonna live this down, am I?" Mason asked.

"Oh, no. Not ever," his nephew replied.

He shrugged. "Good. No excuse not to have a T-shirt made, then. By the way, breakfast in five minutes. Give or take."

Jeremy shrugged and said, "I'm taking the puppy out to pee. And we're calling him Hugo, by the way." Then he crossed the room and reached into the cupboard for a box of puppy treats, took a couple out and dropped them into his pocket.

"Hugo, huh?" I asked. "That's cute. Where'd you get it?"

"Josh. He was looking up potential names on the internet last night, and that's what he came up with."

I heard the snuffling and thunder of Myrtle hurrying down the stairs. Her toenails skidded noisily over the hardwood floor at the bottom, and then she galloped into the kitchen, and bashed her head into Jeremy's shin.

"Ow!" He jumped up and down on one foot, rubbing the other leg. "Jeez, Myrt, what the *hell*?"

"Language, Jere," Mason said.

"Me?" Jeremy asked with a nod toward me.

"Hey, I haven't cussed once so far this morning. In front of you, anyway." He grinned at me, and I finally managed to scoop some coffee into the filter basket, slide it home and hit the brew button. "Looks like Myrtle's demanding equal time, kid. You mind taking her out, too?"

"Sure, why not? C'mon, Myrt."

"If you give that pup a treat and not her, she'll eat him," I added, glad for a distraction from last night's emotional overload.

"This I know," Jeremy said. "She needs to eat first, get attention first and be spoken to first, consistently, to keep her from feeling the need to fight for dominance."

"Internet again?" I asked.

He grinned. "I read a whole ebook on adding a new dog to the family last night." He headed out the door with Myrt walking alongside him, touching his calf to keep herself on track.

Family. Good grief, even Jeremy was feeling it. The dynamic between me and Mason and the boys, and even Myrtle, had changed. Everything had changed. Drastically.

There had been a time bomb inside me, I realized, and it had been ticking away ever since Mason had come into my life. It had detonated when I'd watched him run into that burning house, thinking it might be the last time I ever saw him, and it had been throwing shrapnel and shock waves through my psyche ever since. I'd only realized the truth when he'd said those words to me. It was a lot to take in. I still needed some more time to digest it all.

The coffee was gurgling. We set the table for four, and Jeremy came back in with Myrtle and the pup.

"How'd they do?" I asked.

"Hugo peed. Then Myrtle went and peed right on the same spot."

"She's letting him know who's boss, right, Jere?" Mason said.

"I don't know. My book didn't cover that."

I had no doubt it was true. Jeremy put Hugo down. The chubby little bulldog pounced playfully at Myrtle, who released a long, low, dangerous growl.

"Myrt, stop being such a bitch." I crouched low, rubbing her head to soothe her. "He's a *nice* puppy. *Nice* puppy." I frowned as I heard a car pull in. "Who's that?" I asked, rising, hoping Myrtle wouldn't eat Hugo as he continued running circles around her and yipping "play with me" in bulldog speak.

"I don't know." Mason frowned, too.

I looked out the front door as a nymphomaniac prostitute in a Nurse Goodbody costume got out of a little red car and Beyonce'd her way to the door.

"I thought it was June. It's still June, right? 'Cause this looks like Halloween to me."

Jeremy said, "If she says 'trick-or-treat,' Dad, give her me."

"Oh, hell," Mason said.

I turned slowly, tearing my eyes off the breast-feeding-mother-sized breasts that were revealed by the open top of her white, button-down, skintight, micro-mini nurse getup. Yeah, it was that bad. Anyway, I looked at Mason, and what I saw there was guilt.

She knocked. Jeremy opened the door to let her in. And she said, "You must be Jeremy. I'm Gretchen. I'm your uncle's new nurse."

"You've gotta be fucking kidding me," I said, not to her, to Mason. And I didn't particularly care that I'd blown my unspoken "don't swear in front of the kids so much" goal.

He shook his head, moving his mouth like a trout with something to say, until he finally managed, "I swear to God, Rache... I swear to God..."

"Uh, yeah. Whatev." I turned to the nurse. "Happy fucking Halloween." And then I scooped up my dog, (forgetting for a minute why I never carry her anywhere if I can help it) and, after suppressing both a grunt and a hernia, walked to my T-Bird without looking back. If we spat a little gravel when we left, it wasn't deliberate. I mean, come on. How immature would that be, right? I'm not the jealous type.

Except my blood was boiling, and I had a quick vision of parking behind some bushes until that *beyotch* left the house, and then stomping the gas and leaving some tire tracks on her tits. They'd probably pop.

Wow. What the hell is wrong with you, girl?

I don't know, Inner Bitch. You tell me. What is this?

Green-eyed monster. No doubt about it.

"I don't *get* jealous." I said it aloud.

You do now.

"No." I shook my head, and tamped down the burst of temper. "No, you know what, no. I'm not doing this. Mason Brown is not a player. I know that. Whatever was going on back there, it wasn't that. So I need to knock it the fuck off and give him a chance to explain."

I took a big breath, nodded hard and pulled the car over. Then I pulled out my cell and called him.

He answered before the first ring finished. "It's not what you're thinking, Rachel. I swear to God, she didn't look like that when she applied for the job."

I sighed heavily. "I owe you an apology. I'm sorry I acted like a jealous...whatever back there. That's not me. I don't know who the hell that was. Some jackass snuck in and took over my body. Temporarily."

"Actually, it made me feel pretty damn good."

"That's 'cause you're a guy. And it fed your ego."

"You're probably right."

"I'll let you get back to the bimbo, I just wanted to tell you that..." I sighed. "I guess I trust you."

"That's nice. You can, you know."

"I know."

"I told her that her outfit was completely inappropriate and sent her home. I'll hire someone else."

"Not because of me," I said.

"Completely because of you. Her showing up like that was an insult to you. And I'm sorry. I'm really sorry. I set her straight."

I nodded, even though he couldn't see me. "Thanks for that. I'm sorry I ran out on breakfast."

"Come back? We didn't eat it yet."

I shook my head. "Actually, no. I have a lot of writing to do today, I'm way behind. And..." *And I need some alone time.* "And stuff," I finished lamely. "I'll talk to you later, okay?"

Gretchen had worn a uniform that was a size too small, unbuttoned low, over a pushup bra. She'd blown her hair dry upside down, to give it that centerfold lift and fullness men loved, had applied flavored lip gloss and smoky eyes. She'd gotten out of the car slowly, one long leg first, and she knew he'd been watching. She'd felt his eyes burning on her thigh.

Men always responded to her thighs. The nurse uniform was a new touch. After all, most of her conquests never knew her real name, much less her true profession. But this one was different. With Mason it would be forever.

He'd watched her, she knew it, as she got out of the car and walked toward his front door, swinging her hips better than any runway model and mesmerizing him. She'd knocked, pretending she didn't see him standing back there with the soon-to-be-former girlfriend, his eyes almost popping as they moved from her head to her manicured toes and back again.

And the teenage boy had practically been drooling when she'd spoken to him in her sexiest voice.

Then, just as she'd planned, the brunette had revealed herself to Mason as an insecure, jealous, controlling bitch.

Gretchen could tell that pissed him off. He didn't even speak to her after that, only sputtered a little. That's how angry he was.

Then, exceeding even her hopes, the brunette had hefted the ugly dog off the floor, snapped at her and stormed out.

Gretchen looked at Mason and gasped, squeezing moisture into her eyes. "Why would she say that to me?"

"Um, 'cause you look like you're wearing the sexy nurse costume from Party City," the horny teenager said, all bravado and pretending he wasn't as turned on as his father was.

"Jeremy, that's not nice."

The kid blushed, then took his puppy and turned around.

"Ohh, is that a puppy?" she asked.

"No. It's a wombat. Escaped from the zoo. I'm taking it back." He didn't turn around, just kept right on walking. "Call me when we can have breakfast, Uncle Mace." His kid brother followed him out of the room.

She knew he was raising his nephews, so this didn't come as a surprise to her. She was just glad the kids were leaving them alone. Good. Just what she needed.

She sniffled and wiped at her eyes, then turned to beam up at Mason full power. "Why is everyone being so mean?"

"I think it's got to do with your outfit."

"What about my outfit?" she asked, looking down at herself. "Don't you like it?"

"It's inappropriate."

She blinked at him, then smiled a little. "Then you *do* like it?"

"It's unprofessional," he said.

Oh, he was grasping. Trying really hard to keep his attraction to her at bay. She knew he was. It was admirable, trying to be loyal to that bitch who didn't deserve him.

"I don't think this is gonna work out, Gretchen. You need to go on home now. I'm sorry.

"Because of my outfit?"

"Yeah and, frankly, your judgment."

Right. He wasn't upset that she'd worn it, he was upset that she'd worn it in front of that arrogant girlfriend of his. "I'm sorry. It won't happen again."

"You're right, it won't. Goodbye, Gretchen."

He stood there holding the door open. Her temper flared up, but she tamped it down. He didn't realize yet that she was his destiny. It was normal for a man to resist a little when he first met his soul mate. Commitment of such intensity was scary for men. He would get used to it. He was already going to be unable to get her out of his mind. She'd made sure of that. He wanted her. She felt it. And she'd done a good job of putting his girl-friend on notice. She would make him hate her before she took her out. It would be easier on him that way.

Things were going perfectly.

His phone started ringing just as she left. It was probably *her*, calling to give him hell. She deliberately swung her ass all the way to the car, knowing he was watching. She even dropped her keys near the car door, then bent over slowly to pick them up.

Yeah. He was eating it up, all right. She didn't need to look back to confirm it. Not looking back would be more effective anyway. He would be eating out of her hand in no time. He was already on fire for her. It wouldn't be long now, and he would belong to her entirely.

6

Jeremy and Joshua helped Mason change his bandages right after breakfast. Then Jeremy drove them both to school in the Jeep, which was practically brand-new, because Mason didn't trust him yet with the Monte Carlo, which was old, but classic.

If something got banged up, he would prefer it to be the Jeep, but that was actually third on his list of reasons not to let Jeremy drive the Monte Carlo alone. First was that it was a hot rod, and Jere would be too tempted to drive it like one. But since he wasn't yet experienced enough to handle that much power safely, an accident would be more likely in the Monte Carlo. He and Josh could get hurt. Second, the Jeep had air bags, antilock brakes and very high front- and side-impact ratings. Not only was it less likely to wind up in an accident, but the kids were safer in it, should something go wrong.

He wasn't worried about the Camaro, because he intended to spend a lot of quality time with Jeremy teaching him how to drive it safely. He also intended to take him to a nearby track and let him cut loose with it on a regular basis, so he would know how to do it right and could let off a little of that teenage steam.

Teenage boys were going to do stupid things with their cars. Best Jeremy know how to do it right.

He was turning into a parent. Knowing that was a relief, too, because he'd wondered if he had it in him.

As he cleared up the kitchen, his bandages came unwrapped and dangled in his way. He was thinking that he would have to try rewrapping them himself when there was a knock on the front door.

He looked, then frowned and looked again. Nurse Gretchen was back, a rectangular plastic container in her hands and an extremely demure uniform covering the rest of her. White scrubs with pink piping. The top was tailored to fit her shape and had a shallow V-neck that revealed nothing, and two big pockets low on either side. The pants fit but were not tight. Her hair was in a neat bun, and if he wasn't mistaken, there were brownies in that container.

He opened the door. She sent him a great big smile. "I'm really sorry about this morning. I didn't know you had a girlfriend. I hope she wasn't too angry."

He lowered his head; this was awkward as hell. He hadn't expected to see her again. "It's fine. We're fine. Apology accepted."

"Thank goodness," she said, stepping inside. "I don't know what I would've done otherwise. I mean, I turned down three other temp offers after you hired me, and those spots have already been filled. I'd be screwed completely if you'd fired me."

But he *had* fired her. Hadn't he? He was trying to recall his exact words when she set the container of brownies on the table and turned to frown at his draping bandages. "My goodness, who did this?"

"I did. With some help from the boys. I guess nursing isn't our calling."

"Well, sit down. I'll fix you right up." She pulled her medical bag from her shoulder, and within a few seconds she was efficiently removing the messed-up bandages and applying a new set.

"Gretchen, I think I might not have been clear with you earlier. When I said this wasn't going to work, I meant—"

"I changed my clothes," she said. "Isn't this better?" She left off wrapping, and took a step backward, looking down at herself.

"It's much better. And if you'd shown up this morning in this, instead of that other getup, then we'd be fine, but as it is…"

"It's your girlfriend, isn't it?" She sighed, then blinked as if there were tears gathering in her eyes. "She's insecure and jealous and threatened by me, isn't she?"

"Um, no."

"I'm so sorry," she rushed on, as if he hadn't spoken. "I really didn't know. But I admit, I *was* trying to get your attention." She drew a shuddering breath and resumed wrapping his arm. "I mean, you're a hero. Saving those kids. Risking your life. I read somewhere that you were single, and I just thought…" She shrugged. "Well, what woman wouldn't try for a man like you?"

He couldn't help feeling warmed by her praise. It was flattering, and he was human. "Thank you," he said.

"But like I said, I didn't know about your girlfriend. I mean, I would never even have tried…and it'll never happen again. I promise." She finished wrapping and taped the bandages into place.

"I think that ship has sailed, Gretchen. I'm sorry. I'll pay you for today. But after that you—"

"Don't say it. Please…don't say it." She sank into

a chair and lowered her head, staring at nothing, sniffling. "If I lose this job, I lose everything. You don't understand."

He looked at the bandaged arm. She'd done a good job, as good as they'd done in the hospital. He could tell it would last all day. He sighed, got up from the table and poured the woman a cup of coffee, because he didn't know what else to do, and according to Rachel a great cup of coffee could fix a whole lot of things. He set it in front of her, and shoved the cream and sugar closer. "It can't be all that bad. This was only supposed to be a three-week gig, after all."

"I know. But I was counting on the extra money."

"Well, what were you doing before this?"

"Psych nurse," she said. "But the third time I was attacked by one of my patients, I realized I couldn't keep it up. I'm too petite. And I was reading this book that said to trust the universe. To take a leap of faith and watch for my net to appear. Some bullshit like that. And I believed it. I believed it. Damn that writer for steering me so wrong."

"What, uh…what writer?" he asked, dreading the answer.

"Rachel de Luca." She shrugged. "She's some kind of self-help celebrity. I heard she lives around here. Anyway, I thought…" She shook her head, took a fortifying drink of her coffee and seemed to get hold of herself. "Thank you."

"You're welcome."

"Stupid of me to throw my life away because of something some writer I never met put in a book, huh?"

He shook his head. "I don't think it was stupid to leave a job where you were getting hurt. You didn't have much choice."

"I still have the home care job waiting for me, but it doesn't start for a few weeks. If I could just work for you until then—"

"Look, I don't need that much. A bandage change twice a day. It's not going to pay enough to make a huge difference in your situation."

She shook her head slowly. "You're paying me about half of what I'd make full-time. Plus mileage. I won't lose my apartment, and I can feed my kids."

"You have kids?" he asked.

"Yeah. A boy and girl."

"How old?"

"Almost the same ages as the ones you saved from the fire." She shrugged. "Maybe that's why I felt so attracted to you."

"You have to stop with that. I can't have you working for me if you're going to—"

"I get to keep working for you?"

He heaved a sigh. "Yeah. Yeah, what the hell. It's only for a couple of weeks. All right."

"Oh, thank you!" She bounced out of the chair and wrapped her arms around his neck, pressing her body against his, and bathing his neck with warm breath and warmer tears. Then she backed away, lowering her head. "Sorry. I'm just...so grateful."

"Yeah. Okay. You're welcome."

"Well, why don't you go lie down? You're supposed to be resting. I'll pick up the kitchen for you and—"

"Not necessary. You're not here to keep house."

"You can't be putting that arm into dishwater, Mason." She shrugged. "Just relax. I only have an hour and then I have to leave. My other job isn't far from here. I'm going to wash up the dishes, and then I'll get out of your hair, okay?"

"Okay." He bit his lip, not liking this at all, and feeling somehow as if things had spiraled out of his control in a hurry. "I'll be in the other room."

"Here," she said, and when he turned, she handed him a brownie. "I made them just for you and the boys." Big smile, laser-beam eyes, the most innocent *blink blink*. She was young and in a bad situation. Two kids, no husband, in between jobs.

He took the brownie, turned and went into the living room, wondering how the hell he was going to make this okay with Rachel. She said she trusted him. He hadn't meant to give her such a challenging way of proving it.

I had lunch with Mason's partner, Rosie, at a sports bar in downtown Binghamton, where Mason was highly unlikely to show up, unless he was more psychic than I was.

I'm not psychic, I reminded myself. *I just have super heightened perception. That's all.*

Rosie came in a few minutes after me, so I'd already gotten us a table, ordered appetizers, and was sipping my Diet Coke when he arrived. I got a table, not a booth, because he was getting bigger around the middle all the time, and I didn't want to embarrass him if he couldn't fit. I hoped he could retire or get promoted to a desk job soon, because he was too out of shape to be chasing down bad guys. Besides, his wife, Gwen, was a friend of mine, sort of. We'd bonded over the holidays while trying to keep from getting killed.

Rosie smiled when he spotted me, a real smile that not only met his eyes, but crinkled up into his shaved head. He really seemed to like me for some reason.

"Hello, gorgeous lady. My partner driven you to murder him yet?"

I thought about the bimbo in the sexy nurse costume and rolled my eyes. "Depends on when you ask me, Rosie. He goes from dreamboat to pain in the ass several times a day. But I think I'll keep him around a little longer. How are you and your lovely bride?"

"Blissful, as always," he said. "We could give you two a manual."

"I think we're better off figuring it out as we go along. How's your leg? You're not even limping anymore."

"Good as new, good as new. Thanks for asking."

A waitress came and deposited two sampler platters with every appetizer they offered—the very best kind of lunch, in my opinion—and Rosie's eyes lit up. "What will you have to drink?" she asked him.

"Iced tea. Decaf, if you have it."

"I'll bring that right out." She hustled away, and Rosie dug in.

"You wouldn't be trying to soften me up with offerings of food for any reason, would you, Rachel?"

"Of course I am. I want to know what you found out about Peter Rouse's mystery woman, Noelle Baker." I took a pizza-shaped helping of quesadilla, dolloped it with sour cream and bit in.

"Apart from the fact that she doesn't exist, you mean?" he said, after he'd downed a riblet and sipped his newly arrived tea.

I lifted my eyebrows and stared him down while he started on a mozzarella stick. "I think she does."

He shook his head, chewed, made me wait. "I've checked everything Rouse gave us, which was precious little. The phone number can't be traced. One of those prepaid deals like the terrorists use. It could've been anybody's. Could've been his, for all we know.

The address he gave us is a vacant lot full of glass an' trash. The place he says she worked at never heard of her. There is nobody by that name who fits the description he gave."

"But you did find some women by that name?" I asked.

He nodded, but he'd popped a chicken finger in, so I had to wait until he'd swallowed it and swiped his mouth with a napkin. "Three Noelle Bakers. One's dead, one's ninety-two, and one's around the right age but doesn't match her description."

I shrugged. "She could've cut her hair, colored it, got some tinted contacts."

"Yeah, but could she have gained fifty pounds in three weeks?"

I had to think on that one and decided that yes, one probably could, if there was enough chocolate around. Of course, I was only speaking for myself.

"I got nothing, Rachel. And when you get nothing, there's usually nothing to get. He made her up."

I ate my quesadilla slowly, savoring every bite, while he continued munching and talking, never at the same time. He had excellent table manners. Gwen had trained him right. If anything, Rosie waited too long after each bite to return to listing reasons why the firebug stalker from hell could not possibly exist outside our suspect's imagination.

Eventually I said, "None of that matters. She's real."

"Rachel, I know you've got great instincts, but I've got twenty years on the force. And I'm telling you, if this chick was for real, I'd've found something. Maybe only just a tiny crumb of something, but something. When I find absolutely nothing, then there's nothing to find."

"I respect that, Rosie."

"Good."

"But I was there. I was there listening to the guy when he told us about her. And I'm telling you, he wasn't lying."

Rosie met my eyes, tipped his head sideways, nibbled on one last chicken wing. After he put down the bones and used the provided wet wipe, he nodded. "Okay, let's say she *is* real. Then she's covered her tracks awful damn well."

I nodded. "What about her car? He described her car. Can we look for that?"

"A silver Chevy Cruze," Rosie said. "One of the most common cars in *the* most common color."

"Hmm." I sipped my soda and racked my brain. But I didn't see any way to track her down. "Is someone watching him? I mean, maybe she'll try to see him again."

"Not 24/7, no. We don't have the manpower."

"Well, what about the hacksaw?"

"Nothing on that hacksaw linked it to anyone. Only to the fire."

I sighed in frustration. "Dammit, I'm sure she's real. Rosie, you know that I know things, right? I need you with me on this. I want to find out who set that fire and see to it that they get put behind bars for what they did to Mason."

"And those kids. And their mamma, right?"

"Naturally." But this was also personal. That bitch, whoever she was, messed up my man. And she was damn well going to pay.

I just had to find her first.

"Thanks, Rosie," I said, finishing my drink and digging out my credit card so I could hand it to the next waitress who passed by. "You'll keep digging, right?"

"I promise. And you're not buying my lunch."

"I invited you. Don't be a chauvinist." The waitress swept over and took my card before he could argue any further.

Mason's cell phone rang at two in the afternoon. He had been working, but that had turned into napping. It hadn't been intentional, he'd just nodded off on the sofa like his sixty-four-year-old mother sometimes did after dinner. She would never admit to it, of course. And he understood why. He felt almost guilty when he picked up the phone. Since when did he sleep in the middle of the day?

"Mason Brown," he said when he finally shook enough sleep from his brain to locate the damn thing, which was on the coffee table right in front of him and nearly dead, by the way. *Note to self: plug in the phone.* He tried to make his voice sound crisp and clear, and not like he was half-asleep.

"Mason? Mason? Is it you?"

That voice blasted any remnants of mist from his mind. "Marie?"

"Are you alone? I have to talk to you. Mason, they're coming. They're coming after you. I know it. And the boys, too! There are demons in their eyes."

"Okay, okay, calm down. Calm down, Marie."

She was crying softly. Sniffling and sobbing into the phone. It sounded messy. "They're coming. The demons. They're coming."

"Marie, listen, it's okay. The boys are safe, all right? They're safe."

"You have to get me out of here!" A very loud whis-

per this time. As if she was desperate and afraid of being overheard. "They know I'm on to them. They'll kill me, Mason. You have to get me out of here so I can save the boys."

"All right, listen, the boys are safe. I'm gonna come and see you, okay? We can talk then. I'll come tomorrow. Is that all right, Marie?"

"Today! Come today. You have to come today!"

He looked at the clock. The boys would be home soon. He couldn't take them to see her, not in this state. He could leave them with Rachel, but dammit, she'd been doing everything for him and the boys lately. He was afraid he was asking too much. Pushing her too fast.

"I'll come today." He would find a way. She was a mess. And she was sick. He didn't hate Marie. He detested her disease, though. "I'll come today, Marie, all right? Just be calm, do what they tell you. I'll come today."

"Bring your gun. They're everywhere. They're inside the walls. I hear them in there."

"Okay, Marie. It's all going to be—"

"Marie?" someone asked from her side of the call. "Where did you get that cell phone?"

"No. No, don't take it away, no. No! Give it back!"

There was a shrill scream, followed by the sounds of a struggle. Mason closed his eyes in pain for his sister-in-law and held the phone away from his head to dull the noise, but he didn't shut it off. He left it on, waiting. And then a sane-sounding voice came on the line. "Is anyone there?"

"Yes. Mason Brown. I'm Marie's brother-in-law. What the hell is going on there?"

"Um, well, Mr. Brown—"

"Detective Brown," he corrected. "I'm on my way there. And if I find that my sister-in-law has been harmed…"

"I promise you, Detective, it sounded a lot worse than it actually was. We just sedated her and took her back to her room. That's all. No one hurt her. We don't do that here."

"Where did she get the phone?"

"I don't know. But when I disconnect from this call, I intend to find out."

He nodded. "I'm coming up there. I need to see for myself that she's okay. And I'm going to want to talk to her doctor."

"Detective, as I told you, we just sedated her. She'll be out for a while."

"It's an hour-long drive, plus I need an hour to make arrangements for the kids. And I can always talk to the doctor first. If whatever sedative you gave her lasts longer than that, then maybe you're using too much."

"I thought you were a detective, not a doctor."

She was getting short with him. Okay, he probably had it coming. But hearing Marie scream like that…

"I'll be there in two hours, give or take."

"Fine. I'll let the doctor know. Is there anything else, Detective Brown?"

He hesitated, bit his lip, then blurted it out. "I want her room locked, and I want you to make sure no one gets near her until I've seen her."

He heard her heavy sigh, knew what she was thinking. That he'd bought into Marie's paranoid delusions. That he believed her crazy assertions that people were out to get her.

He didn't.

But he was a cop. You just didn't brush that kind of claim off without checking into it first. Period.

And dammit, if he could manage it, he was going to take Rachel with him. But how could he ask that of her, when Marie had drugged her, tried to kill her and damn near gouged out her eyes while she lay paralyzed and helpless, unable to fight back?

How, after that, could he ask her to come with him to make sure Marie was safe and getting the care she needed?

He made a face, but he dialed her number anyway.

She answered with a chipper "hey, Mace" that made him unwilling to spoil her great mood. "What's up?"

He didn't want to dive right into it, so he said, "I miss you. How has your day been?"

"Right. What's going on?"

"You don't believe I miss you and want to know how your day's been?"

"I would, if the undertone in your voice and your phone vibe weren't screaming 'liar, liar, pants on fire.' You know you can't fool me easily, right?"

"I'm not trying to fool you. Jeez, Rache, can't you let a guy ease into things now and then?"

"I don't believe in wasting time."

"So telling me about your day is a waste of time?"

He could almost see her backing down, settling herself. "I walked Myrtle this morning, and we saw a pair of red-tailed hawks sort of dancing around each other over the lake. Well, I saw them, anyway. It was pretty amazing."

"Nice."

"Then I had lunch with a friend, came back here and wrote a whopping thirteen pages on the new book."

"Does it have a title yet?"

"Not yet. I'm mulling."

"Hmm. Who was the friend?"

"Excuse me?"

Aha! Now *she* was the one trying to gloss over something she didn't want to discuss. "Who was the friend you had lunch with?" he asked, curious now.

"Um…Rosie."

"My partner Rosie?"

"Yeah. I wanted to pick his brain about our mystery woman."

"You get anywhere?"

"He doesn't believe she exists. But he's still looking into it. How's your arm?"

"It hurts, but if I take anything I zone out. Actually fell asleep on the couch this afternoon. Like an old person."

"Well, you're not twenty anymore."

"I'm the same age as you, Rache."

"Like I said, how bizarre for a young stud like you to be napping by day."

"Yeah, I thought that's what you said."

"Okay, charmer, you've buttered me up sufficiently. Tell me what's going on."

She was smiling now. He could hear it in her voice, in her breath, and see it clearly in his mind. He hated like hell to wipe that smile off her face, but he didn't have a choice. Not really. "I had a phone call today… from Marie."

She was quiet for a beat or two. Then, "They gave her telephone privileges?"

"No. They didn't seem to know where she got the phone. It was a cell. She was ranting about demons being after her, and me and the boys. Said they live in the walls. Something like that."

"Ah, hell, Mason. I'm sorry." She sighed heavily into the phone. "You know, in all the spiritual systems out there, everything I've researched to write my books, everything I've read, every guru I've talked to, no one seems to have an explanation for mental illness. It's miserable. And Marie is not a bad person."

"She tried to kill you."

"Well, yeah. But it wasn't her. It was whatever's wrong with her. Hell, Mason, it's clear why they used to think this kind of thing was caused by demon possession. It takes over entirely. It changes people into someone they're not."

"That's generous of you to say."

"Not really. It's just the truth. So what else did she say?"

"She wasn't lucid, really. She was begging me to get her out of there."

"I don't blame her."

"I told her I'd come to see her tomorrow. She was crying and saying 'today' over and over."

"So then we should go today."

It felt as if every muscle in his body relaxed. He didn't even realize they'd all been tensed up until she said that. "We, huh?"

"Yeah." The word was heavy. As if everything that followed it had all been condensed into those four letters. He heard what she didn't say in that one word— that they were a team, that when he faced tough things she wanted to be beside him—and it made the load he'd been carrying feel lighter.

"I'll get Mom to stay with the boys."

"Or they can go stay with her."

"Either way, I'll pick them up at school, and then we'll head out."

"Are you going to tell them where you're going?"

"No. It's torture for me to know what she's going through. The fear she's feeling, the confusion. No point in putting that into their heads. She's still their mother."

"Always will be. I'll be ready whenever you are. Can we bring Myrtle?"

"Yeah, we shouldn't be inside more than an hour. She'll be okay in the car that long, right?"

"With the doors locked, motor running and AC on," she said. "What car are we taking?"

"Jeep," he said. "I want to drive."

"Yeah, yeah. You hate me looking at interesting sights while you're in my passenger seat. Fine. You can drive."

"I only hate you looking at interesting sights when it means you're ignoring what you're supposed to be looking at. The road."

"I like looking. What can I say? I went twenty years without being able to. Cut a chick some slack, will you?"

He smiled and realized how much better he felt. Rachel had that effect on him. "I'll see you soon."

"Okay."

She hung up. He hadn't, he realized, told her about the return of the home care nurse. In his head, he heard Rachel saying "Sounds like the title of a slasher flick. *Return of the Home Care Nurse.*" Her imagined dramatic tone had him smiling again, despite the thunderstorm Marie's call had unleashed in his head. Rachel had a way of cutting right through shit like that. She got to him.

A knock at the door had him heading through the kitchen with the phone still in his hand. His nurse was standing on the other side of the door, smiling and carrying what looked like a Crock-Pot. It was as if thinking about her had summoned her.

Mason Brown opened the door to let her inside. "I was just going to call you," he said, by way of greeting.

So he'd been thinking about her nonstop, too. "I know I'm early," she said. "I was passing by anyway, and I wanted to see if you needed anything from the grocery store."

"No, but thanks for asking. We're fine. My mother's been keeping us pretty well stocked." She'd brought another batch of premade meals before leaving on her cruise. She'd wanted to cancel when he'd been hurt, but Mason had insisted she go and promised they would all be fine without her.

"Okay." Gretchen set the Crock-Pot on the counter. "Chicken and dumplings," she said. "I made enough to feed an army, so I figured I'd bring the excess over here."

"That was thoughtful. Thank you."

"Oh, it's nothing." She reached up to pick a speck of lint off his shirt and let her fingertip accidentally brush over his neck. "So…why were you going to call me?" she asked softly.

"Um, to tell you not to come over tonight. I won't be here. I have a…an errand."

An errand. More like a date with that horrible woman he was seeing. He was going to feel so much better once he was rid of her. "Good thing I came early, then," she said. "I can change those bandages now, so you'll be all set for later."

He looked at the clock. She did, too. "You have to pick the boys up from school soon, don't you?"

She was certain he was amazed by her insightfulness. He didn't know she'd been watching him, and watching those nephews of his, as well. "I could sit with them tonight, if you need someone."

"I was going to ask my mother—"

"Don't be silly. I'm right here, and I'm at loose ends. I could use a few extra bucks, to be honest."

"Who's staying with *your* kids?" he asked.

She lowered her eyes quickly, thinking even more quickly. She'd forgotten for a second that she'd told him she had kids. It made her seem more womanly. More trustworthy. She would have to come up with a way to explain their absence once she and Mason were together, but she would cross that bridge when she came to it. "Their father has them for a few days." She managed a few on-demand tears, then lifted her head and looked into his eyes. "It's so hard for me when they're with him. They're my life, you know?"

"Yeah. I do know." He heaved a sigh, and she knew he was trying to figure out a way to explain her presence to his bitchy girlfriend later. Then he said, "The boys think they don't need a sitter. Frankly, I'm not sure they do, either. Jeremy's practically an adult, and Josh just turned twelve."

"I get it. So if I'm going to sit for them, we have to come up with some kind of cover story to explain my presence here." She looked around, drumming her forefinger against her bottom lip as if she hadn't already concocted a plan. "I know," she said eventually. "We can say you paid me a little extra to do some housework. They can't argue with that. It's not like they want to do it themselves, and you're not supposed to be exerting yourself, so…it's perfect, don't you think?"

Mason pressed his lips together and nodded. "Ten an hour work okay for you?"

"Works great. I'll run my errands and be back here in about an hour."

"Thanks, Gretchen. I appreciate the help."

Oh, yes, this was excellent. The ideal opportunity. She would be the one home with his boys, prettying up the house and watching over the children who meant so much to him. She would be the image of the nurturer until she found the right moment to get rid of the little rug rats altogether.

This was perfect.

7

I sat in a visiting area that contained an ancient, fat-assed television and several round tables with plastic chairs around them. Comfy I was not. Wouldn't have been even in an easy chair, what with the two oversize orderlies at the door and the patients wandering the hall, coming right in sometimes. Either staring and listening, or pretending we weren't there.

They wore regular clothes. But they had a dulled energy around them. Like a sheet thrown over a lamp. Something was smothering their light. But that something was also the only thing keeping them from going up in flames. I know it sounds bizarre, but that's what I picked up. Volatile, explosive energy being smothered because the only other option was to let it blow.

Mason sat beside me, with Marie across from us.

The last time I'd seen her, I'd been paralyzed, slowly suffocating because my lungs couldn't move, staring up into her face while she got ready to cut out my eyes. She knew that my new corneas had been her husband's. And she'd told me, at what was almost my end, that she also knew he was a serial killer. She'd kept his secret, and it had proved too much for her.

She'd lost it.

I almost did, too.

Mason's hand closed around mine like I was weak and in need of comforting or some sappy shit like that. I rolled my eyes and focused on Marie. She looked back at me. Not guilty. Not remorseful. Not murderous. Just sort of blank.

"I don't have to be here," I said to Mason. I'd said it before. But he'd had a death grip on my hand all the way through this place.

"Yeah, you do," he said. And I heard the rest, the part he didn't say. *I need you here.* And I almost got choked up over it. Yes, I'm a sap where he's concerned. No point denying it.

Then he said to Marie, "You were doing so much better."

Her dull gaze shifted to his. She was skinny. Her cheeks were sunken, which made her vacant eyes seem bulgy.

"What happened to change that?" he asked.

She just looked at him for a second, tipping her head a little to one side. Then she looked past him instead. It was a longing look, that one. And it didn't take a rocket scientist to know who she was looking for.

"I couldn't bring the boys, Marie," Mason told her. "You wouldn't want them to see you like this. When you're better."

She swallowed hard.

"Can you talk, Marie? Can you tell me what's going on?"

Mason's voice was thicker than usual. But I didn't need to hear it to know how he was feeling. I felt the emotion rising off him in waves, like heat off a race-horse.

She looked at him. Just looked at him. There was nothing there. Nothing.

"She was so agitated she was a danger to the staff." The nurse's voice startled me. I'd hadn't sensed her presence, because I'd been completely enmeshed in Mason's feelings. Not just knowing them, but feeling them myself.

Her name tag said Vee Davis, RN.

"She stole the cell phone from one of the CNAs," the thirtysomething redhead went on. "Nurses' aides," she added when I frowned at her. "Donna knew she wasn't supposed to bring her phone onto the floor, so she didn't report it when she realized it was missing." She shrugged. "She's new, was afraid she'd get fired."

Mason nodded. "So the way Marie's acting right now is because she's medicated?" he asked.

"Heavily," Nurse Davis replied. "We didn't have a choice, Detective."

I looked from the two of them to Marie again. There was a little dribble of drool at the corner of her mouth, and my heart ached for her. She'd had it tough. No one knew how tough. Her mind just wasn't strong enough to take it, and it broke.

I leaned a little toward her, and her lazy gaze came back around, rested for a second on mine. "It wasn't you, Marie. You were sick, like your brain had a cold, and what you did was a sneeze. A cough. A symptom. It wasn't you. I've let it go. I want you to know that."

I felt her reaction like a ripple through calm water. She heard me. I hoped it helped her a little.

Mason put a hand on my arm. "We should go."

I nodded, stood up.

"The boys are fine, Marie," Mason told her. "They're

doing really great. You'd be proud of them. And I'm taking good care of them. I got Josh a puppy."

I felt the little leap in her heart when he said that, and I smiled at her. "Wait, I have pictures." I took my phone out, glancing at Mason, and then the nurse, as well. She nodded, but watched Marie like a hawk while I scrolled through recent photos and found the ones I'd taken of the boys with Myrtle and Hugo. Then I held it in front of her almost blank eyes. They shifted a little, and then there was a light in them. Like for just a second she was fully there, a dolphin arching out of the waves. But she submerged again, just as quickly.

I leaned closer, so I could see the phone as I swept my finger across the screen to move to the next picture.

She struck like a cobra, grabbing a handful of my hair in a clawlike hand and yanking my face close to hers so my ear was mashed to her face. "She'll kill you first." Her whisper was wet and rancid, and I cringed away as Mason grabbed hold of Marie, the orderlies lunged into action and the nurse extricated her fingers from my hair. I lost a few strands, I'll tell you that much.

I stood up and stumbled a little, but Mason had my back, literally, arms wrapped around me, holding me steady and moving us both away from Marie, who was by now in the firm grip of one of the orderlies. She'd gone limp, though. No more struggling. I thought it had taken all she had to grab me like that. There wasn't anything left in her.

And then I realized that was an accurate statement on every level. She was like a hollow shell, for the most part. Brief glimpses of emotion, and then nothing again.

We stumbled into the hall, the nurse accompanying us. I was looking back, but Mason turned me around. "You okay?"

"Yeah."

"You sure?" We stopped at the elevator. The nurse swiped a keycard to call the car. Mason smoothed my hair.

"Yeah. I'm sure. We need to talk to her doctor. Find out what the hell they're giving her. 'Cause it's too much, whatever it is." I said it with a quick look at the nurse.

She shook her head. "I'm telling you, she was out of control. I'm not going to let my staff get hurt. I'm sorry she couldn't talk to you, but my people come first. I don't know what to tell you." She shrugged. "Give her some time to calm down and try again. She's not usually like this, you know."

"That's why I want to know what instigated it," Mason said. "Did anything unusual happen before this…break?"

"Nothing I'm aware of."

The elevator doors opened, and Mason and I got in.

"Dr. Cho's office is on One East," she said, then stood there while the doors slid closed on us.

Mason let his breath out all at once.

"Man, that sucked," I said. "Come here." He did, and I slid my arms around him and hugged him close. "You heard the nurse. She's not usually that bad. This could be just a temporary setback."

He nodded against my shoulder. It surprised me the way he kind of curled into me, let me comfort him. I couldn't remember that ever happening before. The guy's only flaw was that he cared too much. And seeing his sister-in-law like that was breaking his great big caring heart.

The elevator stopped, the doors opened, he straightened up and turned around, and we stepped out into the lobby. A quick look at the directory on the wall sent us in the direction of Dr. Cho's office.

He was as small as a jockey, with the shiniest blue-black hair I'd ever seen and a perfectly centered soul patch beneath his lower lip, and he answered our knock himself. "Come in, come in. I've been expecting you." He opened the door wider and waved us inside. "You're Detective Brown, yes?" he asked as we walked in. He looked Mason up and down, sizing him up and not hiding it one bit.

"Yes. I'm Marie's brother-in-law," Mason said, extending a hand. Dr. Cho shook it, then looked at me just as thoroughly. Not like he was leering, more like he was truly interested in people in general and us in particular. "And, you are Ms. de Luca. The writer."

"Good to meet you, Dr. Cho," I said.

"Here, sit down." He hurried toward the desk at the end of the room but didn't sit down behind it. He just paused to grab a file off it before heading to a sitting area with four leather chairs and a glass-topped coffee table with magazines scattered over it. "Can I get you anything?"

"No, thank you," Mason said, speaking for both of us as we sat in side-by-side chairs. I didn't know antiques, but I had a feeling the massive desk was one, and a valuable one, too, as elaborately carved as it was.

The doctor stood behind one of the chairs and flipped open the file. "Yes, I see both your names are listed here on the form."

Mason had insisted my name be added to Marie's privacy forms while he'd been in the hospital and I'd been caring for the boys, just in case anything happened to him and decisions about her care needed to be made. She hadn't even argued. It had touched me that he trusted me that much.

"Your sister-in-law's condition is apparently in flux," he said. His accent was barely there. I'd only just noticed it myself. "She's been lucid, calm and stable for quite some time. But suddenly…there's a whole new set of delusions."

"What kinds of delusions?" Mason asked.

"She saw a demon. Claims it was in someone's eyes. And that it's after you, Detective Brown, and her sons, as well." He nodded at a monitor on his desk. "I was watching your visit with her, hoping to get a clue to what has triggered this setback. What did she whisper into your ear, Miss de Luca?"

Mason looked at me, and I knew he was waiting for the answer, as well. "She said, 'She'll kill you first.'"

"She?" Mason asked.

I nodded. "Apparently we're dealing with a demon-*ess*."

"Dr. Cho," Mason asked, "has anything happened that could've caused this shift in her condition?"

Cho sighed heavily. "I wish I knew. Things happen among the patients, of course. The staff don't always know everything that goes on between them. And that's to say nothing of what might be happening inside her mind."

"Yes, but what about her sessions? What was she talking about?"

Cho took a breath. "Just one thing, really. Her son Jeremy's graduation. She's very upset that she can't attend."

"Do you think she was upset enough to have brought on this setback?"

Dr. Cho rubbed his soul patch with his thumb. "I

didn't think so. But then, who's to say? I suppose it's possible."

"I want you to ease back on the medication," Mason said. "The condition she's in right now is inhumane."

"And yet she still managed to attack Miss de Luca," he said. "The medication is necessary, Detective. Not just for the protection of our staff here, but for Marie's safety, as well."

"Come up with something else, I don't care, but don't drug her into catatonia. Don't make me bring in a team of experts to review your practices, Dr. Cho, because if I do, half of them will be lawyers."

I put a hand on his arm. "Mason, he only wants to help her."

Dr. Cho sent me a grateful nod, but my focus was on Mason. I let him know without a word that I was reading Dr. Cho, not guessing.

Mason read me loud and clear, just like he always did. He relaxed a little.

"Let me reassure you that this isn't Marie's usual state. She was only this heavily sedated because she became violent, Detective. She's normally fine when she's on her antipsychotics."

Mason nodded, softening visibly. "I want her lucid. I want to be able to sit down and talk to her."

"Your sister-in-law is psychotic, Detective Brown. That's about the disease, not about her meds. You might never be able to sit down and talk to her."

Mason sighed heavily. "I'm coming back here tomorrow. Have her clean by then."

I got up, too, certain the doctor would comply. Hell, Mason even scared *me* when his voice got all deep and commanding like it had been just now. Gave me goose bumps. I settled a hand on his biceps and went with him out the door. He let his anger carry him out through the hospital and across the parking lot while I ran to keep up, and he only stopped at the Jeep.

"I hate this," he said.

"I know."

The keys were in his hand, but he seemed to have forgotten what to do with them, so I took them from him, tapped the button to unlock the Jeep, opened the passenger door and shoved him in.

"It's awful," I said. "She's not even the same person anymore."

"Not just that. I mean seeing her like this is hell, but…"

I had my hand on his shoulder, and I was trying to see what he was getting at in his face, or sense it in his aura, but I was striking out big-time.

He picked up his head, met my eyes and let it out. "I keep getting the feeling there's a grain of truth in there somewhere. She's trying to warn me about something." He waited, and when I didn't say anything he said, "Did you get any of that?"

"All I got was crazy, Mason. I mean, sure, it feels like the truth, but that's because she believes her own delusions. They're not lies to her, they're her reality."

He lowered his forehead into his palm. "She's gotta get better. I can't have the boys seeing her like this, but what if that means not seeing her at all? How do I explain that to them?"

"She was fine a week ago. Well, you know, for a lunatic. And she'll be fine again."

"We don't know that for sure."

"Whoa. Where did this big pile of negativity come from? 'Cause I know it ain't *my* detective."

He shook his head a little, like I exasperated him.

"There's no point mourning her loss until she's actually gone, right? For the moment, and until you have reason to believe otherwise, you have to believe she's going to get back to where she was before this setback. Understand?"

Slowly, he nodded. "You're right."

"Duh. Spiritual self-help author and guru to the masses here, remember?"

He smiled into my eyes.

Inner Bitch woke up from a blissfully long nap. *Say it! It's the perfect moment. Just say it!*

I opened my mouth. I closed it again. Then I turned and walked around the Jeep, got in behind the wheel, buckled up and started the motor.

He turned, closed his door and faced front.

I put the Jeep in gear. And then I blurted, "I love you, too, by the way." Then, while he gaped at me, I held up a hand. "I've known it since you almost got killed rescuing those kids. So just accept it, okay? We don't need to *talk* about it. Right?" I widened my eyes at him. *"Right?"*

"Right! Yeah, of course we don't. What's to talk about, really?"

"Exactly. It doesn't have to *change* anything."

"Of course not. I just…"

"Just what?"

He shrugged. "I'm really glad to hear it."

"Cool. So…we're good, then."

"Better than good, Rache. I think we have been for a while now."

I rolled my eyes. "Don't get all mushy on me."

"Oh, *hell* no. Not gonna do that."

"Nothing's different. We've just…said it, that's all. Everything's just the same."

It was a stupid thing to say, and he was only nodding so enthusiastically because he didn't want to call me an idiot at this delicate point in our *relationship*. But I *was* an idiot. Because you couldn't say that shit and not have it change anything. Hell, it changed *everything*.

Marie was struggling not to let the tranqs drown her. It had taken every bit of concentration, every bit of will she possessed, to grab Rachel and try to warn her.

But they just thought she was crazy.

Hell, that's because I am.

She'd been stupid, trying so hard to get them to listen, the doctors, the staff…anyone. But they would never listen to a murderous lunatic like her.

She'd become frustrated, lost her temper. She'd raged against them, forgetting, for a moment, that she had no power here. They had all the power. She had to play their game.

So she wasn't going to act out anymore, because she couldn't dodge the injections. The pills, yes. But not the injections. So she had to act as docile and lamblike as she could possibly manage. Until the drugs left her system and she regained control of herself. Then she could take action. Not now. Now she was a rag doll with a brain. A broken brain, but still…

She should have played it this way to begin with. Why had she ever thought they would believe her?

No one would believe her.

No. Someone would. The boys. They would listen. She was still their mother.

I have to get out of here. I have to get to my boys.

Marie caught herself gripping the arms of her chair until they were vibrating. The drug's effects were beginning to fade. She couldn't let the agitation take hold or they would just give her another shot. She took deep breaths and pretended to be relaxed. Sometime overnight she would get her strength back. Until then, she decided, she would make her plan.

Gretchen cleaned Mason's house, imagining herself living there. Oh, she didn't think it would happen anytime soon, but certainly that was where things were headed. She was acting like a partner, not an employee. He would see that, and then he would understand.

She vacuumed the entire place, cleaned the kitchen till it sparkled and was about to start on the bathrooms when Jeremy, the older boy, stepped into her path at the foot of the stairs.

"Can I help?" he asked.

He was tall, very lean. His collarbones showed through his "Grand Theft Auto" T-shirt. His hair was too long, and it curled at the ends. He was an obstacle. He was in the way between her and Mason.

"That's okay. I'm getting paid to do this."

"Yeah? I think you're getting paid to babysit. Even though I'm seventeen and my brother just turned twelve. Uncle Mason's overprotective."

She smiled. "Well, he's also kind of laid up and in need of help with the housework."

"But he has no prob making us do that. And I'm feeling guilty sitting on my ass and watching you work, so...?"

She smiled at him, but she wasn't about to have his uncle walk in and see the kid scrubbing a toilet. She had to be the nurturer. The mother figure, in Mason's eyes.

"I just put some cookies in the oven. You can watch them for me while I clean the bathrooms."

Jeremy tilted his head as he studied her. "Look,

I don't want to butt in, but it's pretty obvious you're crushing on my uncle."

"What?"

"I just don't think it's fair not to tell you that it's never gonna happen. He's crazy about Rachel. You should know that."

"What makes you think I'm interested in your uncle?"

He shrugged. "I'm just saying—in case. Anyhow, there's no way I'm letting you clean our bathroom." He crossed his arms over his chest.

He was *defying* her? Her eyes narrowed, and she spoke in a taut staccato. "As I said, *Jeremy,* I'm getting *paid* to do this. Don't get in my way."

She saw his eyes widen in surprise, and he took a step away. At the same time she heard the front door-knob turning. Quickly, she plastered a smile on her face and said, "Had you going, there, didn't I?"

The kid sighed in relief as Mason walked in. "Wow, something smells fantastic in here."

Gretchen turned her smile up to high beam and tried to look surprised. In her mind, she was in a scene from an old sitcom, the dutiful and cherished wife, wearing a red-and-white-checked apron, a wooden spoon in her hand, the kids content and cookies in the oven, basking in the adoring gaze of her hardworking husband, just home from a day at the office. He came farther inside, smiling at her as she'd known he would.

Then the fat, ugly dog came snuffling in, stopped and looked in her direction, though oddly, not *at* her, and growled deep and low. Right behind the dog, *she walked in.*

Rachel stepped into the kitchen, took one look at

Gretchen, and then shot a look at Mason. "Are you fucking kidding me?"

"I was just getting to that," he said.

The bitch smiled, sort of, like she thought things were so absurd it was funny, and lifted her hands. "So get to it, then."

"Rache, come on," he said, leaning close to her and trying to speak softly. Gretchen had to strain to hear. "She needed the job, she'd been *hired* for the job, and she'd have been in a financial mess without it. We talked about the dress code."

"Mason, a woman who shows up dressed like that has more on her mind that her financial status."

He lowered his head and smiled suggestively at her. "Luckily all I have on *my* mind is you."

Gretchen's fists clenched at her sides. And then that woman looked her way, gave a self-deprecating shrug and said, "The cookies smell good."

But then she got this look in her eyes. They were a striking light blue, and the contrasting dark brown of her hair made her eyes look almost backlit. But it wasn't the way they *looked* that sent apprehension trailing up Gretchen's spine like an icy finger. It was the *feeling* they gave her. She felt naked. Exposed. As if the top of her head had been peeled back and Rachel de Luca could look inside and see everything. She'd done her homework, knew all about Mason's girlfriend and her work. But she hadn't been prepared for that feeling.

"Excuse me for a minute, my phone's vibrating." Gretchen pulled a cell from a pocket and pretended to answer a call, then held up an "I have to take this" finger and hurried through the living room to the back door, and then outside. She closed the door behind her, yapping to a nonexistent caller as she walked around the house until she was out of their sight.

Then she lowered her hand and stood there, trembling.

That woman—Rachel—she was dangerous. She was going to have to go sooner than originally planned.

8

"I think you scared her, Rachel," Jeremy said, staring at the door the woman had just gone through. "She's *weird*."

"I got that feeling, too," Rachel said. Mason noticed that she was still frowning at the door Gretchen had exited. "Something's off about her. And I mean something besides the fact that she'd like to tear your clothes off and bang your brains out."

"Really?" Mason asked. "I didn't pick up on anything."

"That's because you were blinded by her boobs," Rachel shot back. "Honestly, Mason, if you can't tell when a woman's gunning for you, you shouldn't call yourself a detective."

Joshua laughed. They all looked his way. He was on the far end of the living room, completely intent on the puppy, who was sitting just as nice as you please in return for a treat. Mason noted the empty cellophane bag on the floor and said, "Uh, Josh, how many have you given him?"

"I dunno. But it worked! He did it! He learned sit!"

"If you fed him that entire bag, you'll soon be learning about sh—something that sounds like sit," Rachel said, with a mischievous look at Mason. "See? I'm working on it."

No sooner did she say it, than they heard the nurse's car starting up out front. Mason looked out the window just in time to see Gretchen driving away. "Huh. I guess you *did* scare her off, Rache."

"Good. If she shows up again, I'll scare her even harder." She poked him in the chest with a forefinger. "Why didn't you tell me she was back?"

"Because I was afraid it would piss you off." He furrowed his brows. "Actually, I was *hoping* it would piss you off. 'Cause you know, it's good for my ego when you get all jealous. Thank you, by the way."

"*De nada.* So why did you hire her back, anyway?"

"It wasn't…*intentional.* I was talking about her unprofessional clothing, and the next thing I knew she was in tears, thanking me for a second chance and promising to dress appropriately next time."

Jeremy said nothing, but he had a knowing expression. Like a teenager could know anything about an adult relationship, Mason thought. Still, he made a mental note to ask Jere just what he thought he knew later.

The timer went off, and Rachel opened the oven, grabbed a pot holder and took out the pan of cookies. "Well, at least she bakes."

"They're probably not as good as *your* cookies," Mason said, in an exaggerated act of placation.

"Just keep it up, big guy, and you'll be wearing them." She shook her head. "Lucky for you, I'm not the jealous type."

"Then why were you looking at her like your eyes contained phasers set to kill?"

"You know I can't stay mad when you use *Star Trek* references," she said.

He dusted off his shoulder in false pride. "I've been brushing up on them just for you. Seriously, though."

"I don't know. She was putting out something pretty high voltage. It was jarring, like nails on a chalkboard, but she ran out of here before I could figure out what it was."

"You sure that wasn't just a 'get up out of my sand-box' sort of reaction?" Mason asked.

"You wish."

"Yes. Yes I do. I'm imagining the two of you mud wrestling over me right now."

"Fuck you, Mason Brown. With a cactus."

His eyes widened, and he sent a look at the boys. Josh was playing with the puppy and out of earshot, but Jeremy was holding his stomach and gasping for air, he was laughing so hard.

"Sorry," she muttered. "You boys should put out a swear jar. I'd fucking make you rich. Oh, shit, I just did it again, didn't I?"

Mason lowered his head, shaking it slowly and trying not to let his smile show. Damn, but he loved this foul-mouthed female of his a lot. And she loved him back. *That* was some development right there.

In an obvious attempt to divert attention away from herself, Rachel called, "Josh?" And when he looked at her, she nodded toward Myrtle, whose head was turned in his direction, a pathetic expression on her face. Josh got her meaning immediately and jumped to his feet, ran to Myrtle and knelt in front of her, wrapping his arms around her neck. "Don't worry, Myrt. You're still my number-one girl."

"That's what *he* said," Jeremy muttered with a wink at Mason.

"You're not helping, kid."

Rachel rolled her eyes. "I'm over it already. I trust you thoroughly, Mason. It's kind of shocking to me to hear myself say it, but apparently it's true. My inner bitch—excuse me, inner beyotch—has decreed that there's just no bad in you. And my NFP agrees with her finding, so you're off the hook. Keep the sexy nurse as long as you need her. I'm cool with that."

"I don't find her sexy at all," Mason said.

"Then you're gay," Rachel replied.

Jeremy slapped his thigh and roared.

"Can we just get some dinner already?" she asked. "My belly button is touching my backbone over here." Mason picked up the phone. "Chinese or pizza?" They had limited options. It was a small town, and those were the only two places that delivered.

"Chinese," Josh yelled. "I'm sick of pizza."

"Ribs," Rachel said. "I'll even volunteer to go pick 'em up."

"I'll go." Jeremy said. "Josh can come with. You guys can call in the order while we walk the dogs. It's time for Hugo to go out again."

Josh grabbed the puppy, ran to hug Mason goodbye, then turned and hugged Rachel around the middle. She hugged him right back and didn't squirm at all. In fact, she closed her eyes and ran one hand over his hair.

At some point, probably while he'd been on his ass in the hospital, Mason realized, Rachel had fallen in love with the boys, too. He felt a swell of emotion she would have denied could exist and tried not to let his smile look too sappy when she met his eyes.

And damned if hers didn't look kind of sappy, too.

* * *

Okay, I talked a big game, but the truth was, I *was* bugged by the return of Nurse Goodbody. I hadn't lied when I said I trusted Mason. Hell, when I told him what I had in the car—you know, the L word stuff—he'd grown two inches taller in his seat.

Not right away. First he'd looked at me, then away, then back at me again, like he was trying to decide if he'd heard me right, and then finally he just said, "I'm really glad to hear it."

And I said, "Cool. So…we're good, then."

"Better than good, Rache. I think we have been for a while now."

I rolled my eyes. "Don't get all mushy on me."

"Oh, *hell* no. Not gonna do that."

"Nothing's different. We've just…said it, that's all. Everything's just the same."

That was pretty much it. The main thrust of our deep and emotional discussion about our relationship's evolution. And that fact served as further proof that he was the perfect man for me. I loved him. I'd told him so. And the earth hadn't turned into a mucky swamp of emotional quicksand and sucked me in.

That really was pretty cool. And it had continued to be cool all the way home, until I walked into the kitchen and saw that nurse bitch playing Suzy Homemaker in my detective's kitchen.

I don't know if it was because we'd used the L word or what, but something unfurled in my belly at the sight. Something that felt like a fire-breathing dragon. It wanted to take her out. I didn't like feeling that way and knew it was ridiculous anyway, so I tamped it down, but damn. It was big and mean and all fired up.

I meant what I'd said about Mason, too. He *was* good.

Not a deceptive bone in his ridiculously hot body. I really did trust him. Hell, I knew his deepest darkest secrets. Worst thing the man had ever done in his life was cover up the fact that his dead brother was a serial killer. And he'd done that out of love for his nephews.

Him I trusted.

Her I did not. Nurse Sexpot had something going on. I'd gotten a whiff of it as soon as I'd let go of my jealous snit long enough to notice what was happening. And I was pretty sure I couldn't drop the issue until I found out what it was. I know. That's like totally the opposite of what any of my books say to do in this situation.

So fucking sue me. I'm wrong, and I'm doin' it anyway.

Dr. Cho couldn't get the things the detective had said out of his mind. Something was bothering him, but he couldn't figure out just what. So he pulled all the day-to-day notes on Marie Rivette Brown's case, focusing on the ones just before this latest psychotic break, and took them home to study them.

Then he hit on it. Marie's first episode of panic and violence had happened outside, in the gardens. A nurse had been with her, and she'd hit her panic button to summon the orderlies. Perfectly in keeping with stated procedure. But the thing was, this nurse shouldn't have been with Marie. She wasn't one of Marie's nurses, wasn't even assigned to Marie's floor.

Her name was in the notes. Gretchen Young.

He picked up the phone and dialed the hospital, then waited to be put through to Human Resources. "This is Dr. Cho. We have an RN by the name of Gretchen Young who was with one of my patients during a recent break. I need a word with her. Can you look up her contact information for me?"

"Hold on, Doctor." There was some clicking of keys, then the efficient female voice returned. "Ms. Young no longer works for us, Dr. Cho. She left two weeks ago."

"Do you know where she went?"

"As a matter of fact…" More clicking of keys. "She took a home care position. And we had a reference check from the Binghamton PD."

"The police department?"

"Yes. She has a temp job taking care of that cop who got burned saving the kids a while back. Nice gig."

He frowned. "Detective Mason Brown?"

"Yeah, that's the one."

"Do you have a telephone number for Nurse Young?"

"Of course." She read the number, and Dr. Cho wrote it down. "Thank you," he said softly. "You've been quite helpful."

He hung up the phone. Well, this was just odd. Surely a coincidence, but he had to make sure, didn't he? Because this nurse had been with Marie when she'd had her break, and now she was working for Marie's brother-in-law. And Marie's delusion had to do with someone being out to harm her family. So if there was some connection between Gretchen and Marie's family, something Marie could have misinterpreted or built up in her mind into something dark and horrifying, that might be the key. He needed to determine if that was what had sent his patient into such a state.

He needed to talk to Gretchen Young. And afterward maybe to Mason Brown again, as well.

Gretchen paced back and forth across the worn linoleum floor of her apartment, chain-smoking and talking her way through the situation. Things were not going as smoothly as she'd thought. It wasn't that he wasn't attracted to her. It wasn't that he didn't want her. He did. It was just that there were too many things coming between them. Too many distractions.

Those kids. And Rachel. That evil bitch was going to be a pleasure to kill.

But the kids first, because that would be easy. She could have killed them today, while he was driving all the way to the psych hospital to visit that lunatic Marie. Of course, if they died the first time he left her in charge of their care, even if it looked accidental, that would have been bound to have a negative impact on his feelings for her.

At least for a little while.

Peter had known she was the one who set his stupid wife's house on fire. He'd blamed her right away. Not that it mattered. Peter was a mistake. He wasn't her soul mate. She'd known that the first time she set eyes on Mason.

Still, the mess with Peter had happened for a reason. Everything did. It had happened so she could learn from it. She wouldn't make the same mistake again. When Mason's kids died, he wouldn't blame her. He would turn to her for comfort instead.

And then she had a brainstorm.

Wouldn't it be great if it looked as if Rachel had done it? Two birds, one stone. Well, three birds. Five if you counted those irritating dogs.

But no, he would never believe Rachel had done it. It had to be someone he already knew was capable of…

Oh. Oh, yes, that was it. Of course.

Marie.

Okay, so she had to take it slow. She had to arrange things just right. She had to—

Her phone was ringing. It was probably Mason, calling to apologize for Rachel's rudeness and invite her back over to share cookies to make up for it. She'd been imagining just this scenario in her mind. He would have been angry at Rachel for acting the way she had. They'd probably argued about it, and she had more than likely stormed out and gone home, petulant and childish. Mason would hate that. Now Gretchen would go over there, and she would be the very opposite of Rachel. And she would end up staying all night long…in Mason's bed. In Mason's arms.

It was so obvious he was the one. She'd never given any of her men her real name before. She'd always used a pay-as-you-go phone from Walmart so she could throw it away when things went bad, and things *always* went bad. This was the first time she hadn't gone into a relationship already sure it was doomed. This was the first time she'd given a man her real name. Her real phone number. The one she used for work and for family. This was the first time she'd shown a man her true profession, let him see inside her world, even a little bit.

The phone was still buzzing in her hand. Her heart racing, she put it to her ear. Her hello was breathless.

"Nurse Gretchen Young? This is Dr. Cho, from Riverside Psych."

Gretchen's glittering bubble popped. "Dr. Cho?" she repeated, her mind shifting gears rapidly. Dr. Cho was Marie's psychiatrist. He was calling her at her personal number only hours after Mason's visit. What could it mean?

"I want to ask you about a patient of mine. You saw her just before you left. Marie Rivette Brown."

Gretchen looked at her own lap, one thigh crossed over the other, still hidden under the ugly white scrubs. "What about her?"

"She had a psychotic break. You were the last person to talk to her before it happened. Do you remember what was said? Can you tell me about your conversation with her?"

"You think *I* had something to do with her break?" If there was one thing Gretchen would not tolerate, it was being accused. It didn't matter if she'd done the thing or not. No one better *dare* accuse her. Ever. "I'm a *nurse*, Dr. Cho. I *help* my patients."

"I know. I know you do. I am not trying to blame you for anything here. I merely want to know what she said, what she heard. Maybe something you had no idea would be a trigger somehow set her off."

"She asked me to check in on her family," Gretchen said suddenly. It had come without her bidding, but as soon as she said it, she knew why. Dr. Cho would have checked on her before making this call. He already knew she was working for Mason. She had to be able to explain that. "I told her I would."

"I see." He was quiet for a long moment while her mind threw out a zillion possibilities of what he might say next, along with ten zillion potential answers, sorting, sorting, which would be best. "And did you do that?"

"Yes. I did, and it turned out her brother-in-law needed a home care nurse. Since I have a few weeks until I start my new position, I took the job."

He didn't say anything.

Gretchen listened for his breathing, wondering if they'd been disconnected, and blurted, "Just to fill the gap."

Yes, there was his breathing. She heard it now. Why wasn't he saying anything?

"It worked out for both of us. The perfect coincidence."

"Yes. Quite the coincidence."

He didn't believe her. She knew that. She'd seen him use that same trick on patients to get them to reveal things. That long silence. Crazy people couldn't stand silences like that.

"I'm sorry to hear Marie had a setback," she went on. "She actually seemed pretty solid when I saw her."

"And she didn't show any signs of aggression toward you?"

"No. No, she *thanked* me."

"Then why did you find it necessary to push your panic button and summon the orderlies?"

She didn't know why she bothered continuing the game. He knew. He was on to her, or, if he wasn't, he would be by morning. The doctor was a genius. He would tell Mason that she had been Marie's nurse. He would tell him that she had been talking to Marie when her most recent psychotic break had begun. Between that and Marie's squawking that someone from the hospital was out to do him in, it would be obvious, wouldn't it? Mason was a detective. He would put it all together.

She heaved a sigh, nodded once, decision made. "Dr. Cho, I wonder if you'd mind if I talked to you. Professionally—as a patient...off the record, you know? I have kind of a confession to make."

A long pause. But she didn't babble nervously. Not this time. This time *she* waited *him* out.

"I could do that. I can see you tomorrow, if you wish. But it has to be in my private office. It can be early.

Before hours. No one will see you here, if that's what you're worried about."

"Eight o'clock?"

"My first appointment isn't until ten. Yes. Eight o'clock."

"I'll see you then, Dr. Cho. Thank you."

"Goodbye for now, then," he said, and the connection ended with her phone's electronic reproduction of a click. *'Cause there is no click. Not anymore. It's space. It isn't physical. It doesn't make a sound. But the computers give us a sound so we feel comfortable. Like it's still the old way. Like things are still physical. Like there's still a click.*

She put her telephone down. She would leave it home tonight, so there would be no telltale line of blips leading out to Dr. Cho's place and back. She had cans full of gasoline in the storage shed out back. It wasn't going to be fancy. There wasn't time for fancy.

Dr. Cho wouldn't say anything to Mason because she'd asked him for professional help. He'd taken an oath. After he talked to her at her appointment tomorrow, he would decide what to do. Whether she met the standard for ratting out a patient. I.e., "patient must represent a clear and present danger to a known individual or group of individuals."

The problem was, there wasn't going to *be* an appointment tomorrow. Dr. Cho was going to be nothing but ashes by then.

I spent the night. We made slow, necessarily quiet and therefore incredibly sensual love at 2:00 a.m. I had to bite the pillow. It might've been the best ever.

Man, I gotta tell you this was starting to freak me out a little. Cozy evening with the kids, curling up in bed with my man—and without my bulldog, I might add—all content and blissed out. What the hell new sort of Rachel was this, anyway? I didn't recognize her. She was like the new girl in town. And I didn't know if I liked her just yet.

Jeremy made us all French toast in the morning, saying Misty had taught him how. He did a damn good job of it, too. Mason said it was far superior to Jeremy's last effort at French toast. So we ate, and then went our separate ways. Jeremy drove Josh to school in Mason's Jeep. After they left, I said goodbye to Mason, called Myrtle and started to head for my car.

Mason caught up to me, though, grabbed hold and spun me around like he was Clark Gable and I was Vivien fucking Leigh. He tugged me flat against him. I grinned, flipped my hair and leaned back. And then he kissed me like that, all bent backward over his arm and shit.

When he broke off and started to straighten, I grabbed a handful of his shirt in my fist and pulled him down again. "You don't want me to leave, just say so."

He sighed. "You can always come back tonight."

"Or you guys can come over."

"Um, yeah, but…we have a new puppy and you have imported Moroccan walnut floors or some shit like that."

"I've been a real snot about my house, haven't I?"

"I did not say that."

"No, you didn't have to. I'll admit, it was a tough adjustment, having the boys there, but the end result was that I had to relax about it. And I'm better off for it."

"Yeah?"

"Yeah. So bring little Hugo. I'll put papers down. That's what normal people do, right?"

"I guess so." He gave me a lopsided smile, flashing only one of the dimples of death at me, but it was enough to make my liver quiver.

"I gotta go," I said, reluctant as hell. "I have a deadline." *And a horny nurse to check out.*

"Okay. We'll come over for dinner. You want us to get takeout?"

"No. I'm gonna cook. Something amazing. Like… pot roast."

"You know how to cook pot roast?" His eyebrows went up. Myrtle barked. She'd left my side to go around to the passenger door and was now demanding someone heft her porky ass into the car.

"Well, of *course* I know how to cook a pot roast. Everybody knows how to cook a pot roast. And stop looking so surprised."

"I'm not surprised. I'm a little bit *afraid…*" He headed around my car, opened the door and obediently lifted the princess into her seat, then buckled her harness. He took her goggles from around the shift and put them on her, then added her scarf and patted her on the head.

I stood there watching him. And you know what, I had to admit, all sarcasm aside, things were pretty damn good in my life right then.

It was a little scary how good they were.

He closed Myrt's door and came around to mine. "Have a good day. And you're not cooking a pot roast, although I have no doubt you'd cook the hell out of one. I'll just have to wait for another time to find out for sure. I'm taking you out to dinner tonight." He kissed me again before I could swat him for doubting my potroasting abilities, much as he might deny it. I got behind the wheel of my T-Bird, ran my hands over her black-and-yellow steering wheel, and forgot all about that.

Yeah. Things were good in my life. I started her up and listened to her purr.

"Later, babe." I told him, then I closed the door and took off, eager to get my day's work done and call my sister to ask her how the hell to cook a pot roast. I'd said I could do it, so I was damn well going to know how. Because at some point, Mason was going to be expecting a friggin' pot roast.

It was too early in the day to put the top down, but I rolled Myrt's window down for her, so she could gobble up the wind like it was made of pizza.

9

"Holy shit," said my right-hand woman, Amy, when I met her on the way to my own front door. Today her work attire consisted of black skinny jeans, a torn, off-the-shoulder T-shirt and a three-foot-tall stack of files. She'd arrived for her day's work on time. I was the one who was late.

"Holy shit, what?" I asked, fumbling for my keys.

"Holy shit, you're…smiling. Almost glowing." She frowned at me over the top of the files, blowing her long, bloodred, sideswept bangs out of her eyes. "Are you pregnant?"

"God forbid."

Myrtle bumped her in the shins, bulldog for *pet me immediately or the next time I'll leave a bruise*. This was unfortunate for Amy, since her arms were loaded down with file folders and she couldn't have petted Myrt if she'd tried. I got the door unlocked, swung it wide-open and quickly punched in the security code so the pesky alarm wouldn't go off. I hated that thing.

Amy trundled in behind me, hurried across the living room and dropped the files onto the coffee table. Then she finally knelt to give Myrtle her due. I could see the front of Amy's T-shirt now. A gothed-out version of Hello Kitty. With fangs. The folders slid sideways, spreading themselves out into what looked like a more comfy position.

"So why are you in such a happy mood?" she asked.

"Why are you accusing me of being happy?"

"It's Mason, isn't it?"

I shrugged. I didn't have any intention of turning into one of those sappy-ass females who waxed on about how in love they were. I mean, really, just shoot me now. "What are all the files about?"

"Maura."

I froze where I was standing. "Maura? As in Maura Kelley?"

"Is there any other Maura?"

I blinked at the files, then at Amy. "So why are we gathering intel on the most successful female media mogul in the world?" Maura was my hero. She owned her own network. She wrote books. She had a talk show, one of the very few I'd never been invited to be on, even though her guests were usually working in my very own field. She had a magazine. She had the ear of the president. I wanted to be Maura when I grew up.

As soon as I thought it, a little frown pulled my brows together, 'cause it felt a little off. Was that still what I wanted? Interesting that it didn't feel quite on target anymore.

"It's the time of year when her people are booking guests for the new season of *The Maura Show*, and I think it's about time you were one of them. The audio versions of three of your books are coming out right smack in the middle of the new season, too."

I smiled. "I'm not gonna argue with that."

"So I've got the stats on every guest she's had in the

past two seasons. You know, the highlights, their bios, who their agents are, that sort of thing. Trying to find a common thread or two so I know what to emphasize when I send her your dossier."

"Do I pay you enough?"

"Well, there's always room for improvement." She arranged the folders into three neat stacks. "I'm going to make coffee. Have you had breakfast?"

"Yeah. Jeremy made French toast."

"How was it?"

"It was very good. Misty taught him how, and Sandra taught Misty, and you know what a great cook my sister is, so—hell that reminds me. Do you know how to make pot roast?"

"Um, no. And what a weird question."

"I've gotta call Sandra real quick. You make the coffee, and then we'll dive into this stuff." I also wanted to check into Nurse I-made-your-man-some-cookies, but one thing at a time.

"Okay."

So Amy went to the kitchen, and I dialed Sandra, took the phone with me to the sofa and fired up my laptop. Then I typed "Gretchen Young, RN" into the search bar and hit enter.

Sandra picked up the phone. "Hey, baby sister, what's up?" she asked.

"I miss you and your disgustingly perfect family, that's what. How about a barbecue or something before summer's gone completely?"

"Only if it's at your place."

"Done. What are we having?"

"How do I know? You're the hostess."

I made a face at her, and I knew she knew it, even though she couldn't see through the phone. "Burgers and dogs. Let's keep it simple. I'll buy the meat if you'll make the salads."

"Deal," she said. "Now all we need to know is when. So how are you, anyway?"

"Scary good." I glanced toward the kitchen. "I said it back."

"You said what ba— You *did*?"

I smiled, because she'd known exactly what I was talking about almost immediately. "Yeah." I had been dying to tell her, though I wouldn't admit it, not even under torture. "It's not a big deal."

"Then why are you telling me about it?"

'Cause I'm feeling like a giddy teenager and I can't keep it in.

"Because you've had your panties in a knot ever since I told you he said it and I didn't say it back. So now you can relax."

She sighed softly. "I'm so happy for you, Rache."

"Yeah, yeah. Whatev. Listen, I sort of bragged that I could make pot roast. And I don't fucking have a clue how."

"I can tell you how. It takes time, though."

"That's okay, I don't have to do it today. Mason's taking me out. But sooner or later, I *will* need to prove my claim that I can make a pot roast."

"I'll show you next time we all have dinner together."

"When you do, you can meet the puppy."

"There's a puppy? Wow!"

"His name is Hugo. And don't sound so excited. Neither Myrtle nor I are overly impressed."

We said goodbye, and I hung up and looked at the search results. There were several images of several Gretchen Youngs. None of them were her. There was a listing on LinkedIn and a couple on Facebook, but they weren't her, either. And then there was the usual ad that offered to find out everything about anyone for a fee. I didn't need that service, since I was dating a cop.

Dating. Was that still the right word? Was it something more than dating now that we'd exchanged the L word? What did you call it at this stage?

"Who are you stalking?" Amy said. She'd come in from the kitchen with my favorite giant coffee mug in her hand, filled and steaming. She'd waited the full six minutes for my Bonavita to brew a fresh pot. Smart girl.

"Oh, it's this irritating little twit of a nurse who's coming in twice a day to change the dressing on Mason's arm. She's got it bad for him. I just thought she warranted a little checking into."

I turned my chair around and took my cup while Amy frowned at me. "Are you worried?"

"What? That he'll sleep with her? No. I'm really not." I grinned. "That's kind of cool, isn't it?"

"It's beyond cool. So why are you checking into her, then?"

"Him I trust. Her I don't."

"Well, you don't have to." I tipped my head to one side like Myrt when she hears a new word that might have something to do with food. She clarified. "If you trust him, it doesn't matter if you trust her or anyone else. He's the only one that counts."

"Yeah, I know that. Duh, of course I know that. I probably wrote that somewhere."

"You did."

"But she's after him."

"Yeah, but, um, have you *seen* him? There's always going to be *somebody* after him."

"There is?"

"Rachel, the man's a hottie. He's a detective *and* a

hottie. He's like Dreamy McDreamboat. Are you telling me you're oblivious to this?"

I shrugged. "I guess I thought it was just me."

"Uh, no. It's anyone with a pair of working eyes." She clapped her hand to her mouth. "Shit, I'm sorry about the 'working eyes' comment."

I made a face at her, then sighed. "I didn't have a working pair when I first met him. He's even dreamy invisible."

She smiled. "Never thought I'd hear you use the word *dreamy*."

"You didn't. And if you ever say otherwise, you're fired."

She zipped her lips, but bent to reach past me, and closed me out of the browser. "Let this go, boss. Trust me."

"Yeah, this from an expert on affairs of the heart."

"More so than you are."

I rolled my eyes and sipped my coffee, then made my way back to the stacks of folders. "All right, let's figure out what Maura looks for in a guest, then." Sinking onto the sofa, I opened the first folder. The dossier on one Dr. Deepak Chopra. "You pull this off, Amy, and you're a freaking genius."

"So I'll get like a bonus or a raise or something, then, right?"

I scowled at her, but you know what, I *would* give her one. She was probably overdue, and man, did I need her. And she knew it, too.

Mason was sipping coffee, going over the files on the arson case and trying to ignore the way Gretchen's breasts "accidentally" brushed against his shoulders while she changed the bandages on his arm.

He hated to admit that Rachel was right, but she was. He'd been slow to pick up on the signals Gretchen was sending, but now that it had been pointed out to him, it was pretty obvious she had more on her mind than basic first aid. Even though he'd made it clear to her that he wasn't interested.

He felt uncomfortable as hell. He was going to have to let her go, and if she cried rivers and pleaded like last time, he was going to have to ignore her.

He was sitting on the sofa, all the way on the left side, his arm extended. She was beside it. She didn't need to lean in as closely as she had been. And then, when the wrapping was done, she continued leaning in, too close for too long, and he turned to look up at her.

She averted her eyes quickly, but he was suddenly, acutely aware that she wasn't just trying to tease him with her breasts. She'd been reading over his shoulder. He slapped the folder closed. "That's not for public consumption."

"I know. Sorry. I just…it was that case, with those kids you saved, huh?"

He didn't say yes or no. Instead he got up, looked down at his bandaged arm. "Nice job. Thank you."

"You're welcome. I'll just do the breakfast dishes for you, before I—"

"No. You don't have to do that."

"You can't have your burned hand in dishwater yet, Mason. It could get infected."

"I know that. But, uh, my mother's lending me her housekeeper for the rest of the week. She didn't really give me a choice in the matter, so…" It was a flat-out lie. He hated lying. And he was lousy at it.

"I see," she said, and he thought she probably did. Why didn't he just fire her and get it over with?

"Okay," she said, and she was smiling brightly again. "I'll get out of your hair, then. I've got *tons* to do today anyway." She did a little pirouette, but somehow tripped and fell against him. His arms shot up instinctively to catch her by her shoulders. Her hands were flat on his chest. She stared up into his eyes, smiling, and then slowly, her smile died and she inched a little closer.

He set her back—firmly.

"I'm such a klutz." She gathered up her bag while he was composing the words to tell her that her services would no longer be needed. Hell, Rachel was going to hold this one over his head for the next ten years when he admitted that she'd been right.

He kicked himself six ways to Sunday for not seeing it sooner. The thing was, Gretchen was sweet, and her attention was flattering. But it wasn't fair to Rachel. Suppose, he thought, she hired some hot young stud to mow her lawn or something, and the guy was constantly hitting on her. How would he feel?

He would kick the punk's ass, never mind how he would feel.

"Listen, um, Gretchen, there's been a change of plans here."

"There has?" She blinked her wide, doe-like eyes at him. And he felt as if he was about to kick a puppy.

And then his cell phone rang. He glanced at it, irritated, but it was Chief Cantone, so he knew it was important. She wouldn't be calling him otherwise. He held up a finger. "I have to take this."

"Oh, it's okay, go right ahead." She said it with an adoring smile and continued packing up her little black medical bag.

"Brown here," he said to the phone, pacing away a few steps, but taking his file with him.

Gretchen helped out by moving into the kitchen, where she rattled around.

"How's the recovery coming?" Vanessa asked. She sounded tired.

"If I say it's complete, can I come back to work?"

"I'd give up half my pay if you could. And frankly, I think you might have to. There's been another arson incident. Another fatality."

He swore softly. Gretchen glanced in at him, her eyes curious, but then her expression softened. She mouthed "see you tonight" and turned to head out the door.

Dammit. He hadn't managed to fire her yet.

"Where?" he asked.

"North of Syracuse. The house was drenched in gasoline and torched."

"So why are we involved? That's a completely different MO from our local firebug, besides being way outside our jurisdiction."

"Because a witness put a silver Chevy Cruze in the area right before all hell broke loose," Vanessa said. "I don't think it's a coincidence. Do you?"

Silver Chevy Cruze. The same as the car seen a couple of blocks from Rebecca Rouse's house the night it was torched. "Who was the victim this time?" Mason asked.

"Dr. Henry Cho. He was a—"

"Psychiatrist," Mason said. "Marie's psychiatrist. I saw him yesterday."

Vanessa Cantone was quiet for a second. "Well, that's a twist. Is this connected to your sister-in-law somehow, Mason?"

"I don't see how it could be, but…what about Peter Rouse? What was he doing at the time?" It might behoove the guy to torch another house, and maybe even see to it that a silver Chevy Cruze was seen in the area, if he somehow found out one was seen near his wife's house that night. It would give his own alibi more weight, right?

"He was home with his kids. His mother-in-law was there, too."

"How's that?" He couldn't have heard her right.

"She insisted on coming out to stay when the kids were released from the hospital and returned to him. Wouldn't take no for an answer. Said she didn't trust him with her grandkids. Turns out to have been a blessing for him. She insists he didn't leave the house all night. Says she would've known. That she's been watching him like a hawk."

"Because she believed he killed her daughter and tried to kill her grandkids."

"She doesn't think so now," Cantone said. "She's his biggest fan now."

"I'll be right in. Just gotta get dressed."

"Good enough."

Gretchen had driven to the psychiatric hospital after setting Dr. Cho's house alight. She had her old uniform and, more important, her old keycard. She'd lost it once, three months ago, and had to go through tons of red tape to get a new one. But she had, and then she'd found her old one again and kept it. Just in case.

With her uniform and name badge on, no one paid much attention as she made her way through the various locked doors and took the elevator upstairs to the locker room. Once inside, she made sure the room was empty, then went from one locker to the next until she found an unlocked one. She checked inside but found nothing, so she moved on. Eventually she found one that was both unlocked and had another ID tag slash keycard dangling from a hook inside. She took it, because she was going to need two, and then she went back through the halls, making her way to Marie's room.

"Hey, Gretchen," someone said. "You back?"

She turned to see an RN she'd worked with before, but didn't really remember her name. "Just taking a per diem shift. Downstairs. Thought I'd come up and say hi."

"That's nice. How's that new gig with the hero cop working out for you?"

She smiled. "Best move I ever made," she said. "I want to check in on a patient. Catch up later?"

"Sure. Doughnuts and coffee in the break room. Sam brought two dozen."

"Can't wait," she said as she walked on.

When she got to Marie's room, no one was around. She used her keycard and opened the door.

Marie was sitting on the side of her bed with her feet on the floor, hands clutching the mattress on either side of her, rocking. She was agitated. It was clear. Then she looked up and into Gretchen's eyes, and grew even more agitated.

Gretchen didn't waste any time. She held up the keycard she'd stolen. "Brought you a present, Marie." She tossed the card toward her. "You want to stop me? You come on out and stop me. Otherwise…" She smiled and drew a forefinger across her own throat.

Marie surged off the bed toward her, but Gretchen ducked back out of the room, closing the door on her way out.

I took Amy's advice and resisted the urge to start snooping around in Nurse Boobsalot's life beyond my earlier cursory and unsuccessful internet search.

What's more, I continued taking that advice even after Amy had gone home for the day.

I'd hammered out half a chapter on the new book, but it wasn't coming easily. I was starting to feel like I'd said all there was to say on the topic of creating your own reality. Then again, I was just getting the hang of actually doing so. And I clearly had a lot more to learn, or that pesky nurse would never have shown up, right?

So you're back to her *again, Rache?*

Yes, Inner Bitch. Yes, I am. Tell me you're not right there with me.

Hell, yes, I'm with you. I want to march up to her face, grab her by the hair and tell her to get off my lawn.

Me too.

Why aren't we doing it, then?

Because we're civilized.

Fuck civilization.

"This is ridiculous. I trust Mason."

Myrtle thought I was talking to her, and picked up her head. She was under my desk, taking up the space where my feet went. It was her usual spot when I was working at the desk. I'd put a round, plush dog bed under there for her. She kept my feet warm, so you know, bonus.

"Hey, I'm done for the day here. You wanna go for a walk?"

"Snarf!" said Myrtle, meaning "It's about freakin' time," and then she smiled.

I pushed away from the desk, and she got up and came with me, straight to the front door where her leash and my sunglasses and flip-flops were conveniently located. I had changed into my writing uniform as soon as I'd arrived home from Mason's this morning: yoga pants, a tank top and my favorite long gray sweater, because the house tended to stay cool in the summer, even without the AC running. I rarely ever used it. I glanced at the flip-flops and decided to go barefoot. I chose a pair of tinted goggles for Myrtle and slid them on. These were much smaller than her car-ride goggles. More like sunglasses. It was still pretty bright outside. I'd have to get ready as soon as the walk was finished. We had decided I should meet Mason at his place for our date tonight, so we could leave Myrtle there with the boys and Hugo. She hated being alone.

We headed out the front door and down the wide expanse of lawn toward the wrought-iron gate that was supposed to be closed. I was terrible about leaving it open. It was just easier to drive in and out without having to stop and open the damn thing every time.

Past the gate, we crossed our one-lane dirt road. I tiptoed to avoid sharp stones till we hit the bank of the lake and then spread my feet in the soft green grass. Myrtle smelled the air, then trotted down to the water's edge, her nose twitching. I knew she was sniffing for frogs. She loved to sneak up on them. She knew when they'd spotted her by the splash as they dove into the water. But she was getting closer and closer every time. One of these days my blind bulldog might just catch one.

She was amazing, my dog was. Blind as a bat, and queen of the universe. She was like a walking life lesson. I hadn't been like her when I'd been blind. I'd been capable, yeah. Successful, even. But I hadn't had fun. Not like Myrt. Every waking minute was a grand adventure to that dog.

I should do a Myrtle book. *A Blind Bulldog's Advice on How to Live.*

Huh. You know, that's not a bad idea.

It's not, is it? Myrtle makes the best of everything, all the time. If she could talk, she'd tell us all a thing or two, I thought, as I watched her sprounce toward a resting frog, missing it only by an inch or two.

She's smart as hell.

Yes, she is.

And even she doesn't like that nurse bitch.

Dogs have instincts about people.

There must be something wrong with her. Myrtle senses it. Hell, you sensed it, too.

I *had* caught of whiff of something around Gretchen Young, but I had no clue what. But enough of that. I thought I'd decided to stay off this subject.

I sat in the grass and let Myrtle play for a solid hour, and my thoughts turned to Mason's nurse only twice more during that whole time. Then we walked the entire fenced-in perimeter of our property, and Myrt found a thousand things to sniff and examine on the way.

Eventually we headed back to the house, and I went upstairs to shower and get ready for my dinner with Mason. I dressed to kill, in a low-cut black number that showed more cleavage than I actually possessed (women, you know what I'm talking about), and was short and tight enough that I'd be fighting the urge to tug it down all night. (Again, women know.) I don't know why.

You know exactly why. You're reminding him what he's got.

I am not the least bit insecure about Mason.

No, but you are *extremely competitive. You want him to notice you're way out of that nurse's league.*

Only because I am.

That goes without saying. Black stockings, btw.

No one wears stockings anymore, Inner Bitch.

No, not unless they want to drive a man batshit.

Good point. I've probably got a pair around here somewhere.

* * *

The stockings worked.

I took Myrtle over to Mason's. He met us at the door, and his eyes did that sexy thing they do every once in a while, where they travel from my lips to my hips and back again. And then he gave a low wolf whistle.

Jeremy was standing behind him, and he grinned. "You dress like that for graduation and I'm not gonna have any friends left." When I gazed at him blankly, he said, "'Cause I'd have to kick all their asses."

"Oh. *Oh*. Thank you. I think."

He patted his thigh and said, "C'mon, Myrtle. We've got cookies." They started toward the living room.

I leaned close to Mason and whispered, "Are they staying *alone*?"

Jeremy popped his head back through the doorway. "I'm seventeen. Josh is twelve. In some states, we can legally marry."

I looked at Mason.

"We'll be gone two hours," he said. "Three tops. Jere's graduating in a week. They're fine."

I nodded. It made sense. They were good kids; they wouldn't get into any trouble.

"Come on, gorgeous. Let's go before you talk me into ordering pizza and staying home. That would be a waste of a killer dress."

"The only person I care about seeing this dress has already seen it."

He was holding the door open for me. I walked through it. "Careful, woman. You're getting sappy."

"I know, that was pretty lame, huh? It's been happening a lot lately."

"To me, too." He opened my car door, like he had manners or something.

"Sickening, isn't it?" I asked, sliding onto the passenger seat.

He was staring at my thighs.

"Mason?"

"What?" He lifted his head up quickly.

I laughed at him. Okay, I was enjoying this romantic crap. I admit it. "You okay to drive?"

"I don't know. Maybe you should throw a blanket over your lap or something." He winked and closed my door, then got behind the wheel and started his beloved Beast. The motor had this deep-throated rumble that you could feel in your sternum. It was one of those cars that run on a mixture of gasoline and testosterone.

Yep, I was having a great time.

And then I wasn't.

It changed in the forty minutes or so between getting into the car, and ordering the appetizers. Suddenly it felt as if my whole body had been injected with Novocain. I looked at my hand, made it move, but it didn't feel like my own. I laid my foreign hand on my foreign thigh, but it was as if my body were a puppet and I was only pulling its strings.

Blinking, I scanned the restaurant's dim, black-and-wine interior, at the nimbus of light around all the little candles, and how they blended into one if I squinted a little. My head felt small and tight, and then I seemed to break out of it and float above, like a balloon on a string.

"Rachel? Hey, Rachel. Are you okay?"

I realized Mason had been saying my name for a while. I looked down to see him holding my hand, but he might as well have been holding a piece of wood. I watched his other hand dip into his water glass, watched it coming toward me, cupping a few wet pieces of ice and moving to run them across the back of my neck.

I sucked in a breath so hard it hurt and slammed back into my body like a skydiver slams to earth when his chute fails.

Everything in me felt the physical shock and then trembled with its reverberations. That was what I felt. What I *thought*, that was more important. I emerged into consciousness again with only one thought. "We have to go home. Something's wrong."

Mason's face went lax. "What do you mean, something's—"

"We have to go. Now, Mason." I didn't wait for him. I grabbed my bag off the table, lunged out of my chair, and started for the door on legs gone as wobbly as if I hadn't used them in days.

I heard his phone go off as he hurried behind me. Heard him answer it and then say, "Oh, Jesus, oh, God."

My blood turned icy as I looked back at him. "What? What is it?" Grabbing his upper arm, I rushed us both out the restaurant doors, speed walking us to his car.

He unlocked my door first, then ran around to his own. "The boys. The house is on fire!"

10

It was a nightmare.

It had to be. I kept telling myself to wake up.

Mason skidded to a stop behind the fire trucks that filled the driveway and spilled out onto the road. He was out of the car and sprinting, the nice jacket he wore flapping like the wings of a frantic bird, his arms pumping, his face contorted in anguish and effort.

I ran behind him, but I wasn't feeling my feet hitting the ground or the strain of my muscles. I was feeling pain. Mason's pain. Overriding my own.

The house was engulfed, every bit of it being devoured by hungry flames that seemed to hiss and snap at the watery cannons that tried to beat them down. Mason was past the fire trucks, cutting such a sharp turn around the front of one that I thought he'd crash. He didn't. I strained to keep up, my eyes on the blazing inferno that used to be Mason's house. The boys were inside! Myrtle! My heart trembled. My lips formed the word *no*. I took the corner after Mason, trying to scan the crowd for any sign of the kids or Myrt. I spotted Vanessa Cantone, looking less like a police chief than ever with mascara tears streaming. I spotted Rosie,

Mason's partner. He stepped into the path of Mason's mad sprint. Mason crashed into him, and they both went down.

"Mason, wait!" Rosie shouted, but Mason was already on his feet again. Rosie moved faster than I'd ever seen him move, springing up like some kind of overweight Chuck Norris, right into Mason's path again. He put his hands on Mason's shoulders.

"The firefighters are already inside, Mace."

"They're my fuckin' *kids*!"

Mason shoved Rosie aside, and then Rosie drew back, punched him in the jaw and knocked him flat on his ass. Before he could get back up, three more cops were on him, and Vanessa Cantone was one of them.

"There's nothing you can do, Brown!" she shouted. "You'll just keep them from finding the kids and getting them out by distracting them with your sorry ass."

"I'm going in, goddammit." He wrestled free of all of them and made it about two more strides before three firefighters ran out the front door and two more came crashing through windows like divers, hitting the ground, springing up again and running like hell toward us. Behind them the house just…it just folded in on itself like a tower of playing cards. The walls fell inward, the roof collapsed to the ground. A giant blast of sparks and flame shot upward. And then there was no more house. Just a mound of burning debris.

Mason fell to his knees, collapsing much like the house had. He said, "Rachel," in this breathless voice like nothing I'd ever heard in my life.

I knelt down beside him, wrapped my arms around his neck. "They're not in there," I whispered, right up against his ear, but it came out all broken up by sobs, and my face was wet against his neck.

He held me harder. "Cantone, did my boys get out?"

"We don't know, Mason. If they did, they're not here. Maybe they went somewhere. Over to a friend's house or out for pizza or—"

He lifted his head, looking around. "The Jeep's here."

I saw it, far from its usual spot. Someone had moved it away from the fire. One of the firemen, probably. Then Mason whispered, "Jesus, this can't be happening."

I clung to him, and then I said it again. "They're not in there, Mason."

He looked at me suddenly, sharply, maybe finally hearing what I was saying. "Are you…getting something?"

"No. I just… I would be, if they were… When they were in danger I felt it. If they'd been inside, I would have felt *that*, too." *Maybe only if they were alive though, right? But no, I've felt things from the dead before.*

Even thinking of the boys and the word *dead* in the same context made my chest spasm. I had to try not to lose it. Mason needed me. I dragged in a few open-mouthed breaths.

The firemen closed in on the flames, manning their hoses, drenching the monster that writhed and raged at them. The men who'd been inside were near the biggest truck, pulling their respirators and helmets off. Mason pushed himself upright and dragged me over to them, one hand still clasped around one of mine. Not that I'd have left his side. "What did you see? What did you see in there?"

"Nothing, man. There was no sign of anyone inside."

"Did you check everywhere? All the bedrooms? Under the beds? In the closets?"

The firefighters looked at one another, then at Mason again. "We checked the ground floor, two of the three upstairs bedrooms and the bathroom. We didn't get to the farthest room back before it started to go bad."

The farthest one back was Mason's room. Would the boys have gone there to hide from the flames? I just didn't think so. They were old enough to know that when there's a fire, you get your ass out. They wouldn't go upstairs to hide in Mason's bedroom. Right?

I felt something, an awareness skittering up my spine, and I turned fast. Then I started sobbing, clutching at Mason's shoulder and pointing with my other hand.

Myrtle was coming hesitantly across the grass toward me, apparently from the wooded lot that ran along the edge of the property, where Josh liked to play. She was carrying Hugo by the scruff of his neck like a mother dog would carry her pup.

I ran to her, dropping to my knees and skidding across the grass, tearing my black stockings all to hell and not giving a damn. "Myrtle! It's okay, baby. It's okay, I've got you." I hugged her neck, sobbing into her fur. Mason came to kneel beside me and picked up the puppy, holding it beneath his chin. His eyes were stricken and wet. The man was devastated.

"I'm sorry," I told him. "I'm sorry." And I think he knew what I meant. Sorry that I was so relieved to see Myrtle, even though the boys were still missing. Maybe dead.

No, not dead. That just doesn't feel true.

"Myrtle wouldn't have left that house if the boys were still inside," Mason said, and he crouched low and rubbed her head. She was trembling, the poor baby. "Would you, girl? No, I know you wouldn't." He met my

eyes. "They're not dead. She wouldn't have left them, I'm telling you."

"They have to be okay. They have to be."

"Jesus Christ, why weren't we notified before now?" The voice was Vanessa Cantone's, and she was hurrying toward us, yelling into her cell phone. Rosie was beside her, hurrying to keep up. "I want every detail waiting on my desk when I get back, and I mean *every* detail." She hung up just as she reached us, looked at me, at my dress and black stockings and shoeless feet. My stilettos were somewhere on the road. I'd run right out of them and only just now realized it. Then she looked at Mason. "Your sister-in-law escaped from Riverside sometime before five this morning. One of the staff reported her blue Ford Focus missing from the parking lot and her keys missing from her locker."

Mason closed his eyes. "Thank God."

"Are you losing it, Mason?" Cantone asked. "Marie's a homicidal maniac. She *had* to have done this."

"Yeah, but she wouldn't hurt the kids. She wouldn't. No matter how crazy she is, she would never hurt her boys."

He looked at me for confirmation, because we both knew there was no telling what Marie was capable of. But he needed it, so I gave it, nodding and sniffling and knuckling my nose. "You're right. She wouldn't."

Vanessa looked heartbroken. She put a hand on his shoulder. "Mason, I don't want you to get your hopes up."

"Oh, no, no, get your hopes up, Mason," I said, standing and stepping around in front of him so he had to look at me and not her. "You always want to have your hopes up, because you know as well as I do that you

get what you believe in. So get those hopes up and keep 'em there. I am. I am, Mason."

He nodded at me. "I'm right there with you, Rache."

"Good."

He looked past me at Vanessa. "Get as many people onto Marie's trail as possible. Get an Amber Alert out on the boys."

"Mason, we can't put out an Amber Alert until we know—"

"You damn well *will* put out an Amber Alert or you can have my badge right now. Now, how fast can they get some dogs and an arson team in here to verify that Josh and Jeremy aren't in that rubble?"

"I don't know. I'll find out." She turned and made a beeline for the fire chief, a short, stocky man who should've retired two years ago. I didn't know his name, but she was shouting "Tony," so I guessed that was half of it.

"I'll get that Amber Alert out myself, pal," Rosie said. "Worst she can do is fire me. And I don't think she's gonna do that."

Six hours. We sat outside the rubble of the house for six miserable hours. I called my sister, and she came over, took Myrtle and the puppy back to my house, and promised to stay with them until we got there. Myrt needed me, but so did Mason. I couldn't leave him, and *he* couldn't leave the fire. Misty stayed with us. We were all sitting on the tailgate of a Castle Creek Fire Department pickup truck. She was on my right, Mason on my left. We were draped in blankets and sipping the hot coffee someone had brought us. There were spotlights set up all around the house, and a small backhoe was sifting through the still-smoking rubble. They pulled

the remains of Mason's house away in layers, spreading the wreckage into shallow piles on the ground nearby so that other men in protective gear could poke through it in search of remains. Bone didn't burn. Not completely, anyway. I knew that from something I'd read somewhere in my lifetime. Or maybe something I'd seen on TV. If anyone had been in that house, they would find bones. It was going to take all night, but they were paying special attention to that rear corner, where Mason's bedroom had been, and so far...nothing.

Rosie came over to us and said, "You should go home. You should get some rest."

"I don't have a home at the moment."

"Yeah you do," I said. I don't know if he heard me. He was all twisted up inside himself. I didn't know if I could get to him there.

No one had left. No one seemed willing to go. All the firefighters were still there, and so, apparently, were a large number of cops from the Binghamton Police Department. Vanessa was still there, too, along with the fire chief, whose name I now knew was Tony Fuscillo. The arson investigation unit from Mason's own department was also on hand. It was a beautiful night. Just a little bit chilly from the steady breeze, but clear. There were a million stars in the sky, and the crickets were chirping like a chorus.

"I can't leave until I'm sure," Mason whispered. Then he closed his eyes. "Thank God my mother's on a cruise. At least she'll be spared this...the not knowing. The waiting." He shook his head slowly and said, for the hundredth time, "I never should've left them alone."

"Mason—" I began.

Vanessa hurried in our direction and held one hand in

the air, snapping her fingers rapidly. "Where? When?" she asked her cell phone.

We looked at her expectantly, and then she lowered the phone. "We have what looks like a credible sighting in response to the Amber Alert."

"Details, details!" Misty shouted, jumping off the tailgate.

I tried not to smile too soon, but my heart seemed to shed a layer or two of ice at her words.

"The car that was stolen from the psych center parking lot has been seen. Same plate number, the whole nine. A woman matching Marie's description, and two kids matching Josh's and Jeremy's, were inside it."

Mason sighed so heavily I thought he'd deflate like a punctured balloon. But he didn't; he turned to me and he whispered. "They're alive."

"I told you."

He hugged me close, and I cried in relief, then peeled one arm away from him and wrapped it around my niece, who was standing in front of us and blubbering, too.

Vanessa kept talking. "They stopped for gas in Cortland, and a woman at another pump thought the older boy was trying to signal her, so she wrote down the plate number, got back into her car and checked her phone for local news. Saw the Amber Alert and called it in."

"How long ago?" Mason asked.

"An hour. Witness said they got back onto I-81, heading north."

He nodded, jumping down from the tailgate to the ground. "Okay. Okay, then. We have to get after them."

"Hey," I said and took his face and turned it toward me, so he would pay attention. "We have to go home.

To my house—and that *is* home for you now, and I don't want to hear it, so don't start. We have to change clothes at the very least, okay? Every department in the state is on this, probably Pennsylvania, too. Come on. You don't steal a cop's kids and get away with it."

"She's right, Mason," Rosie told him. "You ought to get some food in you, too, and then try to rest some."

Mason nodded at me. "We'll change clothes. Grab some food."

"Takeout," I said. "And then we'll go after them."

"You're crazy. You both need to get some sleep," Rosie said. "Mason, you've only been out of the hospital for—"

I jumped off the tailgate. "Let's go!" And that effectively silenced Mason's worried partner, who could sometimes nag like a housewife. Then, with Misty beside us, we headed back up the road to where Mason's car was still parked where he'd left it. Someone had closed the doors. Misty got into the backseat, I slid into my customary spot in the front passenger side. I'd been in this car so much the seat was starting to shape itself to my butt.

Mason started it up, looked at me and smiled. "They're okay."

"I know they are. And they're gonna stay okay until we can get them back. Marie's a lot of things, but she loves those kids."

Neither of us acknowledged that we were pretty sure she had intended to kill both the boys last Christmas so she could to reunite her family in heaven. Or that she'd framed her own son for her crimes so she could keep on committing them while we were distracted. Neither of us brought it up, but we were both thinking about it. We could pretend we trusted Marie with the boys' lives, but we didn't. We couldn't. And she was so fucking crazy, she could hurt them unintentionally just as easily as not.

But we were choosing to stay positive. To believe the best of her. There was a mother underneath Marie's insanity. A devoted mother who loved her kids even from within the hurricane of madness in her mind. She loved them. I was praying that love would shine through and keep the kids safe long enough for us to find them.

He turned the Beast around and started for home.

Jeremy had been second-guessing himself ever since his mom had shown up at the farmhouse shortly after Mason and Rachel had left on their date. He was sure he'd made a huge mistake coming with her, but she hadn't given him a choice. Even in hindsight, he couldn't come up with a way to get out of it.

She'd knocked on the front door barely a half hour after Mason and Rachel had left, and when he went and opened it, he had so many reactions all at once that he still hadn't sorted them out. But despite everything, she was his mother. And his first reaction had been a surge of gladness to see her that had brought tears springing to his eyes.

He hugged her, and she melted against him, laying her head on his chest and whispering, "Oh, Jeremy, Jeremy, my Jeremy, I've missed you so much." She was shaking all over, as if she was very cold, and she was bone thin. He could feel her shoulder blades and her ribs.

He heard a soft gasp and knew that Josh had come into the kitchen behind him. His mom heard it, too, and she lifted her head and looked around Jeremy, then stepped out of his embrace and opened her arms.

Josh ran right into them, shouting "Mom!"

Jeremy looked down at her as she hugged his brother. She wore scrubs, like a nurse would wear, and as he glanced past her to see if she was alone he saw a blue compact car in the driveway, a Focus, he thought.

She was sniffling, wiping away tears as she straightened up. "I need you guys to come with me. I need to talk to you." She took Joshua's hand and started out the front door, and Josh went right with her.

Jeremy grabbed his brother by the arm and stopped him. "We can't leave, Mom. Uncle Mason will be right back."

"Don't lie to your mother, Jeremy. He's out for the evening. And you're not safe here alone."

"Yes, we are. We're fine, Mom, it's—"

"No. No you're not. There's something you don't know. She's after you. She's going to hurt you. And it's going to be now. Tonight."

"Who?"

She muttered something that sounded like "the demon" but then bit her lip and averted her eyes. "Your uncle is in danger, too. We have to help him, don't you understand? But first we have to make sure you're safe."

In the distance, headlights approached.

"Oh, God, she's coming! Hurry! Hurry!" She gripped Josh again and ran for the car. Josh looked back helplessly, with a "What do I do?" expression on his face.

Jeremy ran after them, leaving the front door open behind him, but he kept one eye on the oncoming car as it passed. It didn't seem like anything other than an ordinary driver just passing by. His mother shoved Josh into the backseat and slammed the door closed.

"Mom, wait!"

"There's no time to wait. Jeremy, come with me.

Please, come with me now. I promise I'm telling you the truth." She raced around the car while she was talking and dove behind the wheel. The engine was still running. She'd never shut it off.

She put the little car into gear, and it began to move.

Jeremy ran as hard as he could, got hold of the door handle and yanked it open. His mother braked to a stop, and he got in. He didn't see that he had a choice.

As his mother sped away, he looked back and saw Myrtle standing inside, her paws on one of the windowsills, staring toward them even though she couldn't see, as if she sensed that something was terribly wrong.

He realized he didn't have his cell phone. Dammit, he should at least have grabbed his phone.

His mother drove onto the highway. He noticed that the built-in GPS was smashed. He kept asking questions, begging her to take them back home or to the police station, *anywhere*, but she had tunnel vision. There was no getting through to her.

He was scared to death, and kept flashing back to Christmas and the people she had killed. He didn't think she would ever hurt him and Josh, but how could he be sure? She'd almost killed Rachel. So he kept grasping at straws, coming up with any excuse he could think of to get her to stop somewhere. Anywhere. I'm hungry, I'm thirsty, I need to use the bathroom. None of those worked, but when he noticed the needle pointing to E on the gas gauge it seemed like a miracle to him. And when he pointed it out to his mom, it worked. She pulled off the highway in Cortland to gas up, warning them not to get out of the car for any reason.

Jeremy didn't want to antagonize her, but he was itching to grab his brother and make a run for it. Then he noticed a woman who was gassing up a minivan at the next pump over. She was visibly pregnant, and there were little kids in the van. He could see them bouncing and wiggling through the tinted windows. His mother's back was to him, so he waved at the pregnant lady until he caught her attention. Then he cupped his hands, breathed on the window and quickly wrote H E L P backward in the fogged glass.

Her eyes widened, and she looked at him and then at his mother, then back at him again. He nodded hard and wiped the glass clean before his mom could see it. The lady nodded, he thought. It was very slight, but he saw her tip her head a little, and he was pretty sure she was looking at their license plate. Then she got back into her car and pulled away.

He hoped she'd understood. He hoped she was even now calling for help.

And then they were back on the road again, still heading north through the night. He had no idea how far his mom planned to take them, or where the hell she was going. He knew she was completely insane. But she was still his mother, and he knew in his heart that she loved him. And she loved Josh. He didn't think she would hurt them.

God, he hoped not.

Never had my place seemed quite so much a haven as it did when we pulled through the gate that night. All the downstairs lights were on, and the house glowed like a beacon, guiding us in from a storm. There was a part of me that wished we could stay. Curl up on my overstuffed sofa, wrap ourselves tightly in the brown fake-fur throw I kept there, Mason on one side of me and Myrtle on the other, and just sleep the horror of this night away.

There had been a while there when we'd thought the boys were in that house, and when it collapsed…

That had been terrible. It had damaged us. Both of us. Because we'd felt the same trauma we would have felt if it had been true, and that kind of thing leaves a wound on your soul. Thank goodness the anguish hadn't lasted very long. It could've been worse. But the damage was probably irreversible.

I'd have to explore that in a book sometime. The actual physical damage done to a person by emotional trauma. And how or whether it could be healed. My inner bitch filed it away for future consideration.

Misty ran ahead of us to the front door. My sister, Sandra, opened it before she got there and folded her daughter into her arms. Christy was right beside her mom, and they group-hugged their way into the living room, making room for Mason and me to walk in behind them.

Jim, Sandra's husband, was right there, too, extending a hand and shaking Mason's, then pulling him closer and clapping him on the back with the other. "Thank God the boys are all right," he said. "How are you holding up? What can I do?"

Sandra released Misty to her twin and wrapped her arms around me. I hugged her back. "I'm okay, I'm okay. How's Myrt?"

"Fine. She hasn't let that puppy out of her sight since we got her home, though. I've never seen anything like it."

She pointed, and I saw Myrtle, curled up in her dog bed with the pup nestled in front of her sleeping. Myrtle was awake, looking my way, but not getting up to greet me. I went to her, got down on her level and hugged her. "She smells like smoke." I sat up a little, and stared at her white fur in dawning horror. "Mason, she's got soot on her face. She must've been inside when——"

"But she got out. And she's okay," he said softly.

Jim said, "We checked her thoroughly. The puppy, too. They don't have any burns, no singed fur. We'd have woken up the vet if they had."

"I've been listening to them breathing, too," Christy put in. She was planning to enter nursing school after graduation. "I don't think they inhaled any smoke."

I leaned close to Myrt's face, scratching her ears just the way she loved. "You're okay, girl. And your boys are okay, too. I wish I could stay here and hug that great big scare away, but I have to go get 'em. Okay?"

She closed her eyes and pressed one ear against my scratching fingers. Then she changed her mind and offered the other ear. Hugo whimpered, and she pulled away from me and pushed her nose into him, nuzzling, checking.

"I thought you hated this little guy?" I asked her.

She lifted her sightless eyes toward me, and then she smiled. She smiled as if to say, "I've got my pup safe and sound. We're good. Now go get yours."

I kissed her face. "Thanks, Myrt."

Then I left her, much as I hated to, and headed upstairs, Mason on my heels. We changed clothes at a speed that had to be some kind of a record, hurrying through my bedroom with our clothes flying off in all directions, like we hadn't done in a while. And for all the wrong reasons this time.

"Thank God I've been leaving some things here."

"Thank God the boys have, too. I think most of their stuff is probably still here."

"It could've been worse."

"Could've been *way* worse, Mason. We were freaking enchanted tonight. It's like there's some kind of protective bubble around us that lets shit get bad, but not *too* bad."

"It is, isn't it?"

"It is," I told him. "I don't know why, but we always come out okay. The boys are safe. We'll get 'em back."

He wrapped his arms around my waist and pulled me close, him in fresh jeans but shirtless. Me in the same, plus a bra. "I couldn't even begin to get through this without you. You know that, right?"

"Yeah. Same here. Fucking disgusting, isn't it?"

"Beyond disgusting, yeah." He kissed me hard, but way too briefly, and then we were pulling on our shirts. Mason donned his shoulder holster, and we started back down the stairs.

"Rachel?" Sandra sounded on edge.

I looked at her standing there at the bottom, waiting for us and scared to death. "We only came back to change clothes, Sandra. We have to go after the boys."

"Rachel, you *can't*."

Jim put a hand on my sister's shoulder. "We know you have to. I'll go with you—"

"No," Mason said. "I don't know how bad Marie is, and—" He glanced quickly toward the twins. "I don't want to see any more kids orphaned." Mason looked at me. "And that means you should stay, too."

"You couldn't make me stay if you drugged me, tied me up and locked me in a room full of cheesecake, Mason. So let's not waste time. You know me."

He opened his mouth, but I locked on to his eyes. "You *know* me, Mason."

Sighing, he nodded.

My sister moved aside to let us off the staircase, then

got up close and put her hands on my face. "Do you *have* to go, Rache? After what she tried to do to you…"

"She's medicated. She's been getting treatment for six months."

"She's not medicated *now*, because she's not in the hospital. Rachel, not six months ago she tried to *kill* you."

"But she *didn't* kill me. And she's not going to. I can help him find the boys, sis. I have to go. If it were your kids and I could help, you'd want me to go, wouldn't you? Well? Wouldn't you?"

She nodded shakily and, head down, took two steps back, hands rag-dolling to her sides. She drew a shaky breath, then said, "Be careful, Rachel. I love you."

"I love you, too." But I didn't hug her, because I was afraid she might not let go. She'd become half big sister, half mom when our parents had died on a second honeymoon so many years ago. She was still trying to protect me, and I was driving her nuts, what with my serial killers and psychopaths and sex slave traders. What with my partner, the homicide detective. What with my penchant for falling into one case after another like I was being pushed there. Like I was being led there. Like I was being *used*, somehow. God knew it wasn't because I was a nice person. I didn't aspire to become a crime fighter. I just wanted to stay the fuck home and write my bullshit-that-wasn't-such-bullshit-after-all books. And love my man and his boys and my dog. Our dog. Dogs.

Damn, things had changed.

"I've gotta go, Sandy." I hadn't called her Sandy since we were kids.

It got to her. She wiped her nose and nodded. "I know."

I hadn't realized that Misty had left the room until she returned, my beer cooler in her hand. Don't judge me. I got the damn thing free in a grocery store promotion and have used it twice in two years. Okay, maybe three times. Or four.

She handed it to me. "Some food for the road," she said.

She'd been paying attention to our conversation on the way over after all.

I took it. Its weight made my stomach growl. "Thanks, honey. Don't worry. We'll bring them back. Both of them."

"I know you will."

Mason touched my arm. It was time. So we headed for the door with everyone telling us to be careful and be safe all at once. And then we were in the car, in the dark, heading for the highway, facing I didn't know what.

It was, I thought, the perfect time for junk food, and I prayed my niece hadn't given in to her health-nut tendencies and had been kind instead.

Oh, yeah. She had a heart of gold, my niece did. There were Doritos, ice-cold bottles of Coke and a stack of leftover pizza. Mmm, sausage and mushroom. This was gonna give me the strength to tackle whatever we were driving into tonight. So I dug in.

Until Mason elbowed me. "You gonna share or what?"

Smiling, probably with pizza sauce on my face, I handed him a slice.

Yes, I was smiling. I was forcing myself to believe the boys were still all right and not in imminent danger from their dangerously insane mother. But deep down, I knew they were. Every tick of the clock was another chance for something horrible to happen. Something tragic. Every second that passed, the nightmare images and fears were bubbling up from a deep, hellish pit inside me. And it had to be just as bad for Mason. Worse.

For once, we were both following the advice I spewed in my work. Not just following it, but clinging to it, literally holding on for dear life.

11

Gretchen watched. She watched all of it. The fire, the beautiful, fierce fire as it devoured the house. She'd poured especially large amounts of gasoline near the front and rear doors, so the kids wouldn't be able to get out. The damn dog had escaped, though. Blind as a bat, that thing was, but it had found a hole somewhere that she must not have covered, and it had carried the irritating puppy out, too.

By then, the first fire trucks had been screaming to a halt on the road out front. She had to back farther into the wood lot across the way.

There had been no reason to make this one look like an accident. Not this time. In fact, this time she wanted it to be an obvious arson that didn't appear related to her usual clever burns. This time the blame would be placed squarely and easily on Marie. After all, she was criminally insane. She'd killed before. And she'd escaped in the wee hours of today. Gretchen knew that because she'd made it possible.

The timing couldn't have been better.

She saw Mason arrive and race toward the house with that bitch writer on his heels. Her plan was to wait until he was completely gutted, on his knees in anguish and all alone. Then she was going to slip away through the woods to get her car, which was parked, well hidden, not far away, and show up as if she didn't know what had happened. She was going to run into his arms, share in his devastation and be his only comfort. She was going to be the one he turned to in this time of grief and loss.

Except her moment never came. Rachel stuck to him like a burdock, and he held on to her as if he would blow away in the next stiff breeze if he let go. Dammit. This was not the way it was supposed to work.

It must have been four o'clock in the morning, Jeremy thought, wishing for his cell phone for about the thousandth time, when his mother finally pulled the car to a stop at the end of a "seasonal use only" dirt track through solid pine forest. They were deep in the woods. Deep. He'd been paying attention, committing every turn to memory—road signs, too, where there were any. He thought he could get them home, or at least back to the nearest town, if they could just get away from her. Better yet, if they could get away from her with the car keys.

"Where are we?" Josh asked from the backseat.

"Your dad's old hunting cabin." His mother smiled when she said it; then the smile turned into a horrible grimace that contorted her whole face and forced tears out of her eyes. She turned away so Jere wouldn't see. But he had. What was *that* about?

"Dad didn't *have* a hunting cabin, Mom," he said. He said it carefully. She was sick. She wasn't evil. She'd never been evil. She was his mom. She wasn't abusive, never hit them, yelled now and then, but who didn't?

She was just sick. And right now she was confused, because he would have known if his father had a hunting cabin.

She sniffed, got herself together, turned to him again with those wide, pretty, "I have no idea what's going on here" eyes that Amy Poehler faked so well. Only on Mom the vacancy signs were for real. There was no one home in there. He didn't know what had happened to his mother, but this wasn't her.

"He *did* have a cabin. *This* cabin. He didn't want anyone to know about it, so he put it in his mother's name."

"Why would Dad need a hunting cabin that nobody else knew about?" Jeremy asked.

The vacant eyes weren't so vacant anymore. There was a spark of some kind of knowing, but she opened the car door and got out before he could figure out what. "A man needs his privacy, Jeremy. When you have a wife and kids of your own, you'll understand." She turned to face the log cabin, a darker shape in the night. Not a light on. Nothing. The place was creepy. A crypt would look cheerful beside it.

"There's power, believe it or not. See the line? I don't know how much he paid to get that strung all the way out here, but he managed it. We just have to throw the main switch. It's in the shed over there, Jeremy, and there's a flashlight just inside the door, to the right, about shoulder level. Go turn it on, will you?"

Jere nodded and turned to his brother. "You're coming with me, squirt."

"Okay, Jere." Josh's voice was shaky. He was scared.

Jeremy took his hand, gave it a squeeze and walked to the shed. Sticks and twigs snapped under their feet, and the grass was knee high. He walked carefully. Behind them, his mother was trying to get the cabin door open. She had a small light of some kind, and he saw her go inside with it, then he crouched down and grabbed Josh by the shoulders.

"We're gonna be okay. You know that, right? Uncle Mason is already looking for us. Rachel, too, and you know she's got that…NFP stuff."

Josh had heard, though he shouldn't have, of Rachel's NFP, and he grinned, just like Jeremy had intended, at the mention of the naughty word in the middle.

"We just have to keep Mom calm, act like everything's fine and not do anything to upset her. All right?" He thought about making a run for it right then but knew it would never work. She was too close, too watchful. He still thought he could talk her down. That would be the best way. The safest way.

"She went crazy before, Jere." Josh's eyes were huge in his freckled face. He looked so scared it made Jeremy's heart ache. "They said she hurt people."

She'd done a lot worse than hurt people. But that wasn't her. That wasn't the real her. Then again, neither was the lady in the cabin. "I'll be keeping my eyes on things, little bro. If she starts acting crazy again, we'll go to plan B."

"What's plan B?" Josh asked.

"We run for it." He pointed. "That dirt road right there is about three miles long. That's not far. Like forty-five minutes' walk. Maybe longer, 'cause we'd walk just inside the edge of the woods, so no one could see us on the road. But we'd keep the road in sight, follow it, so we don't get lost. Then at the end we turn right onto a paved road and do the same thing, stay in the woods but follow the road. Five more miles. Another hour and a half or so, then take a left. Then the first right, and then left at the Y. A mile past that, there's a little town. The last one we passed. That's where we'd go."

"Yeah." Josh nodded hard. "Yeah, that would work."

"Straight, following the dirt road till it ends, then right for five miles, left at the Y, then right again. Go straight until you come to the town. Inside the woods, not on the roads. You got it?"

"Why do *I* have to get it?" His eyes were wide, and Jeremy turned away, looking for the electrical box. "Jere, I'm not going without you, am I?"

"Not unless you absolutely have to. But you might have to. You might be my only chance."

Josh took a deep breath and nodded. "I sure hope Myrtle and Hugo are okay."

Jeremy found the switch and threw it. Then he looked back toward the cabin and saw lights coming on. And his mother in the cabin's doorway, looking out, watching his every move. "You never told me why you decided to name him Hugo. It was one of the names you found on the net, right?"

"No. I was looking, but nothing seemed right. And then I just decided."

"What made you decide?"

"I don't know. It just showed up in my head. It happens sometimes."

"Now you're starting to sound like Rachel. You sure you don't have NFP, too?"

Their mother stepped out onto the porch. "Boys, c'mon now. Get the groceries out of the back of the car and bring them inside for me."

In that moment she sounded perfectly normal. Like Mom again. It made Jeremy's heart hurt. "Coming, Mom," he said, pretending for a minute that they'd gone back in time. That Dad was still alive and Mom was still pregnant with their baby sister, and that life was still normal.

"They could've got outside," Josh said as they started back toward the car. An outdoor light came on, making the journey a lot easier and giving Jeremy a wider view of their surroundings, and giving his mother, he realized, a better view of him. But this wasn't the time to make a run for it. Not yet. They were safe with her. For now.

"*Who* could've got outside?" he asked.

"Myrtle and Hugo. I left the door into the back room open when I put my basketball away."

The back room was a half-finished lean-to slash porch attached to the rear of the farmhouse, accessible via a door from the kitchen. The previous owner used to stack firewood out there. There was still half a pile of it left.

"I don't think you need to worry about Myrtle," Jeremy said. "What's she gonna do, run away from home? She's too lazy."

"She might try to come after us," Josh said.

Jeremy lifted his eyebrows as he opened the car's rear hatch. "Yeah, she might. But she won't get more than a hundred feet from the house. Uncle Mason and Rachel would find her on their way home. She's okay. And so is Hugo."

They took several bags of groceries out of the back of the car and carried them inside the rustic log cabin. It wasn't much. But there were a couch and a couple of chairs, a sagging cot, a big potbellied wood-burning stove, and a kitchen off to the right with an ancient fridge, stove, a small table and two chairs.

Marie took the groceries from their hands. "Shut the door, Jeremy! Before they see!"

He frowned at her, but he closed the door. Then he took the bags back from her and carried them to the kitchen. Josh walked so close he was practically stepping on Jeremy's heels, clutching the small bag he carried like a shield. Jeremy hated seeing his little brother so afraid.

He started unpacking the grocery bags.

His mother looked at him and smiled, her little outburst forgotten. "That's a good boy. You've always been such a good boy."

"You've been a good mom, too," he told her. His throat got so tight that it practically cut off at the final word.

"Well, let's get something to eat. I got everything you love. All your favorites."

Jeremy looked at the items lining the counter. There were twenty-four cans of Campbell's cream of mushroom soup, five loaves of bread, three jars of peanut butter, coffee, a three-pound bag of trail mix, some toilet paper and a bottle of shampoo. Great. This was going to be just great.

Mason's mood was lighter, but only by comparison, because it had been so dark mere hours earlier. Knowing the boys were alive was about a million times better than thinking they'd burned to death. But knowing they were with their mother, that wasn't all sweetness and light, and as the night wore on, that knowledge weighed on him more and more.

Their first stop was the gas station in Cortland, where he checked the restrooms and talked to the employees, but there was nothing to be found. The boys hadn't scrawled a note on the bathroom mirror in soap.

The video surveillance footage was already being

reviewed by the State Police, and the woman who'd phoned in the tip was being interviewed. He would soon know if there was anything new from either source.

After that they got back on I-81 and drove steadily north, and his mood headed south.

It was starting to rain. The drops hit the windshield in a fine misty drizzle. He snapped on the wipers. "This is pointless, isn't it?"

He looked at Rachel. She was sleeping. Head back against the seat and tipped slightly to the right, eyes closed. Dammit, he knew she was exhausted, but how could she sleep?

"Pointless," he muttered, and reached for the radio.

Her hand covered his, but when he looked her way, she hadn't even opened her eyes. "Keep going," she said.

"What do you mean, keep going? We've got nothing to go on. No further sightings."

"There will be. Keep going. We're going the right way."

And that was when he realized she hadn't been sleeping at all. She'd been...doing that thing she did that wasn't ESP. His heart got to beating a little faster than before, fueled by hope. He didn't doubt Rachel's abilities. They were uncanny. They were sometimes even scary. But they were almost never wrong.

So he kept driving.

An hour later she abruptly said, "Stop."

Mason didn't even waste time asking why. He gave a quick glance in the rearview mirror and pulled onto the shoulder. They weren't near an exit, and there was hardly any traffic this time of night, this far north. They were smack in between Syracuse and Watertown. There just wasn't much there.

"We went too far," she said, and twisted in her seat to look behind them.

"When?"

"I don't know. Just…I think we should go back a little ways. Back to the last exit and get off there."

"And *then* what?" he snapped, then wished he could suck the words back in.

She shot him a look. "What do I look like, Nostra-fuckin-damus? I don't know what. I just know what I know, and what I know is that we were closer, and then were farther away, so we have to go back."

"Okay, okay. I'm sorry. I didn't mean—"

"I know." She put a hand on his cheek. "It's okay, I'm feeling pretty bitchy, too."

He pulled the car into motion again, making an illegal U-turn at the first break in the median that they came to, and heading back the other way. He saw the way Rachel relaxed in her seat, nodding to herself.

Hell, he didn't know how she did it. She didn't seem to have much control over it, or she certainly wouldn't have let him leave the kids home alone tonight. She couldn't predict the future, exactly. But she sure as hell was good at finding people. Like a bloodhound. She'd led them to Amy the same way when she'd been kidnapped last year.

They drove another five miles before he saw an exit sign for Parish. He glanced her way, and she nodded. So he took the exit ramp to the end, then sat at the stop sign.

"Don't shoot me, but…which way?"

She pointed at the Dunkin' Donuts sign in the window of what looked to be a gas station and convenience store. "I don't know what else to do. I guess we get some coffee and park this thing somewhere for a few minutes. You can make some calls for updates, and I can…think. And *feel*."

It was, he thought, as good a plan as any.

Jeremy had made them peanut butter sandwiches and mushroom soup for dinner, and then Marie, who hadn't eaten a bite, had insisted it was bedtime and gone outside to shut off the power. He didn't know why but presumed it was either part of the Looney Tunes show going on inside her head, or to make it more difficult for the two of them to slip away.

As soon as the lights went out, Joshua surged off his cot, smashing himself against Jeremy, who hugged him tight. Josh was shaking. Gosh, he must be scared.

Still holding his brother close, Jeremy moved toward the front door and looked out through the dingy glass. His mother was out there, standing in the rain and having an animated conversation with no one. She was slipping.

"Mom's crazy, Jere," Joshua whispered. "She's *crazy*. I love her and everything, but—"

"It's not her fault. Her brain is sick."

"I know that, I just don't want to be here. We've got to go, Jere."

"Not yet."

"Why?"

"'Cause I'm gonna try to talk to her first. Try to get her to take us back on her own."

"But I want to go *now*."

"We'll have a better chance if we can get her to take us to a town. Look, if we run away and she catches us again…it might get bad."

"You think…you think she'd hurt us?"

"I don't think so. But just in case, we don't want to

do anything to upset her. We're gonna do everything she says, and be respectful and nice to her. Just keep her calm until we have our chance. Understand?"

"I guess."

"Just hang in there a little longer, okay, Josh?"

"Okay."

"Here she comes, get back in bed now."

Josh did as he was told. Jeremy's eyes hadn't adjusted to the darkness yet, but he could hear his little brother scrambling onto the cot. A hint of some musty scent floated into the air when he burrowed beneath the covers. Then the door opened and Marie came inside.

"Jeremy?"

"I'm right here, Mom." He was already in the process of lighting one of the old kerosene lanterns on the mantel, feeling his way through the process. It didn't take him long.

"Where's Joshua?"

"He's in bed. Let him sleep, it's been a hard day for him." Jere turned to face her and held up the lamp, so its glow spilled onto Joshua's head. He'd turned to face the wall. Jeremy knew he was awake but hoped his mother would buy that the kid was asleep and not pester him.

He poured the last cup of coffee out of the stove-top percolator, set it on the wooden table and sat down. "Sit down, Mom. We need to talk."

"My goodness, don't you sound all grown-up?"

"That's because I am. I'm graduating next weekend. You remember that, right?"

"Of course I do." She sank into the chair, took the cup, sipped the coffee, but didn't seem to be tasting it. "I've been trying to get them to let me out so I can be there, but they just don't listen."

"You're not well, Mom."

She sniffled. "I'm not as sick as they think I am."

"Yeah. I can see that." He knew it was better not to antagonize or challenge her, and he intended to do just what he'd told his brother to do. Placate her and try to keep her calm. "But I thought it was a pretty good hospital. When we visited you, it was peaceful there. Green and sunny."

"It's a prison. And they give me meds, and I can't talk to your father anymore."

Jeremy lifted his eyebrows, opened his mouth, closed it again, then whispered, "Is that who you were talking to outside just now?"

She met his eyes, then smiled. It was a wide smile, but not a happy one. It didn't match the haunted look in her eyes. "Yeah. He came back. It's been so long."

"That's great, Mom." He reached across the table and put his hand over hers. "So how long do we have to hole up here, do you think?"

She pulled her hand away, shot a look in Josh's direction.

"He's okay," Jeremy reassured her. "He's sleeping. But he still has school. And I have graduation rehearsal and—"

"Do you want to be *dead* for graduation?" she shouted, jumping out of her chair and standing over him.

Josh sat up in bed and stared at her, wide-eyed, but Jere held out a hand, down low by his side, and tried to subtly tell him to be still.

"Is that what you want? Because if we don't stay here, I'm telling you that's what's going to happen! The demon will get you." She went to Jeremy in a single step and hugged him to her chest. He was still sitting in his chair, but his head was about level with her chin.

He caught a faint whiff of sweat and wondered when she'd last had a shower, or a change of clothes or a decent meal. God, she was skinny.

"I can't let anything happen to you. I can't. I just can't, baby."

"I know, Mom. It's okay. I know."

She rocked him a few times, then reached back to pull her chair closer to his and sank into it, all without letting go of him. Her arm was still around his neck, and she laid her head on his shoulder.

Jeremy kept his voice very soft, very calm. "I just… you know, I don't want Uncle Mason to be too worried."

"He left you home alone. He never should've done that."

"Mom, I'm almost eighteen." Why was he reasoning with her? She wasn't reasonable. Not by a long shot. But he couldn't lose his patience. He had to be careful with her. "But that's not the point. You said Uncle Mason is in danger, too, didn't you?"

She nodded, her face still mashed into his shoulder.

"So shouldn't we warn him?"

"Of course we should. But I had to get you two. That was first. I had to break out. I had to get a car. I had to save you boys, and then I had to find this place again. It's been so long. Years." She lifted her head and looked around the cabin. "I wasn't even supposed to know about it, but I followed him once. I thought he was having an affair."

It took him a minute to realize she was talking about his father again. She jumped around so much it was hard to keep up. He could see, though, why she might have been suspicious. His father had been a secretive man, always closed up inside himself. You always got the feeling that everything about him was an act. He was never genuine. You could almost feel him always trying too hard. But for Jeremy that had been normal. He'd decided at about the age of fourteen that his father didn't know how to act like a normal person, so he faked it. He was always uncomfortable, always super-self-conscious. He was just awkward, that was all.

"Dad loved you, Mom," he said, because it seemed like a good thing to say.

"He did. I loved *him*, too. That's why I never told."

Jeremy blinked. "Never told what?" He glanced toward the cot, wondering if Josh had fallen asleep. He doubted it.

His mother looked at him. "We do have to warn Mason, honey. We'll figure it out tomorrow, okay? It'll be easier now that you're here. It's hard for me to think, sometimes. I'm so glad I have you here to help me. So glad."

"Okay, Mom. I'll come up with a plan while I sleep, then, and we'll talk about it in the morning. Okay?"

"Yeah. Okay."

"You should eat something," he told her.

She looked at him and smiled a little crookedly. "You're growing up, you know that?" Reaching out, she ran her fingers through his long hair. Then she went still, and her eyes widened a little. "You look like him."

"Do I?"

She nodded twice, then bent closer, peering into his eyes as if she was looking for something. "Don't you be like he was, Jeremy. I won't put up with it again. I'll kill you myself."

Jeremy's throat went so dry he couldn't answer her. Had she really just said that?

She squinted at him, hard, as if she was trying to see inside him, and it sent a chill right down his spine. For the first time he was afraid of his mother. Afraid she might actually hurt them. He didn't say another thing, just got up and went to the cot where his kid brother was trembling under the blankets. He crawled right in beside Josh, on top of the musty blanket, and wrapped one arm around him.

"Good night, boys," Marie called, sounding completely normal again. She went to the lamp and blew it out, plunging them into pitch-darkness. And then she moved around the room, and Jeremy braced himself, wondering what she was doing. Picking up a knife or a hammer to come at him with? To kill him because she thought he was like his father? And what the hell did that *mean*, anyway?

He shifted position a little, making sure he was blocking his brother's head with one arm, in case she missed. Jeremy knew he had to get Joshua the hell out of here. If she fell asleep, he would do it. He had to. The kid could end up dead here. As soon as she slept, Jeremy thought. As soon as she slept.

As long as she didn't kill him first.

We had coffee in the car, and it was good coffee. Moreover, it was *needed* coffee. Then Mason phoned Chief Cantone to get filled in.

That still slayed me. Vanessa as chief. The job I'd wanted for Mason but he hadn't wanted for himself. It was almost too perfect, the way it had worked out. Like it was how things were meant to be or something.

You know, if you believed in that sort of thing.

Which I never had, even though I'd made my fortune writing about it. Until very recently, that is. Since Mason Brown had come into my life, everything I'd ever known, or even *been*, had experienced complete particle reversal. Is that a thing? I think that's a thing. If it's not, it should be. I wasn't the same, is what I'm getting at. I didn't know what I believed anymore. I was starting to think that maybe I'd been telling the truth the whole time, in some weird cosmic, karmic way. Not believing it, but spewing life-changing shit to the masses. And helping them.

Sometimes I wondered if I'd been used somehow. Which was both an honor and an insult. I was one pissed-off egomaniac. I had to work through that before moving on to what was real and what wasn't, and what I made up and what I was…*given.*

Jesus, this was too deep for me.

Mason was in soft conversation with Vanessa, so I fished out my own phone and called my place. Sandra picked up on ring number two, so I guess she wasn't getting any sleep, either. "Hey," I said. "Did I wake everyone?"

"No. What's happening? Have you found the boys?"

I heard a plaintive "Mom" in the background, and then my sister said, "I'm putting you on speaker for Misty."

"Okay." I gave it a beat, then told her what there was to tell. "All we have is my gut telling me they're somewhere near Parish."

"Where's that?" Misty asked.

"North of Syracuse, off I-81," her mother filled in. "So where are you?"

"Parked at a gas station drinking coffee. Mason's talking to the chief, and I'm talking to you. Have you heard anything from your end? Any tips leaking out to the media?"

"I've got every TV in the house tuned to a different channel," Sandra said. "The Amber Alert is going off at least every half hour on one channel or another. All of the Binghamton and Syracuse stations are airing it on a crawl at the bottom of the screen. They'll probably make it a custom graphic if it goes beyond tomorrow morning."

"No rampant rumors we can follow up on? No speculation so wild it just might be true?"

"No, honey. They have almost no details. The police either don't know anything or they're keeping things to themselves."

"If they are, they have a reason. Thanks, sis. How's my dog?"

"Restless. It's weird, Rachel, it's like she freaking *knows*."

"Well, she was there. She must've seen it happen." I shook my head and muttered, "Bitch, leaving my dog inside like that. I find her, she'll be lucky I don't—"

I heard Misty swearing, and then the click as Sandra took me off speakerphone. "Insensitive much, kid sister?" she asked me.

"What? She tried to kill my dog."

"She kidnapped the boys."

"And I'm out looking for the boys. Aren't I?"

Sandra sighed. "I'll call you if we hear anything you can use. You call me as soon as you know anything, okay?"

"Yeah. Okay."

"And be careful."

"I will." I disconnected and saw that Mason was ending his call at the same time. He looked up. We locked eyes. "What?"

"The car she stole has a built-in GPS."

"That's fantastic! Did they trace it yet? And if not, what the fuck are they waiting fo—"

"It's been partially disabled. Marie must've realized. It's pinging every now and then, but the signal is very weak and inconsistent. Last ping they picked up was more than three hours ago, near Syracuse. They're just waiting for it to send out another."

I closed my eyes, lowered my head.

"The car's owner was a psych nurse. Her locker was empty and her car was gone when she got off her shift this morning. Another nurse reported her keycard missing when she arrived for work. And a security guard in the parking lot was found dead. His head was bashed in with his own nightstick."

I looked up quickly. "She killed again."

"Yeah. And she was on meds, presumably, when she did it. Meds she hasn't had for an entire day now."

"God, Mason, we can't assume the boys are safe with her. Not with this."

I clapped a hand over my mouth. That wasn't what he'd needed to hear. God, how could anyone be so great at feeding people positive Pollyanna encouragement in print and so freaking *lousy* at it in person? I heaved a sigh, racking my brain for something we could do besides sit here waiting for a lead. And then I thought of something and blurted it out before vetting it first.

"Let's get a map of the area."

He sent me a puzzled look. "What are we going to do with it?"

"I don't know, exactly, but I'll figure it out. This is a gas station slash convenience store slash restaurant. They'll have maps. Let's get one."

"All right."

"All right."

So we got a map. Then we unfolded it on a table inside the restaurant, and I got a red pen and made an X near the spot north of here, where I'd felt we'd gone too far.

He watched me, waiting. I got it now. I knew what to do, or else my imagination was making shit up and throwing it at me for lack of anything better to do.

"Are you…you know…getting something?"

I looked at him. He needed something to hang his hope on. So I nodded, even though I wasn't as sure as my nod was. "We drive south until I sense we've gone too far, and then I mark that spot on the map. Then we head to a point dead center between the northern X and the southern X and we head east. Mark that spot, then try west and mark that one. Then we connect the dots, and we have a search perimeter."

He reached across the table, grabbed me by the front of my shirt and pulled until I met him in the middle, where he kissed my mouth. Then he let go and said, "You're brilliant. You do know that, don't you?"

"Well, duh."

He smiled at me. That told me I really had given him hope, which was what I'd been going for. And then we spent the rest of the night driving around, first creating our perimeter and then searching inside it.

At least it gave us something to do.

12

Jeremy stayed awake. It wasn't hard, because he was half afraid his mother would murder him if he fell asleep. So he stayed awake and hugged his kid brother, and he hoped he was going to live long enough to graduate from high school. He realized as he lay there that he didn't just hope it for his own sake. He hoped it more for Josh's sake. The poor kid had lost his father and his baby sister to death, and his mother to this terrifying monster that had taken her place. He couldn't handle losing his big brother, too. Everyone else would be okay. Uncle Mason would be devastated, yeah, but he would recover, because he had Rachel. She could get him through anything. Jeremy thought she would be pretty broken up by his death, too. She was a part of their family now. He hadn't given it much thought before now, but he guessed he kind of loved her. She would survive it, too, though. She would be strong for Uncle Mason and for Josh. She would be okay.

But Josh... Josh was just a kid. He couldn't take another hit so soon. It would do him in.

Eventually the steady, even sound of her breathing told him that his mother was asleep on a worn-out old couch by the door. She even snored every few breaths, which meant she was really deeply asleep, right?

He thought so, and he nudged his brother. "You awake, Josh?" he whispered, close to his ear.

"Yeah."

"We have to activate plan B. You remember what I told you? That you might have to go on your own?"

The kid nodded. "But I don't want to leave you."

"You have to. You're the only one who can save us."

Their mother rolled over, and they went dead still and silent. But soon the soft breathing started up again. Jeremy waited a full minute to make sure she was sound asleep and not faking them out. Then he spoke even more softly. "Get the flashlight out of the shed. Stay off the road, but follow it. All the way to the end, then go right." He gripped his brother's right hand, just in case he had any question about which way that was. *"Right,"* he repeated, just in case the kid got mixed up. He was already so scared he barely knew down from up. "Another hour and a half, then go left. Then the first right, then left at the fork. End, right, hour and a half, left, first right, fork left. Got it?"

"It'll take you a couple of hours to get to that village we passed on the way in. You got it?"

Joshua nodded firmly, then sat up, quiet as a mouse.

"Are you sure, Josh? There are like five places where there are turns in the road. You take any of those, you'll be lost. Have you got it for sure?"

"I've got it."

"All right. We've got to be quiet." Jeremy got out of bed at a snail's pace, picked up Joshua's shoes off the floor. He'd taken note of where they were before his mother had blown out the lamp. As Josh followed, Jeremy walked through the cabin to the bathroom in the

very back, which was more like an attached outhouse.
There was a window in there. He'd scoped it out earlier.
They crowded into the tiny room, and Jeremy closed the
door softly. "Here, put these on, but be quiet," he whispered, pushing the shoes into Joshua's hands.

Josh sat on the closed toilet seat and put them on,
barely making a sound while Jeremy was opening the
little window. There was no screen in the way, but the
opening was awfully small. He wasn't listening for his
mother anymore. There was no point. They were committed, and there was no turning back now. Josh was
getting out of here.

"Come here, buddy."

Josh hesitated. "Why can't you just come with me?"

"Because if we're both gone, she'll come after us.
But if I stay behind, I can distract her. I can keep her
from going after you and give you time to get help. It's
the best chance for both of us."

"How are you gonna do that, Jere? How can you
keep her from—"

"Don't even worry about it. Just trust me, okay?" He
didn't want to think about *how*, but he knew he could
keep his hundred-and-one-pound mother in check if he
had to. He was practically a grown man, almost as big
as Uncle Mason.

He picked his brother up, giving him no more time
to argue. The kid was heavy. Josh stuck his feet out
the window, and Jeremy continued to hold him while
he wriggled his body through, then lowered him until
he couldn't reach any farther. Before he let him go, he
said, "You're a pretty awesome brother, kid. Don't think
I don't know that."

"You too," Joshua said, and it sounded like there
were tears in his voice. Jeremy couldn't handle that, so

he let him go. His eyes were adjusting a little, and he could see Josh land, then scramble to his feet. He waved once, then turned and headed toward the shed, around the cabin and out of sight.

Jeremy closed the window carefully, then he opened the bathroom door and tiptoed back into the main part of the cabin.

"What are you doing up?"

His mother was a dark silhouette sitting upright on the ratty sofa. Jeremy's eyes darted to his own rumpled cot. The covers made a lump where Josh should be, sort of. He got back in fast. "Shh. Don't wake Josh," he said softly. "I just had to pee."

"Oh." She spoke much more softly then. "Okay, then. Good night."

"Night, Mom." He tugged the pillow underneath the blankets, spooning with it as if it were his kid brother, closing his eyes, and praying with everything in him that Joshua would find his way, fast and safe, and send help.

He also wished for his phone, so he could tell what time it was. He lay in the bed for what felt like a long, long time. Maybe an hour. Maybe two or three. It was impossible to tell. But it was still dark when his mother came over, aiming a flashlight beam at his face.

"Where is he?" she demanded. "Where is your brother?"

Jeremy jumped off the mattress and stood close to her. "Mom, you've gotta listen to me."

"Where is your brother?" She aimed her light around the cabin.

"You're not right, Mom. I know it's not your fault, but you're sick. Josh wasn't safe here with you. You told me to take care of him. That's what I did."

"No. No, dammit! You don't understand!" She slammed him in the chest with both hands so he fell back onto the cot, and then she was surging toward the front door and through it, aiming her light high and low, shouting Joshua's name.

Jeremy ran out behind her. "He's gone, Mom. He's long gone. It's no use. He's probably already found help out there."

"No. No he can't! It's not *safe*! Out there all alone. In the dark, in the woods! He's just a baby! God, Jeremy, what have you done?" She headed to the car and got in, starting it up, still in the nurse's scrubs she'd worn yesterday. She'd kept the keys in one of the big pockets. "Come on!" she shouted at him, her door still open.

Not yet. Not yet, he thought. He couldn't be sure enough time had passed. Josh might not have made it far enough. Jeremy sat down on the top step. "No. I'm sorry, Mom, but...no."

"We have to get to your brother. Jeremy, his *life* is in *danger*."

"Then call Uncle Mason and tell him where we are."

"I can't do that!" She got out of the car and ran to him, grabbed his shoulders and shouted in his face, "Jeremy, he's in danger! She'll find him."

"The demon?" he asked, averting his face from her morning breath.

"Yes."

"Mom, there are no demons."

"Oh, baby, you don't even know." She let go of him, lowered her head. "Your own father was one of them. But I loved him. I should've stopped him, but I loved him."

Jeremy got a cold chill down his spine. It made him shiver so hard he had to stand up. He wanted to ask her what she meant by that, but there was something inside him, something way down deep, warning him that he didn't really want to poke at this particular dark hole.

And then it was too late, because his mother had him by the arm, tugging him toward the car. "We're going after him. We're going after Joshua."

"No we're not." He pulled free, but she grabbed him again. It occurred to him that he was bigger than her, stronger than her, and saner than her. It shouldn't be this hard. He could just overpower her and tie her up. He could punch her in the face and knock her on her ass, throw her into the back of the car and drive them both to the nearest police station.

Except that she was his mother. And he didn't want to hit his own mother. There was a part of him, too, that was afraid of what she would do if he tried. Because he couldn't hurt her, not really. He could never bring himself to.

She could hurt *him*, though. And after last night, he didn't think the part of her that wouldn't harm her own son was still in charge.

So what was he going to do? He kept pulling free, and she kept grabbing his arm again, dragging him closer to the car every time. She finally managed to get him to the passenger door, and she opened it, tried to shove him inside. He pulled away, slammed the door shut. "We're *not* going after Joshua!" he shouted.

"Yes. We. Are!" she shouted back, and wrenched the door open again. She gripped a handful of his hair and part of his ear, as well, and pushed with all her might. She was freakishly strong, especially considering how thin she was. He couldn't get free of her without hurting her. She shoved his head into the car, and he saw the keys in the ignition and let himself be pushed into the seat, even pulled his feet in on his own.

She slammed the car door, breathless, panting, and raced around the front of the car to get into the driver's side. Before she got her door open, Jeremy yanked the keys free and jumped out on his side. He ran for all he was worth, aware she was on his heels, and then he drew back and threw the keys into the woods.

His mother came to a stumbling stop beside him. "Oh, God, Jeremy, no! No!" Then she went charging into the woods in the direction he'd pitched the keys.

There. That would do it, he thought. It would take an hour, at least, to find those keys. And he wasn't going to help her. He went back to the shed and flipped the switch to turn the power in the cabin back on, and then he called, "I'm making us some coffee, Mom. You might as well come in and get some."

He went into the cabin, expecting her to give up and follow.

He was running water into the coffeepot when he heard the car start up, dropped the pot and ran.

Gretchen showed up at Rachel de Luca's home before 8:00 a.m. She knew she probably should have waited a little longer to be believable, but she was impatient. She knew where the *famous author* lived. She'd scoped it out. The pretentious wrought-iron gate was closed. It had been open every other time she'd come by. Probably Rachel and Mason were afraid Marie was going to come after them now that she'd supposedly murdered Mason's nephews. Gretchen smiled slowly and looked for a bell to ring or a button to push or whatever. But there wasn't one. Apparently Rachel was famous enough for a gated home but not enough for an intercom.

But wait, a pair of blonde teenage girls was coming down the long paved driveway toward her, the two pain-in-the-ass dogs trotting along beside them. She'd intended for both mutts to burn with the house. She'd intended for Mason to have nothing and no one left to turn to—except for her—by the time she was finished. And that was why she was here: to remove Rachel from the equation, as well. And since it was only a matter of time before Marie was caught and stuck back in her padded cell, time was of the essence. Rachel had to die, and Marie had to be blamed. Period.

And then there would be no more barriers between herself and Mason.

The blondes stopped at the gate. They were almost identical, except that one of them had a curvier shape and had been crying so much that her eyes were red-rimmed and puffy. The other one was stick thin and bitchy-looking.

Gretchen plastered a worried look on her face, and said, "I've just come from Mason's house and it's…it's just gone. What in the world happened? Where is he? Is he…?"

The old blind bulldog started growling.

"He's fine. He wasn't home when it happened," the weepy one said. "It's the boys we're—"

The skinny one clamped a viselike hand on her sister's arm. "I'm sorry, but who are you?"

"Gretchen Young. I'm Mason's nurse."

Bitchy lifted her pale, perfectly arched brows. "His *nurse*?"

Weepy put a hand on her shoulder. "For the burns on his arm. I know about her, it's okay." She reached for the gate and started to pull it open. The older bulldog started barking like mad. A short, snuffly sound more like a series of powerful sneezes than an actual dog sound. "It's all right, Myrtle. Calm down, okay? You can go ahead and drive your car in, Ms. Young. My folks are inside, they can fill you in."

"I just…wait, Mason's not here?"

"No. He and Rachel are out looking for the boys."

Gretchen didn't move to get back into her car. She just stood there by the partially open gate, looking from the weepy girl to the still growling dog. The little puppy was growling now, too, looking at the big dog as if for approval, then growling, then looking at her again. Mimicking her.

"What do you mean, out looking for the boys? I thought… I mean, if they were home when that fire happened, then… I mean, how could they have survived?"

"We don't know how, but they did. It looks as if—"

"Jeez, Misty, why don't you show her where Aunt Rache keeps the silver while you're at it?" The skinny sister pushed the gate closed again. "Look, I'm sorry, lady, but I don't know you from Adam. When Mason gets back I'll tell him you came by. He can decide what he wants you to know and what he doesn't. All right?"

"He would want me to know about the boys," Gretchen said, trembling in the effort to hold her temper.

"Then he'll tell you himself. See ya."

"Christy—"

"Uh-uh. No way." Bitchy flipped a lock from the inside of the gate, gripped her sister's arm and firmly turned her around to start hoofing it back toward the house. Their two blond heads leaned close, and they whispered as they went. The dogs trotted along beside them, and the weepy twin looked back with an apologetic shrug.

Gretchen narrowed her eyes. Something was going on.

She hadn't watched any news reports, because it would be easier to feign surprise, shock and horror if she hadn't heard any of the spin the press were putting on the fire. But maybe it was time she started listening. She got into her car, tuned the radio to a local all-news station, then turned herself around and headed back the way she had come.

"...so far, no human remains have been found at the scene of the fire. Detective Brown's two nephews are being treated as missing persons..."

She snapped the power button off. Dammit. If the kids weren't in the house when she torched it, then where the hell were they?

"Marie," she whispered. "It had to have been Marie." She stomped hard on the gas pedal, sending up a cloud of dust in her wake.

"Mason, we've got a sighting of what looks like a young person walking alone along a deserted stretch of road near Parish. Fisherman headed out for an early morning trip saw him and found it odd enough that he called it in to the local sheriff. Are you still in the area?"

The voice was Vanessa Cantone's, and it came from Mason's cell phone, set to speaker and resting in the spot that used to be an ashtray when the car was new and was now a cell phone holder.

"We're still here, Chief," he said, sending me a hopeful look. I thought it was unlikely just any local kid would be out walking the back roads of this nowhere place in the predawn hours. "Where?"

"Barclay Road."

I snatched the portable GPS off the dash and keyed in the road in question. "U-turn," I told him, slamming the unit back onto its holder and then unfolding the map to verify.

"We're on our way," Mason said, swinging the car around in a one-eighty, then flooring it.

We'd been driving in an approximation of concentric circles, and I'd been trying to feel Joshua and Jeremy's vibe or whatever you want to call it. But my NFP wasn't doing a hell of a lot to help me, which was odd. If the boys were in trouble, I'd feel it, wouldn't I? When Amy was in trouble, my NFP was practically screaming inside my head. It was like there was a magnet pulling me right to her.

I was as close to Josh and Jeremy as I was to Amy. Maybe closer. Yeah, probably closer. Okay, *definitely* closer. Much as I hadn't wanted to, I'd become a kind of a mother figure to them, I supposed. Until I'd walked onto the scene of Mason's burning home, I hadn't realized how much the brats meant to me.

So why wasn't I getting anything stronger? Why was their signal so weak?

"There'll be a right just up ahead," I said. "Then a quick left. Slow down a little."

He did, but not enough. The car rocked up on two wheels when we took the corner and barely touched all four down again before he took the next.

"This is it, this is the road."

He braked to a crawl. I dragged my finger along the map. "It's only a two mile, road, Mason. Let's park the Beast and walk it."

He pulled onto the shoulder, and we jumped out of the car, slammed the doors and started walking, him on the right shoulder, me on the left. I called the boys' names and wished Myrtle were there. She'd sniff them out if they were close.

We walked and we shouted, and we walked and we shouted some more.

And then I heard something rustling in the woods along my side of the road, and a soft voice said, "Rachel?"

I looked up, my heart clenching in my chest just as Joshua burst out of the trees and into my arms. I hugged him to me, picked him right up off his feet, and hugged him, and yeah, there was a sudden floodgate that opened behind my eyes, but so what? Jeez, I'd gone from being sure he'd died a horrible death to thinking he was kidnapped by a homicidal maniac to having him all wrapped up in my arms. So yes, I bawled. Sue me.

Mason crossed the road in two long strides and wrapped his big arms around us both, and Josh sobbed and tried to twist around to hug his uncle, too. And then eventually we untwined ourselves and set the poor kid on his feet.

His face was dirty and wet, and he was sobbing almost too hard to talk.

"Have to…get…Jeremy."

"We will. We will, don't worry. Do you know where he is?" Mason asked.

He nodded. It was jerky but firm. "With Mom. In a c-c-cabin."

"Can you find it again?"

"I can try. I don't know. I think I took one of the turns Jere told me not to. I thought I was lost for sure." He wiped his eyes. "Sh-she's crazy, Uncle Mason. I was scared she'd k-kill us."

"I don't think she'd do that," Mason told him. "She's sick, but she still loves you."

"It's like…some s-stranger. In Mom's body. I d-don't know *what* she'll do. And Jeremy thinks she might hurt us. That's why he made me sneak away." His face contorted and fresh tears spilled. "He saved me."

Mason crouched down and hugged the kid again. "You've got a hell of a brother, kiddo. Let's go get him, okay?"

Josh nodded, wiping his eyes with his knuckles.

"Come on, pal, and we'll head back to the car. It's not far, and then we'll go get Jeremy. Okay, pal?"

"Thank God you weren't in the house," I muttered.

Josh frowned and looked over at me. "Why?"

I blinked and slid my gaze to Mason's, stunned that Josh might not be aware of the fire. Mason gave me a subtle shake of his head, and then I focused on Josh again. "Myrt's gonna be so glad to see you. She's been out of her mind."

"Is she okay? I was so worried about her and Hugo."

"Why were you worried?" Maybe he *did* know about the fire.

"'Cause I left the door out to the back room open. Mom took us so fast, I didn't have time to go back in and close it. Did they get outside?"

"Yeah, kid. They got outside." I ran a hand down his back. His forgetfulness had probably saved Myrtle's life. And Myrt had, in turn, saved Hugo's. "And they're both just fine. Now we're gonna go get your big brother, and then everything will be okay again. All right, pal?"

He sniffled, nodded. "I knew you'd come for me. I knew you *both* would."

He reached sideways to take hold of my hand. My damned eyes burned again. What the hell had happened to hard-ass, independent, "don't even think about making me a mother figure" Rachel? Where was she?

Burned up in that fire, I guessed.

* * *

Jeremy had barely managed to grab hold of the car door handle and jerk it open as his mother pulled away. When he did, though, she braked sharply, and he banged his head on the open door. He didn't even pause, though, just dove into the passenger seat. "Dammit, Mom, you're losing it! Let him go."

"Don't you think I would if I could?" She had tears dripping from her chin, and her nose was running. "God, I'd let you both go if I could. I can see you're terrified of me." Her lips pulled into a tight grimace. "You hate me. You do, don't you?"

Something in Jeremy's stomach knotted up tight. "I hate what you did. Killing people, Mom. Trying to kill Rachel."

She nodded rapidly. "I know. I know. I know that now."

"And leaving my pocketknife in the snow. So Uncle Mason would think it was me."

She sniffed hard. "Only to divert him. I never would've let you go to prison, Jeremy. Never. I'd have died first."

"Why did you do it, Mom?"

"Your father told me to." She blinked, frowned hard. "Only my doctors say it wasn't really him. It was some kind of sickness in my brain." And then she shook her head rapidly. "But it wasn't sickness. It was him. It was your father. I know it was. And I shouldn't have listened, but I just love him so much that—"

"Mom, no. It was the illness. It wasn't Dad. Dad's dead."

"Demons don't die, honey. It was him. I know you loved him, but your father wasn't a good man." Again, the grimace that pulled her mouth so wide it was almost a smile. "He was evil, and he made *me* evil, too."

"Dad wasn't—"

"He killed a lot of people, Jeremy. Thirteen before he died. More after. I don't know how he did that, but like I said, demons don't die."

Jeremy sat there, staring at his mother, knowing she was insane. And yet there was something. There was something way down deep inside him, some weird kind of awareness. "That's not true," he said.

"You should know. You deserve to know what he was. Your father was the Wraith."

He shook his head. "That's not right, Mom. The Wraith was that lunatic I shot when he tried to kill Uncle Mason."

She shook her head. "Your father just made you believe that."

"My father was already dead."

"You don't understand. Maybe it doesn't matter." She pulled the car to a stop. "I wonder which way Joshua went from here. We have to find him, Jeremy. We have to. There's another demon, and she's after him. After you both." Then she started forward again, driving until she spotted a rutted track off the road into the forest. A logging road or something. It had a sign on it that said No Trespassing, but she took it anyway, and drove several hundred yards before she stopped again, got out of the car and started walking as the sun rose over the horizon.

By 7:00 a.m., after they'd walked and searched for more than an hour, Jeremy was sure Josh had either found help and was somewhere safe, or had gone off track and was hopelessly lost. Otherwise they would have found him by now. Apparently, his mother had given up on finding him, too. As they made their way back to the car, she said, "We have to leave here now.

We can't go back to the cabin. Josh will tell them where we are, and they'll find us. We have to leave."

Jeremy sighed, his hopes for imminent rescue dashed. But he was too relieved about Josh to be too upset. If they left here, then Josh was home free for sure. And that was more important. He didn't want his kid brother within reach of his crazy mother and her wild delusions about their father.

The Wraith. The only serial killer their area had ever had, the one Jeremy had come face-to-face with on what was still the most terrifying day of his life. His mother was even crazier than he'd realized.

13

Mason drove, while Josh told him where to go. I don't know how many times the kid changed his mind, and we had to backtrack and start over. The kid had gotten himself so turned around it was a miracle we'd found him. Thank God he'd stuck to the roadsides and hadn't wandered off too deeply into the forest.

I manned the phone. The first call was to Chief Cantone, who had the State Police dispatch choppers and every cop within a reasonable distance to our location.

My second call was to my sister, but I only had time to say, "We've got Joshua. He's safe. Marie still has Jeremy. But I think we're close" and for her to reply with a predictable "Be careful, Rache" before the cabin came into sight.

Mason stopped the car, left it running and got out. "Take the extra gun out of the glove compartment, Rachel. Lock the doors and stay in the car."

Like I was gonna shoot the kid's mother in front of him. I scooted over behind the wheel. "If we have to run, we'll run, but I'm not going to shoot anybody."

Josh was in the backseat, leaning forward, looking

hard for his brother. "Her car's gone," he whispered. "She had a car. A blue one."

I saw Mason's face fall, but he closed the door and crept forward anyway. I watched him, realizing after a few seconds that I was holding my breath. He moved fast and easy, kind of edging his way along the tree line. The log cabin was tiny, couldn't have been more than two rooms, or maybe just one big one. Two little windows in the front with no adornment. And a door that had been painted a dark shade of green that was hard to distinguish from the moss growing over it. The place had an abandoned look to it.

And something bad. Something real bad. Something that made me want to grab Mason and pull him back into the car, only he was out of reach now.

I looked again at the cabin, those two black windows like dead eyes staring back at me.

And then there *were* dead eyes staring back at me. A young man's dead, wide-open, brown eyes, with blood trickling across his forehead and dripping into one of them. And I was standing over him, holding a bloody framing hammer in my left hand. It was a big hand, stuffed into a leather glove that strained at the seams, and it was attached to a thick, hairy forearm.

I'm Mason's brother again. I'm Eric. I have his corneas. I'm seeing what he saw.

He'd killed here.

Josh was shaking me, one hand on my right shoulder. "Rachel? Rachel? Come on, Rachel, please?"

I blinked back into myself and gave a full-body shudder that felt like a dog shaking off water. It was Eric I was shaking off. I wanted a shower. God.

He'd killed here. I'd seen it. Here in this cabin no

one but his wife had known about. Now that I knew what had happened here, the stench of death was hard to miss. I wanted to get out of this place.

"Where's Mason? I lost track," I said, my eyes jumping from one part of the clearing to the next. "Where did he go?"

"He went behind the cabin a second ago. I don't think there's a back door, though. I had to climb out the window."

I felt a sudden stab of fear. Josh's fear. Jeez, the poor kid. "He'll be okay," I promised. *Joshua shouldn't be in this place. It's bad for him here. His father murdered innocent young men here. And I can still feel it. It's like I breathe it every time I inhale.* God, *I want to get out of here.*

"Something moved inside! Rache!"

"I see it, I see it." I squinted, leaning forward in my seat. Why the hell didn't we have a pair of binoculars as standard equipment in every vehicle? A shadow moved. I traced the curve of its neck into its wide, sturdy shoulder. "It's Mason. I don't see anyone else."

Almost as soon as I said it, Mason came out the front door and walked toward us. I opened my door but couldn't bring myself to get out, to set even one foot on this polluted ground.

"I found a couple of windows in the back, one big enough to get in through. They're gone. Left in a hurry, it looks like. Lots of stuff left behind for Forensics to go over." He braced his hands on the open door and hung his head in between them.

I had a perfect view of the anguish on his face. On impulse, I reached up and ran my palm over his stubble. "We'll find them," I said. I heard a chopper overhead and the first sirens in the distance. Then I looked Mason right in the eye and willed him to feel what I was sending. "Mason, we have to get away from this place. I can't *be* here. Okay?"

He heard me, understood what I was saying—that bad things had happened here and I was feeling them. I could tell by the way he frowned hard, searching my face like he was worried about me, because he probably was. I was amazed all over again at how we could communicate without any words at all. The enormity of this thing kept hitting me full-on over and over again, amazing me every time.

I know, great timing, right?

"Slide over, I'll drive," he said.

We drove until my spine unknotted itself and started to elongate again. I don't know what to tell you, that's how it felt. Then he stopped at a pull off alongside the road, in plain sight of the police vehicles that screamed past us toward the cabin. If they wanted us, they would know where to find us.

"What was it?" he asked me. "About the cabin?" He slid the shift into Park, and turned off the engine.

My window was down. I could smell the pine all around. Everything was dappled in early-morning sunlight, the way it filtered through those boughs. I breathed deeply, then looked at him and then Josh, and back to him again. He got the message: *Not in front of Josh,* and acknowledged it with a slight nod.

"Where do you think she took Jeremy?" I asked Josh, to distract him from the unspoken conversation I'd just had with his uncle.

"I don't know. Anywhere. She's crazy, Rache. I've never seen anything like it." He was shaking his head in a way that was far too old for him. He had seen too much in his life, things a kid should never see.

"It's awful, how sick your mom is, Josh," I told him, 'cause my heart was breaking for him and I just wanted to say something to make it better. I looked for words, and they were right there. I don't know who put them there, but they started spilling out, like when I'm on a roll with my writing, like I've tapped into a well. I reached around, put my hand on his shoulder. "But it's not her fault. I want you to remember that. She's not the woman you just spent last night with. She's the mom you remember from back when things were good. That's who she is. You hold on to that, okay? Because you know what? Your holding on to that memory of her when she was at her best is gonna help her as much as it helps you."

"It is?" He sniffled—unashamed, I think.

"It is. Don't ask me how I know it, but I do. I wouldn't lie to you, Josh. I love you."

He snapped his arms around my neck, almost launching himself out of the backseat and into the front. "I love you, too," he said against my jaw. His cheeks were wet.

Great time for an emotional meltdown, right?

I let him go, wiped my eyes and turned to Mason. "Let's find a diner, get some breakfast and wait for another lead, okay? Jeremy's smart. He's going to find a way to let us know where he is. Or the team will find some clue in that cabin. Or I'll get another inkling. We need to get some sustenance into us."

"Okay." He looked from me to Josh, then back at me again. And he smiled, but it was a shaky smile. Finally he started the car and drove back toward the nearest town.

* * *

Jeremy couldn't believe what he was seeing.

His mother had driven them into a nearby little town, and she hadn't spoken a word the whole way. Then she pulled into the parking lot of a retro-looking diner that was apparently just called Diner. That was all the sign said, at least.

She'd gotten out and gone inside, and he'd had no choice but to follow her. They sat down, and when he asked her what she was doing, she held up a finger and calmly ordered two breakfasts of ham and eggs, and coffee with cream and sugar.

And then she sat there, staring over his shoulder at the TV in the corner, answering every question with a finger aimed at his food. She wanted him to eat. So he ate. She didn't. She only pretended to.

"Look," she said at last.

He turned, frowning to see what was on television that was so important. Didn't she know she shouldn't be here in public? She would be caught.

But that was what he wanted. Wasn't it?

The question went unanswered as his brain registered what his eyes were looking at. News footage of a house on fire. Of Mason's house, *his* house, on fire. He leaned forward, listening now and motioning to a waiter. "Can you turn that up?"

The guy did.

...the fire that destroyed the home of Binghamton Police Detective Mason Brown last night was deliberately set, according to arson investigators. The whereabouts of Brown's two young nephews, ages twelve and seventeen, are still unknown; however, investigators say there are no signs of human remains at the scene, and

there are indications the boys may have been abducted. An Amber Alert has been issued.

At that point Jeremy saw photos of himself and Josh flash onto the screen with the words *Missing Boys* underneath them. He lowered his head, turned back around and felt more than one pair of eyes on him.

"We've got to get out of here, Mom," he muttered without looking up. He picked up the menu to shield his face.

"No," she said softly. "You've got to go back home. And I've got to find another way to stop her." She leaned across the table, put a palm gently against his cheek. "You be careful of that demon, okay, Jeremy? Don't let her get to you before I can get to her. Do you hear me? Be careful of Nurse Gretchen."

She got up and calmly crossed the diner, heading into the restroom, while the words *Nurse Gretchen* were ricocheting through his tangled-up brain like stray bullets. His home had been burned down. His mother knew the name of the his uncle's nurse and said she was a demon out to kill him, but then again, she also said his father was a serial killer whose crimes had continued long after his dad's death. And he was certain everyone in the diner was looking at him, knowing he was the face on the news. He sat there a second longer, trying to figure out what to do first. Then someone cleared their throat, and he looked at the people around him. The only ones not gaping at him were the ones tapping on their cell phones. Three familiar digits, he bet.

Yeah, this took priority. He stood up and said, "Yeah, it's me, I'm the kid on TV, but it's okay. She's my mother. Everything's fine."

Before he could say anything more, a screaming cop

car skidded to a stop out front. It was the first of several. God, they must've been close.

"Ah, hell," he said, sinking into his chair and covering his head with his forearms.

The cops came running into the diner, guns drawn. Jeremy stood up, raising his hands. "It's okay."

"Where's your mother, son? We know she took you and your brother."

"Don't hurt her. All right? She gave up, she was bringing me back. She already let my brother go. And she doesn't have a gun or anything."

But one of the customers was pointing urgently at the restroom door, so Jeremy wasn't sure the cops were even hearing him anymore.

Five of them converged on the ladies' room like a SWAT team.

"Mom, they're coming!" he shouted. "Mom, just do what they tell you, all right? Just do what they say and—"

They kicked the door open and crowded inside while Jeremy held his breath and listened for gunfire he prayed wouldn't come.

And it didn't. The men came back out again, shaking their heads. "It's empty. No one's there."

Jeremy sank back into his seat. He hadn't even remembered standing up.

As we neared what my smartphone told us was the nearest diner, something in my gut went jittery and my heart skipped. Literally skipped. "Something's happening. Jeremy's—"

I clasped Mason's arm, felt it flex as he clenched the wheel. The flashing lights and crookedly parked police SUVs and sedans said the diner wasn't serving. He pulled in among them and got out so fast he didn't even shut off the car. I started to follow, but Josh clutched my hand before I made it all the way.

"Stay with Josh!" Mason called over his shoulder. Then he paused, looked at me. "Keep him safe."

"I will. Go on."

He nodded and headed toward the diner door, only to be met by a flow of cops coming out like some cop dam had just busted. One stopped to talk to him, and the flow split and flowed around them. And then, last of all, Jeremy came out. I saw him a split second before Mason did.

"Josh, look!" I said.

"I see him, I see him!"

And then Mason did, too, and he torpedoed through the officers, grabbed Jeremy hard and hugged him right off his feet, even though the kid was taller. I had tears on my face again. They had me, didn't they, this fucked-up little bunch of males? They had me as hooked as the ring in Amy's nose. They had me.

Mason looked back at us and motioned us over. It was a good thing, because Josh would've split a gut if I hadn't let him out of that car soon. I got out of the car, stepped out of the way to let him rocket past me, then jogged to catch up. The cops had cleared out, mostly jumping into their vehicles and speeding off in different directions. A few had jogged away on foot.

"Get your family inside where they're safe," the cop who'd been talking with Mason told him. "We'll leave a few men here, just in case."

Mason nodded as Josh crashed into his brother, almost knocking him back through the diner doors. "I did it, Jere. Just like you told me. And I found Uncle Mason and Rachel."

"You did great, Josh," Jeremy was saying. He put an arm around his brother. "I knew you could do it." He looked at me over Josh's head, and then his face fell. "I saw the fire on TV. Are the dogs…?"

"They're fine. Both at my house with my sister. Her whole family is there. Misty's been out of her mind." As soon as the words were out, I keyed a rapid-fire text to Sandra to let her know Jeremy was safe and I'd call soon.

"What fire?" Josh asked.

Jeremy crouched low, just inside the diner's front door. "There was a fire at our house. It was pretty bad. But we're okay. So are Myrt and Hugo."

"Oh, no!" Josh blinked rapidly. "'Member, Jere, I left that door open?" he said, letting go of his brother and bouncing in time with his words. "Myrt must've got out that way."

"That's exactly what happened," Mason said. "So you saved them, kiddo."

"Yes," I added, "and when I first saw Myrtle afterward, she was carrying Hugo in her teeth, like a mama dog carries her puppies," I said. "I bet Myrtle carried Hugo outside. I bet she saved him."

"I bet she did," Josh said.

"And your aunt Sandra says Myrt's been sticking to that pup like glue ever since." Had I just called my sister his aunt? Huh. That came pretty naturally.

"Mason?" I put my hand on his arm so he wouldn't be distracted. "Why did he say to bring us inside where it's safe?"

"They just…"

"They don't know where Mom is," Jeremy said. "She went into the bathroom. Must've climbed out a window or something. She was gone before they got inside. But she's not gonna hurt us. She wouldn't."

"She scares me," Joshua said softly. Then he looked Mason right in the eyes. "She's crazy."

"Not as crazy as everyone thinks," Jeremy said. "That demon she thinks is after us? The one she escaped to try to save us from? Right before she went to the restroom she called it Nurse Gretchen."

"Holy shit, I was right about her after all."

Mason elbowed me for the language, but I could see he was dumbfounded. Blinking slowly, he walked across the diner, pulling out his cell phone and dialing a number. I heard him say, "Chief, I need someone to run a background check on that home care nurse I hired. Gretchen Young. And just for the hell of it, check and see if she ever worked at Riverside." He paused, then, "Yeah, that's where Marie is. Was. And yeah, it's connected. Maybe. I've gotta go." He hung up the phone.

I looked at the boys. "It's late, and I don't know about you, Jeremy, but the rest of us haven't had breakfast, so I think it's time for some food." I turned to the nearest person with a name badge and an order pad, who turned out to be a buxom blonde with cleavage I would've killed for. "Any chance we could get a meal, as long as we're all stuck here for the time being?"

She nodded. "You bet you can, and it's on the house." She eyed the boys. "You kids had a rough night, I hear."

"The roughest," Jeremy said. We slid into a booth, Josh next to me and Jere on the other side with Mason.

"Is all our stuff gone, Uncle Mace? The Xbox? All the games?"

"Yeah, pal. It is. Our clothes. Everything that could burn, burned. And I know that hurts a lot, but we're gonna be okay. Stuff isn't what's important. People are. Stuff can be replaced."

I had my arm around Josh, and I squeezed him a little. My eyes were on Mason, though. He had this intense look I'd never seen before. This protective, passionate look. I could see his heart in his eyes.

"Josh," he said, "when we came home and saw the fire, I thought you guys were inside. And I never felt pain like that in my life. Never. I hope I never feel like that again, I'll tell you that much. What we lost…" He opened his palms. "It's nothing. It's nothing. What we've got, no fire can take away, and it's worth everything. We've got each other. You guys are okay. The dogs are okay. We're still together. We're still…"

"A family," I said, when he hesitated. It was a moment. I felt my heart swelling with it, and I thought I could feel each one of theirs doing the same. It was getting a little too mushy for my blood, but then again, I was the one who'd started it.

"It's a good thing Mom came and got us, huh?" Joshua asked. "If she hadn't, we would've been in there when the fire happened."

I frowned at Mason. We'd been working under the assumption that Marie had set the fire herself, but I realized now that didn't really make sense. If she'd set it, wouldn't Josh have known about it?

Mason looked at Jeremy. "There was no sign of any fire when you left with your mother?"

Jere shook his head. "And she didn't go back, either. She was there like ten seconds, Uncle Mace, just long enough to get Joshua into the car. I had to either get in, too, or let her take him without me."

If it wasn't her, I thought, then who?

Gretchen?

Had Marie been right all along?

* * *

The police didn't find Marie, so eventually they let us go home, though only after extensively questioning the boys and extracting our promise that we'd bring them into the station to go over their statements the next day. We had company all the way to my front gate, lights flashing but sirens silent.

God, it was good to see home again. The boys got out and ran for the front door. Mason and I were a little slower, watching them run inside. The door opened, and Jeremy scooped Misty off her feet in a hug that carried her inside. Josh was on his hands and knees in the doorway, being thoroughly adored by two happy bulldogs. Myrtle kept nosing the pup away and planting her girth in between him and Josh, but Hugo was younger and faster, not to mention sighted, and would just attack from a new direction.

I stopped walking, turned to look up into Mason's face. "I want you to live with me."

He smiled, nodding, his face so scruffy that I wanted to drag him inside and upstairs to my room. "Thanks. I know it's a lot. You've already had them for weeks. But it'll only be until we can—"

"I want you to *live* with me," I said again. "Permanently."

He didn't speak, and that made me nervous, and when I'm nervous I talk. A lot.

"We've said the L word already. Living together is the next step, isn't it? Isn't that what people do? We've been dragging our feet. We've been going at a snail's pace so we don't mess this up. But, Mace, we've had a lot of big, bad things—I mean really *huge monstrous things*—trying to mess this up, and none of them have.

Maybe what we've got going on here is stronger than we've been giving it credit for."

"I'm pretty sure you're right about that." He pulled me closer, right up against his chest, and he kissed me on the mouth, right there in front of the still-open door, which currently housed my gaping sister and grinning brother-in-law.

14

We tried to make the day as normal as possible. Sandra and Jim went out for supplies, and we cooked burgers and dogs on the grill, picnicked on the back lawn and did some fishing from the dock, and later on, went swimming, too. Myrtle chased froggies, and Hugo watched, picking up the game quickly and joining in to help. Mainly he just scared them off, but Myrtle seemed to enjoy teaching him.

We had dinner together, too. Rosie and Gwen showed up with vats of Chinese takeout and a brand-new Xbox for the boys. It was a model newer than the one they'd had, and they were overjoyed.

Things seemed almost normal. Except that both Marie and Gretchen, who might or might not be truly evil, were still out there somewhere.

That night I slept like the proverbial log, waking up briefly only when Mason got in and out of bed. He was up over and over again, pacing the halls like a restless ghost, checking on the kids, the locks and I don't even know what else. He was worried.

Once the sun came up, he got up for good. I knew because he headed for the shower and got dressed. I dozed on and off while he did, but once he finished up, I took my turn, and by the time I was dressed he had a pot of coffee brewing in the kitchen. I followed its aroma through my home, wondering how many accidents Hugo'd had around the place, but I didn't see or smell any. Then again, my sister would've been on top of that.

Mason had sent Sandra, Jim and Christy home with a police escort. Misty had spent the night in one of the guest rooms.

I was standing in front of the open fridge, staring inside, brain-dead and wondering what to make for breakfast, when Mason came inside through the side door from the garage. He had both dogs with him, and a couple of giant-sized take-out bags in his hands.

I closed the fridge and sniffed the air. "If you do this every morning, I'll get fat."

"How do you know it's not something healthy? Could be a six-pack of fruit-and-yogurt parfaits," he said. Then he set the bags on the table.

"Could be, but it's not. It's Egg McMuffin sandwiches. Sausage." I sniffed again. "And hash browns. And...French toast sticks?"

"Right on all counts." He started unloading one of the bags, so I quickly poured the coffee and we sat at the breakfast table together, munching and sipping. Myrtle lay down underneath the table for a nap, and a possible crumb or two. The pup climbed up on top of her back and gnawed on her ears, growling ferociously. She didn't mind a bit. In fact, she seemed more content than I'd ever seen her.

"I checked in with Vanessa this morning," he said.

I glanced at the clock. 8:30 a.m. "Did you wake her up to do it?"

"She was already in the office. Gretchen Young's previous job was at Riverside."

I stopped with a sandwich halfway to my mouth. "Where Marie was?"

"Yeah."

"So Gretchen is the demon Marie thinks is after you and the boys. And now we know Marie actually knew her."

"Did you say Gretchen?" Misty asked from the doorway. She'd come in quietly, still in jammies and a robe, apparently lured by the smell of fresh coffee. She poured herself a cup and sat at the table. "There was a Gretchen here yesterday looking for you, Mason, and asking about the boys."

Mason raised his brows. "What did you tell her?"

"Not much. Christy sent her packing before I could say anything. She said we didn't know her and shouldn't be talking about that kind of stuff with a stranger. Wouldn't even let her through the front gate." She shrugged. "She told me afterward that she didn't like her on sight, but I have no idea why. She seemed okay to me. Maybe it was just because she seemed so surprised that Jere and Josh didn't die in the fire."

I looked at Mason. "What do you make of all this?"

"I don't know. But she did work at Riverside. She must've had contact with Marie for Marie to know her name. Maybe Marie's warped mind decided to build some delusions around her, or…"

"Or…?"

"Or what?" Misty asked.

"Or Marie has a good reason to be suspicious of her. Gretchen didn't tell you she'd worked at Riverside, did she, Mason? Why would she keep that from you?"

"Because I didn't ask."

"Right. She showed cleavage instead of a résumé. I forgot."

He made a face at me. "She did have a résumé. She either left that part off or I skimmed it a little too quickly. She was between jobs and about to lose her apartment. I felt sorry for her. I should've run a background check."

"Well, at least you've run one now." I shook my head. "Something about Gretchen has felt off to me right along. But she skitters away before I'm in her presence for any length of time. Like she knows I can read her if she hangs around too long."

"Now I think you're reaching," Mason said.

"Weird, though," Misty said, "that Christy felt something, too."

I thought of Misty as the good twin. But I was beginning to think of Christy as the twin most like her aunt Rachel. I wondered if she'd inherited more from me than my less-than-sweet nature.

"How the hell could Marie know she was working for you, though?" I asked Mason. "That's what I can't figure out."

He shrugged.

Misty said, "Maybe Josh mentioned it. You know how the kid talks. It's almost nonstop when he gets on a roll."

"No, we haven't been out to see Marie since before she came to work for me, so that can't be it," Mason said.

"I'm going to question her this morning. See if she remembers any interaction with Marie at Riverside. It would be great if you could come, too, Rachel, but I'm scared as hell to leave the boys alone with Marie and this arsonist, whoever it is, still on the loose."

Chills ran up my spine at the words *leave the boys alone.* The memory of coming back from a date to find the house on fire, and thinking the kids were still inside, was too fresh. "I'll stay, it's all right. We'll lock the gate and arm the security system."

"You'll have a cruiser outside, too," he said.

"Do me a favor, though, and take Rosie with you. I'm telling you, there's something off about Gretchen. If I think it, and Christy thinks it—and even Marie thinks it—maybe you should pay attention. Be careful."

"I will. You too."

He got up as if to leave, and Misty said, "One sec. Um…" She looked from me to Mason and back again. "I think there's something wrong with Jeremy."

Mason sat back down.

I said, "He's gone through a lot. His mother—"

"It's more than that. I don't know what it is, he won't tell me. But there's something really wrong. Something big."

Nodding, Mason said, "I'll go up and talk to him."

"Maybe you should stay with the boys and I should go talk to Nurse Gretchen," I suggested.

"You're already biased, Rache. You couldn't trust your own NFP, given how much you dislike her. No, I've got this."

I couldn't even argue with him on that, so I just sighed and broke off part of my sandwich, handing it under the table to Myrtle, who jumped up to grab it so fast the pup flew off her back, hit my shin and landed on my feet.

I gave *him* a nibble, too, as Mason headed back through the house and up the stairs. "What do you think it is, Misty?" I asked. "What's your intuition telling you?"

She shook her head slowly. "I'm not you, Aunt Rache. No NFP here." She tapped her head. "But it's got something to do with his father."

My heart skipped a beat. "His...father?"

"He has a picture in his wallet. He had it out and was staring at it in the middle of the night."

I lifted my brows. "What were you doing with him in the middle of the night?"

"Not having sex. God, Mason was up prowling the halls so often we couldn't have gotten away with that even if we'd tried. Which we didn't."

"You'd better not."

"He's messed up, Aunt Rache. It feels like he's got something rumbling around way down deep inside him, getting ready to erupt. It scares me."

"Scares you how?"

"It doesn't scare me for me. It scares me for *him*."

It scared *me*, too. The kid was seventeen. How much more of a beating could his psyche take?

Mason was back, leaning into the kitchen where I sat with my niece. I was glad it was the weekend and no one had to go to school. "He's sound asleep, and I think he needs it. I'll talk to him later." He ducked back out, but told me with his eyes to come with him.

I took my coffee with me, and Misty was smart enough to stay put and give us a minute alone. Myrtle remained where she was, but in her case, it was all for the potential handouts. The legend of canine loyalty evaporates in the presence of fast food.

I followed Mason all the way out to the front steps, pulling the door closed behind me.

"Arm the system. Keep the gate closed and locked. If Marie didn't set that fire, then we still have an arsonist on the loose, one with a grudge against me, apparently. Maybe it's connected to the Rouse investigation. Maybe it's personal. And maybe it's Gretchen. Whoever it is, they're out there."

"I'll be careful. Believe me."

He lowered his eyes. "You're scared. I don't blame you, but—"

"Scared? Yeah, scared I'll have to kick some firebug's ass in front of the kids." I sighed, pissed that he could see right through my bravado. Fortunately, he pretended not to. What can I say? The guy was almost perfect. I mean, aside from having the world's most fucked-up family. "Mason, what do you think is going on with Jeremy?"

"I don't know. It could be just spending time with Marie. Can you imagine being that afraid of your own mother?"

"No. I can't." I swallowed hard and brought up the thing we were both avoiding. "What if she told him? About Eric?"

"She didn't. She *wouldn't*."

"He was so quiet all the way home." I lowered my head, trying not to imagine what the poor kid would be going through if he knew. "And all day yesterday, too."

"Whatever it is, we'll deal with it. I've gotta go, Rache. Rosie's meeting me at Gretchen's apartment."

"All right. Be careful."

"I will." He looked down at me, then, with a crooked half smile, bent down and kissed me goodbye. "This is starting to feel kinda domestic, isn't it?"

"Get out of here before I show you I'm still feral." I made a claw and swiped it at him, then added, "But pick up milk and bread on the way home."

He laughed out loud. I hoped he knew I wasn't kidding. Those boys of his could pack away food like a small army. I'd learned that while he'd been in the hospital and they'd been guests in my home. I hadn't stocked up since he'd been out of the hospital, and that was going to be crucial and probably urgent.

Mason drove away, stopping outside the gate to close it and turn the lock. I should really have it automated, with a speaker system I could answer from the house. I mean, if we were going to have to use the damn thing all the time, we might as well make it easy.

I turned and went back inside, straight to the kitchen to refill my coffee mug. Misty was still there. "Have you thought about how neat it is, the way things worked out, Aunt Rache?"

"How do you mean?" I asked. I knew she didn't think Marie escaping, the boys being kidnapped or Mason's home being torched were cool.

"If Mason hadn't saved those kids in that other fire and gotten hurt doing it, he wouldn't have been in the hospital. If he hadn't been in the hospital, Jeremy and Joshua wouldn't have had to spend so much time here. If they hadn't had to spend all that time here, half their stuff wouldn't still be up in their bedrooms. They've got clothes, games, even their old PS3."

I was only half listening, because something in my brain had stalled at the mention of *that other fire.* It hadn't been the *only* other fire. There had been one in between. The one that killed Dr. Cho. Marie's psychiatrist.

That was another person Gretchen Young would've known from her job at Riverside. Or *could've* known, anyway.

"Aunt Rache?"

"Yeah. Yeah, I hear you." I went to the phone and dialed a number I knew pretty well by now. It rang only once, and then the chief of police answered herself with a crisp, "Cantone."

"Hey, Vanessa. It's Rachel." I was supposed to call her Chief in public, but I didn't consider a phone call from my own living room to be public.

"How are the boys?" she asked. "They okay?"

"Remains to be seen. They're sleeping in."

"They probably need it."

"Yeah. Listen, um, I just…I just have an inkling here. It's probably nothing but—"

"Since when are your inklings ever nothing? What is it?"

"Gretchen Young. Is there a photo of her anywhere around there you can get your hands on?"

"I can probably pull one from state records. DMV, nursing license. Why?"

"I'm just curious what Peter Rouse's reaction would be to seeing it."

It took her a minute. Then she sucked in a breath. "The mysterious other woman he says set the fire that killed his wife?"

"Maybe. He said his girlfriend from hell was a brunette. Gretchen's a blonde, but it might be from a bottle. She worked at Riverside, and Marie knew her. Dr. Cho's house burned, too, and he was Marie's shrink. And then Mason's house."

"But Marie set Mason's fire."

"Did she? Do we really know that? The boys said the house was fine when they left it. No fire. And that she was with them the entire time from then on."

Vanessa sighed. "It was crude. She splashed gasoline all around the place and set it off. Maybe she started it in the back, and took off with the kids before they could get a glimpse of the flames. The Rouse fire was clever, careful, made to look accidental."

"Look, I know I'm reaching here, but it bears a look, doesn't it?"

"Why am I even arguing with you? If you say she's the one, then she's the one. Is she the one, Rachel?"

"I don't know. I haven't been around her long enough to get a handle on her, but something about her makes me uneasy."

"I'll show Mr. Rouse the photo."

"Let me know, okay? Mason's out with Rosie, questioning her now."

"I'll keep you posted. Thanks for the tip, Rachel."

She hung up, and I turned to see Jeremy slogging tiredly down the stairs. He hadn't showered or dressed yet, and his hair was sticking up every which way.

God, I was glad to have him back. Myrtle was in her dog bed in front of the fireplace already, having deduced that breakfast had ended. But her head came up when she heard his footsteps, ears perked. The puppy danced little circles at the foot of the stairs until Misty came out and picked him up. "There's coffee," she said. "And your uncle brought us breakfast. Come on."

He let her take his hand and tug him toward the kitchen, but his eyes were on mine.

"Morning, Jere."

"Morning."

"Mason wanted to talk to you before he left, but he also wanted to let you sleep in. He'll be back soon, though."

He nodded, but he was still searching my eyes. I don't know what he was looking for. Then he let himself be pulled into the kitchen by his adoring girlfriend. Myrtle got up, heaving a huge sigh that said, *You know, you people could make my life a lot easier if you'd just all eat at the same time.* And then she lumbered slowly into the kitchen to resume her handout-gathering position.

Gretchen saw them arrive. Mason, in his black car, the one she knew very well, and his partner, Rosie, who she'd only seen from a distance while watching Mason, in a bright yellow Hummer. They parked right in front of her building, got out and spoke to each other before coming to the door.

They must know. They had to know. It had been a mistake to give Mason her real address. Her other lovers had never known anything real about her. Not her real name. Not her real job. Not her real address. But he knew it all. He knew because she'd wanted to work for him, so she'd had to give real details, even if she had left a few things out.

Mistake, mistake, mistake.

She took her emergency bag off the hook near the door. It was a backpack-style bag with the Riverside logo on it. She kept it packed and ready for quick getaways because there was always a chance she would need it. Then she moved quickly through her apartment, sweeping a few extra things into the bag. Her address book. Her laptop. The calendar off the wall, where she'd marked dates and times. Then she took her jacket and her purse. Just before she left, she set the delayed start button on the microwave and put the gift she had just mixed up inside.

Mason must know it was her. He was coming to arrest her for setting his house on fire. That bitch Marie had ruined everything. She was supposed to escape, yes, but only take the fall for the fire and the deaths of her own two kids, and later, Rachel. She was *not* supposed to snatch the brats before the fire was even set.

Hell.

Mason and his big partner were pressing the buzzer down below. Gretchen hit the button that unlocked the building to let them in, and then she left her apartment, leaving the door open and heading down the hall to the stairwell no one ever used. It wasn't obvious from the ground level. Besides, they would take the elevator. Everyone took the elevator.

She jogged down the stairs three floors, and then she was on the ground level, near the rear entrance, which opened onto the parking lot. She had her keys in her hand, ready. Unlocked the car. Threw her bag inside. Then, getting into her little car, she checked her watch and turned to stare at her own apartment window.

The explosion went off just as she'd intended. A window shattered outward, raining glass and debris down on the parking lot as she calmly drove away.

When Mason pushed the buzzer with Gretchen's apartment number on it, there was no answer. He gave her a minute.

"So the kids are still okay?" Rosie asked while they waited.

"Yeah. They were more worried about that Xbox than anything else. You did all right with that, partner."

"Gwen's idea. She loves the bunch of you. So the boys... Marie didn't hurt 'em?"

"She didn't hurt 'em. I was afraid she might, but she didn't. I'm starting to have a hard time believing she would, but—"

"I don't. Not after seeing her handiwork. Marie's a dangerous kind of crazy, Mace. You gotta know that."

"I do know it. But she loves those boys. In her way." He hit the buzzer again. "I'm not sold on Gretchen's innocence, but at the same time, Marie's still on the loose, so if she's targeted Gretchen, then we need to warn her. And we need to know how she knows Marie, what her connection is to all this, too."

"You think there's more going on here, don't you?"

"Yeah, I do. Gretchen worked at Riverside. No reason for her not to tell me that. And Rachel's been uneasy about her from the get-go. I thought it was just jealousy at first, but—"

"Rachel?" Rosie interrupted. "I can see her angry, but not jealous, pal. If she thought you liked some busty nurse better than you liked her, she'd probably kick you in the balls and send you packing."

"Yeah." Mason smiled when he said it, then hit the buzzer again.

This time the lock disengaged with a noisy clack, and he pushed the door open and went inside. The elevators were front and center, so they got in, and he punched the number three button, then waited. The car moved like it was being cranked by hand.

"What do you think about her, Mace? The nurse?"

"I think I was an idiot not to run a background check myself." The doors finally opened. He looked left and right, then headed in the direction the letters told him to go, toward 3-F. As he approached the door, he saw that it was standing open.

"That's odd." Rosie knocked on the open door.

"Gretchen?" Mason called. "Gretchen, it's Mason Brown. Are you in there?"

"Shit, I hope Marie didn't get here first," Rosie said. He pulled out his gun.

Mason did the same, then shoved the door open

wider with one arm, holding his gun in the other hand, and turning to step inside.

There was a sound. The hum of something running.

Rosie grabbed Mason's shoulder and jerked him backward into the hall just as the place exploded. The shock wave sent them smashing into the opposite wall and slammed the apartment door closed. On the floor, Mason held one arm over his face as debris fell like hailstones and the building's fire alarm screamed him deaf.

He pushed himself up off the floor, still holding one arm in front of his face, because the apartment was on fire. Looking around, he spotted Rosie on the floor, up against the wall, nodding that he was okay. Then he spotted a fire extinguisher and smashed the glass so he could yank it off the wall. "Get out to the parking lot, see if you see her anywhere."

"Marie?" Rosie asked, getting to his feet.

"No. Gretchen. I don't think Marie has the know-how to do this. Could be Rachel was right."

"Isn't she always?" Rosie jogged down the hall as Mason blasted his way into the apartment with the extinguisher.

Misty came stomping into the kitchen while I was cleaning up the breakfast mess and making myself a fresh pot of coffee. "I need a ride home," she said, slamming herself into a chair.

I had just pressed the brew button and turned around to eyeball her. She was working up a good fit about something. "I can't leave the boys, hon. I'm sorry."

"Fine, I'll walk, then." She shot to her feet. "I'm not staying here."

It was a few miles, but she could probably manage it. I wouldn't let her, of course, given all the crap we had going on and the fact that my nearly three-mile-long road was a dirt track that wound through county-owned forest before hitting the village of Whitney Point. "You want to tell me what's wrong?"

"Jeremy's being a jerk." She crossed her arms and paced my big kitchen. "Says he's not in the mood for company. Says he wants to be alone."

"Yeah. I imagine when you get kidnapped by your own mother, who's criminally insane, and you risk your own life to get your kid brother to safety, and then you watch an army of cops kick in the door of the bathroom where you think your mother's hiding while you sit there helplessly waiting to hear the report of the bullet they're probably about to fire into her skull, you need a little downtime. So again, I ask you, what's the problem?"

She stopped long enough to glare at me. "I knew you'd be on his side."

"Of course I'm on his side. Jesus, Misty, when did you turn into one of those stereotypical teenage girls who can't see beyond her own makeup mirror, anyway? I never pegged you as one of those."

Her mouth dropped open. She snapped it shut again. "I know he's been through a lot, but he doesn't need to take it out on me."

"Telling you he needs some time alone isn't exactly taking anything out on you. It's being honest with you. And you're falling into the trap of the ignorant. Letting what he says or does decide your mood for you, instead of picking it for yourself."

She rolled her eyes. "It's 'quote the latest book' time, isn't it?"

"Yes, it is. Now sit your impossibly tiny ass down.

We'll have coffee and hash this out. And don't even think about arguing."

Sighing heavily, the poor, put-upon teenager returned to her chair and sank into it.

"Three cleansing breaths," I told her. "You know the drill."

I got fresh cups and my favorite pumpkin spice creamer, which contained a ridiculous number of calories, and plunked them on the table. Then I dug around for the leftover doughnut I knew I'd stashed in the bread box, took it out and broke it in half. The coffeemaker took six minutes. It was one of my favorite miracles of modern science. So I was pouring almost before she'd finished taking the three deep, cleansing breaths. I know, I used to roll my eyes at the method, too, but you couldn't argue with success, and it worked. It always, always worked.

I sat down with my mug, pushed her half doughnut toward her (doughnuts always work, too) and said, "So do you *like* being mad enough to choke him?"

"No." She sighed.

"Sometimes you do. Admit it. Sometimes the drama is fun. Sometimes you're just waiting for your boyfriend to screw up so you can bitch him out. Sometimes you're practicing your bitch-out before he even screws up because you're so sure he's going to."

She looked me right in the eyes. "I don't do that." But she was nodding all the same. "Other girls do. I've seen it. A lot. But I really don't do that, Aunt Rache."

"Then you're a rare female indeed. Most of us do it well into our thirties."

"Mom has called Christy on it so many times that I guess I know better." She shrugged. "She still does it, though."

I nodded. Sipped my coffee. Gave her time to get a little sugar into her bloodstream, where it could trigger happy endorphins to spill into her brain. Then I said, "I don't think Jeremy could hurt more if you spent the next hour slicing his skin with razor blades. He spent the night afraid his own mother was going to kill him, honey. I don't think we can even begin to imagine what that does to someone. I don't think *he* even knows."

She nodded slowly. "You're right. God, I'm an idiot."

"No you're not. You're almost as enlightened as your auntie."

"Oh, please. Believe your own PR much?" But she was smiling, teasing me, so it was okay. She dunked her half doughnut and took a big soggy bite, nodding and mulling. After she swallowed she said, "There's something else bugging him, though. Something his mother said to him, but he won't tell me what. I think that pissed me off more than anything."

I nodded. "Just because you love someone doesn't mean they're obligated to tell you everything the second you decide you want to know, though."

"Yeah."

"He might be working through it himself. He might tell you someday, or he might not. You have to be okay with that. You have to be okay with the fact that not everything is about you. This is his journey, and it's been a rough one. Whatever he has to do to get by, that's got to be his call. You get to decide if you can live with that or not. But you don't get to decide what *he* can or can't live with."

She was looking at me as I spoke, nodding slowly. "Wow. That's good stuff, Aunt Rache. No wonder you and Mason are so good together."

I had to clap a hand over my mouth to keep from

spitting out my doughnut. Lowering my head, I tried again to swallow, with an assist from my mug of deliciousness. *Oh, pumpkin spice, how I love you.*

"What?" she asked, looking at me, amused.

I shrugged. "Just because I can dispense wisdom doesn't mean I can practice it. Look, I'd probably get all pissy if I thought Mason was keeping secrets from me, too." *Although in hindsight, it's kind of easy to see why he did. And if Jeremy is keeping the same secret, that his dad was a serial killer, well, can you blame him for not wanting to tell his girlfriend?* "I mean, I'd know I was being an unreasonable bitch, but I'd probably do it anyway. At least until I got over myself. Which seems to take less time these days than it used to." I patted her hand across the table. "I'm a work in progress. We all are. The trick isn't to be perfect, the trick is to recognize where there's room for improvement and then to improve."

She heaved a heavy sigh. "I should apologize to him."

"Yeah. But you should do it later. He asked for space. Maybe we should both let him have it for a little while."

"Okay. Yeah, you're right."

"I know I am." I got up from the table, taking my by now nearly empty mug back to the pot for a refill. Halfway there, I stopped dead as I felt a bomb go off inside my head. No other way to describe it. There was a blast, flashing light, a shock wave that hit me square in the chest so hard that I staggered backward, and my mug smashed to the floor.

The next thing I knew, Misty was in front of me, shaking me until I blinked away the vision of flames and fire and saw her. I didn't know when she'd gotten up and come to me. I'd missed that part.

"Aunt Rache! What the *hell*?"

I took an openmouthed breath. Then I took another. And then I felt a sickening clarity come over me. "Mason. Oh, Jesus, Mason."

15

Mason managed to douse the flames before choking to death on the smoke. The explosion had been huge, but the resulting flames were just getting started. Having learned respect for them the hard way, he ducked back into the hallway as soon as he was done, meeting the firefighters who came trooping into the hall from a stair door at the far end. He absently registered that the stairway was at the rear of the building. Probably led down to a parking lot.

He blocked the firefighters' paths, holding up his hands. "It's out. Before you head in there, just know we've gotta preserve evidence as best we—" *Hack cough choke.*

The firefighters, there were five of them in the hall now, radioed their chief. "We've got a cop up here says he put the fire out. Apartment's a crime scene."

"That him coughing?"

"Yeah, Chief."

"Give him some fucking oxygen and stay where you are. I'll be right up."

True to his word, Fire Chief Tony Fuscillo arrived a few minutes later, almost as winded as his EMT seemed to think Mason was. He was past due for retirement, but fighting it hard, and he was built like a taller Danny DeVito. He had as much attitude as you'd expect from a gangster, which, he claimed, he had plenty of in his family, *you know whaddahm sayin'?* He saw Mason and shook his head. "You decide to make running into burning buildings a fuckin' hobby or somethin'?"

Mason took off the oxygen mask and sent a quick look at the EMT reaching down to put it back on. It was enough to make the guy back off. "Screw you, Chief," he said affectionately. "It's a crime scene. I had to try to preserve the evidence."

"Yeah, but my job is to protect the residents by making sure this bitch is out. *Capiche?*" He crooked his head to one side. "I'll send one guy in alone."

Chief Tony nodded at a firefighter thirty years his junior whose badge read Kenneth Howe.

"You know the drill, Kenneth," Mason said "This could be the arsonist we've been looking for."

"Yes, sir." Kenneth Howe went inside. Mason stood in the doorway, watching him move almost catlike despite his heavy gear, through the apartment. He stopped every few steps and took a careful look around him.

Mason's cell phone rang. As he picked it up and saw it was Rachel, the elevator doors opened and Rosie, who'd gone out to look for Gretchen, emerged, Chief Cantone at his side. She had a worried-mother look on her face, which she came by honestly since she had a kid with her partner, Sally, but also a little surprising, since she was younger than he was. Go figure. Women baffled him.

That was why he liked Rachel. She was brutally honest, straight up telling him what she thought, like it or not. In fact, he liked it. There was no guessing, no wondering where you stood with her.

He held up a finger to the chief and took Rachel's call.

"Was there…some kind of explosion?" she asked the second he answered.

"Hell, has it hit the news already?"

"No," she said. And she didn't say more. She didn't have to. Sometimes the shit she knew sent shivers right up his backbone. This was one of those times.

"Yeah, we had a little blast at Gretchen's apartment. I'm all right," he told her. "Everyone's all right."

"Do you think Marie…?" She stopped for a second, then whispered, "Or Gretchen?"

"I don't know, but I hope we'll find some evidence." He was looking in through the open apartment door again; Vanessa Cantone was behind him doing the same, like his shadow. It looked as if the kitchen area was pretty blackened and the windows back there were blown out, but the rest of the place seemed almost intact. "I put… I mean, the fire was put out fast. Not too much damage."

"You put it out, didn't you? Mason, did you walk into another burning house?"

"Of course not." *It was an apartment.* "I've gotta go. I'll call you when we finish up here, okay?"

"All right." She paused, then, "You're okay? Really? All the way?"

"Not even a blister," he said.

"Okay. Go, then. Do your cop thing."

"See you soon." He disconnected. Vanessa had moved up beside him in the doorway, crowding him so she could get a look for herself, but they parted to let the young firefighter out.

"What did you find in there?" Vanessa asked.

Howe stood up straighter when he saw her and introduced himself, pulling his mask and helmet off as he came out the apartment door. Several more cops had arrived. "C'mon," Howe said. "It's too smoky up here." He nodded toward the stairs, then headed them down the hall.

Cantone called out over her shoulder to the other officers who'd arrived by then. "Just tape it off and come downstairs until the smoke clears out. No one inside until the arson investigator arrives."

Then she led the way, with Mason and Kenneth right behind her, down the first flight of stairs. The fire chief came behind them, as did Rosie. The two of them had to take the stairs single file, both being big guys.

The air on the landing was clear. Smoke rises, after all. Four of them stood on the landing, way too close for Mason's comfort. Rosie stayed on the step just above, because there was no room for him to squeeze in. Firefighter Howe ended up looking directly down into the cleavage of the Binghamton police chief, and he clearly appreciated the view.

"Quit looking at my tits and tell me what you saw in that apartment, Howe." Vanessa was 100 percent in police chief mode. Mason had seen her step into the role as if she'd been born to it. She commanded respect, and she got it in spite of her good looks and killer figure, not because of them.

Howe's cheeks got red, but he jerked his eyes up to meet hers. Poor kid was moonstruck. Maybe thunderstruck was a better term. He didn't know, or maybe just didn't care, that she was not only married but to another woman. Ah, youth.

"Chief Cantone," Howe blurted. "Um, sorry about

that." He shook his head as if he'd been about to say more and then thought better of it. "There's no one inside. The origin point seems to be the microwave oven on the kitchen counter. Looks like whatever was inside it exploded."

"What, exactly, makes you so sure the microwave is the source of the blast?" she asked, slightly sarcastically. Clearly she was pissed about his unprofessional behavior.

"Its door is in the living room."

"Oh." She lowered her head, seemed to regroup, then leaned close to Mason's ear. "Was this Marie or was this your nurse? Because I'm damn sure it was one of them. It sure as *hell* wasn't an accident. Not with that kind of timing."

"I don't know. I don't see how it could be Marie. I just don't think she would've known how to rig something like that. She certainly didn't before she went in. And it's not like she's got access to that kind of information from inside."

"No, it's not." Vanessa took a deep breath. Mason didn't notice the way it expanded her chest until he saw Howe gaping at it. Then he edged himself in between them, blocking the view. The kid was either stupid or he had a death wish.

"At your significant other's suggestion," Chief Cantone said to Mason, either not noticing or choosing to ignore the exchange, "I showed Gretchen Young's photograph to Peter Rouse today. I called him to the station, showed him four other photos along with it, random female mug shots I pulled. I asked him if he knew any of them."

Mason's heartbeat sped up. "Did he?"

"Yeah. He picked out your nurse without even look-

ing at the other four, even though she used to be a brunette. Said she was the other woman, the one who went
stalker on him when he tried to break it off. The one he
said set his wife's house on fire and killed her."

"Holy fucking hell. Rachel was right. It's Gretchen.
It's been Gretchen the whole time."

"It's beginning to look that way. I've got a full investigation into her history under way. Ran into some
sealed files from when she was a minor. Got a judge
unsealing them for us as we speak."

Mason looked at Rosie on the step above them. "You
see any sign of her outside?"

"No, and her car's not in the parking lot. At least,
not the one you mentioned. But there *is* a silver Chevy
Cruze out there."

There was probably a silver Chevy Cruze in every
parking lot in town, Mason thought. But it was too much
not to check out, since there'd been one seen at two recent fatal arson fires.

"Mason," Chief Cantone said, "you and Rosie get
outside and start talking to the residents before they're
allowed back in. I'm going to wait for the arson team
to get here, then see what they think happened in that
apartment."

Mason continued downstairs with Rosie. When they
got outside they circled to the front of the building,
where about twenty people were standing around.

"Everyone, if I can have your attention for a second.
I'm Detective Brown, this is Detective Jones. We're
gonna need a few words with each of you."

"Is the building on fire?"

"When can we go back inside?"

"What's going on in there? Was it a gas leak?"

He held up his hands. "There was an explosion, but it

was contained to one apartment. The fire didn't spread. Your stuff is safe. Your homes are fine. We still don't know the cause, and you'll be able to go back inside as soon as the fire chief says it's safe."

They nodded, muttering.

"First question, who owns the silver Chevy Cruze in the parking lot out back?"

People looked at each other. One guy raised his hand. He was blond, obese and had an unfortunate case of acne.

"Okay, I need to talk to you, then," Mason said. "Rosie?"

Rosie nodded and took over. "All right, this explosion was in the apartment of Gretchen Young, and she wasn't home at the time, so I need to get hold of her so we can tell her what's happened. If anyone knows Ms. Young or saw her today, I'd like to talk to you. Let's take this one by one, all right?"

As he started sorting through people, still talking in his friendly, easy way, Mason made his way to the blond guy and extended a hand. "You can call me Mason," he said. "You are…?"

"Ross Van Deusen. Did my car get damaged in the blast?"

"No. It's fine," Mason said, leading him a few steps away for privacy. "I'm just wondering, does anyone else ever drive it?"

"No. Well, not as a rule."

"That sounds like a yes."

"I did loan it out once."

"Yeah? To who? Relatives, I'll bet."

He frowned. "No. To Gretchen"

Mason tried a casual smile and shook his head slowly. "Why would she borrow your car, Ross, when she has one of her own?"

Ross shrugged. "Her inspection sticker had expired and she had a home care visit to make one night. It wasn't for long. I didn't mind."

"And what night was that?"

Ross lowered his head, furrowed his brows. "Gosh, it was three or four weeks ago. A Friday night. I remember that much."

"I'm gonna have to know which Friday night."

Ross pursed his lips, then held up a finger and pulled out his cell phone. "It was the same week the new WoW expansion pack was released."

"Wow?"

"World of Warcraft. I downloaded it on release day, which is almost always a Tuesday, and was looking forward to the weekend so I could really get into it. I started it the same night Gretchen borrowed the car."

He thumbed through screens on his phone, until he said, "There it is." He turned the phone to face Mason, the calendar date highlighted with a bright red *WoW*.

The date was the night of the fire that had killed Rebecca Rouse. "What time did she take the car?"

"Around seven, I think. I told her to just leave the key in my mailbox." He pointed at the building, and Mason turned to see a grid made up of neat rows of black mailboxes each with an apartment number in gold foil stickers on the front. They hung on the wall beside the door, four rows of six. "So I have no idea how late it was when she brought it back."

"Okay. She borrow it at any other time?"

"No. Just the once."

"And do you leave the keys in the mailbox a lot?"

Ross shrugged. "Almost always. I lose them around the apartment. It's easier if they're on the way out."

Mason nodded. "What about a few nights ago?" He

had to think to remember the night of the fire that had killed Dr. Cho. "Wednesday night?" he asked. "Were your keys in the mailbox then?"

Ross shrugged. "Probably."

"So, Ross, how did she manage to drop your car keys in your mailbox? They're all locked, aren't they?"

Ross nodded. "I gave her an extra key so she could. I *really* didn't want to be interrupted in the middle of game night."

"I see. And, um, did she ever return it? Your extra mailbox key?"

Ross frowned. "You know, I don't think so, now that you mention it."

Mason nodded. "I might need to talk to you again. Do me a favor and jot down your contact info for me." He was reaching into his pocket for a pad and pen, but the kid pulled out a business card and handed it over. Geek Squad.

Mason tucked it into his pocket. "Thanks." Then he said goodbye and headed back to help Rosie interview the other residents.

When Mason came home, I was hard at work at my desk, trying to focus on outlining *The Ultimate Guide to a Luscious Love Life*, and I was staring hard at the screen, which is what I do when I'm really staring into the depths of my mind, trying to spot an answer. I'd started the book like I do all of them, by listing the questions I figured your average reader would have on the subject, then shorthanding my answers underneath one, and finally scribbling the further questions those answers would elicit. When I untangled it all later, it would make sense. In the beginning it was chaos. Darkness upon the face of the deep. It was freewriting.

But I'd come to question number thirteen and hit a snag.

What happens if my significant other and I want completely different things?

It was a great question, and it brought me to a grinding halt. So far, Mason and I had been pretty much sympatico. But now that we were cohabiting, there would be decisions about how things should go. Every single day.

What if we disagree? What if I want red satin sheets while he has his heart set on plaid flannel? What if I want to take a cruise to the Caribbean and he wants to take one to Alaska? What if he wants six more dogs and a pony? Or a motorcycle? Or to grow a full beard, for the love of God?

"Hey," he said near my ear, just as a warm hand curled around my shoulder. "Everything all right? You're staring at the computer like you're trying to melt it with your mental heat ray."

I looked up at him. "You're like a freakin' ninja, you know that? How did I not hear you come in?"

He shrugged, looking not at my eyes but at my screen and blinking cursor.

"No. Uh-uh. No way." I clicked Save and closed the document at the speed of an embarrassed author, then faced him again. "Never do that, okay?"

"Read what you're writing while you're writing it?"

"Yes. That."

"Okay. That's cool. I'm good with that." He shrugged. "I mean, if you don't want the answer to the questions you were sweating over, then far be it from me to—"

"You know the answers?"

He met my eyes, wiggled his brows up and down. "Aren't you going to tell me?"

"Nope." He turned and started a casual and totally

fake saunter toward the kitchen. "You don't want my input, so I'll just go and—"

I sprang from my chair and caught him in two strides, tugged him around by his shoulder, and said, "I snapped at you, didn't I? I didn't mean to. I was in deep."

"You did snap. A little. It's okay. How else am I going to learn not to interrupt when you have that particular expression on your face?"

"I'm sorry anyway."

"I'm sorry for reading over your shoulder. I can see where that would raise your hackles." Then he frowned. "What the hell are hackles, anyway? Exactly where, on the body, are hackles located?"

"You can hunt for them later. First, tell me the answer you think you know, oh, wise guru of relationships."

He smiled slowly. "The answer is simple. Compromise. Satin sheets one night, flannel the next. Alaska one year, Caribbean the next. I promise not to ask for six more dogs and a pony, but I refuse to surrender the possibility of a bike and/or a beard, because, hey, you never know."

I frowned. "Did I write all that?"

"You tend to think with your fingers. Where are the boys?"

"The new Xbox needed breaking in, and luckily Rosie and Gwen bought a bundle that included a couple of games," I said. "I made them hook it up in their bedroom, 'cause I like to work down here during the day. Sandra picked Misty up a couple of hours ago, and the Brown boys have been fighting terrorists in foreign lands ever since."

"Jeremy still sulking?"

"He seems a little better."

"Gaming does that for him."

"Really?"

He nodded. "Shuts the brain off for a while. Like getting wrapped up in a great book or a really good movie."

"Makes sense. I never thought about it that way."

"See how much you're learning, having me around?"

I smiled slowly. "Let's try this again," I said, and I slipped my arms around his waist, hugged up close to him. "Welcome home, Mason. How was your day?"

"It was a revelation. How was yours?"

I gave a shrug. It hadn't been very productive, but I would adjust. "So what did you learn? Tell me everything."

Nodding, he surrounded me with his big strong arm and walked me into the kitchen. It was only four-thirty, so there wasn't anything happening as far as dinner. He went to the sink, cranked on the faucet and washed his hands while he started talking.

"Biggest headline of the day is that it was Gretchen."

I blinked. "What was Gretchen?"

"All of it. The Rouse fire. Dr. Cho. Probably even my house."

"Holy…"

"She rigged her apartment, left the door open. As soon as Rosie and I started to walk in, the microwave exploded. Freaking brilliant, too. She used a balloon."

I blinked, because he was speaking Dutch. "How does one blow up a microwave with a balloon?"

"According to the arson investigator, she did it by putting gasoline and sulfuric acid inside said balloon, and taping a little potassium chlorate and sugar to the outside. Then she set the delay start timer. Not for long, either, or the stuff inside might have eaten through the balloon. But before it could, the microwave turned on, the balloon popped, the chemicals mixed, and..." He flicked open the fingers of both hands. "Boom."

I swore, and when he turned from the sink I looked him up and down for signs of damage. He had some tiny black holes in his shirt, like he'd been peppered by hot sand. And there was a smear of soot across his gorgeous neck.

"Son of a—"

"I'm fine. Rosie's fine, too."

Not that I'd asked, but I would have, I swear.

"How bad was the fire?"

He smiled that time. "Not as bad as she wanted it to be. I grabbed a nearby extinguisher and—"

"Saved the building and everyone in it." I was not amused. He would get himself killed with this hero bullshit of his.

"I kept the evidence from going up in flames."

"What evidence?"

"Don't know yet. We have a team going over the place now. Technically I'm still off duty, so they sent me home." He poured himself coffee, and I wondered if he'd had any lunch. I opened the fridge to peruse its contents. It was filled to bursting, because I'd bribed Amy to give up her Saturday to do some massive grocery shopping, and she'd taken her mission seriously. "I could make you a sub, if you want."

"I need a shower and fresh clothes."

"Cool, I'd rather help with that anyway."

He smacked me on the ass, gave it a squeeze, then sank into a chair and sipped his coffee. "We found the silver Chevy Cruze. Belongs to a neighbor. He loaned it to Gretchen the night of the Rouse fire."

"And again the night of Dr. Cho's?"

"Not knowingly, but by then she knew where he kept the key. I suspect she helped herself."

"She really thought she had everything covered, didn't she?" I frowned. "But why did she do it?"

"Well, Dr. Cho might have caught on to her. And according to Peter Rouse, she was obsessed with him, so she probably wanted to take out everyone she perceived as standing between them."

"And she was crushing on you pretty hard," I said. "Probably had the same idea." I blinked. "God, Mason, she tried to kill the boys. She probably thought they were inside when she set that fire."

He nodded. "She's still out there. We can't let down our guard. Okay? We need to stay on top of this. And the kids…I don't even know what to do about the kids. It's not like they can go to school with all—"

Of course Jeremy chose that moment to walk into the kitchen. He looked a little better than he had earlier in the day, but he still wasn't his usual self. It was like he was hiding under a thick cloud of something.

"We can't not go to school, Uncle Mason. I graduate next weekend. It's the last week. We've got Senior Prank Day, one more Regents test, graduation rehearsal, Senior Legacy Day, Senior Skip Day—"

"You need to go to school on Senior Skip Day?" Mason asked.

I rolled my eyes. "God, didn't you even *have* a childhood? You go to school, meet the rest of your class and then bug out together to raise hell all day." I met Jeremy's eyes. "Grown-ups, right?"

He smiled just a little.

"We'll figure it out later," Mason said. "You've had other things on your mind besides school. I'm sorry I couldn't stay home today, but I'm here now. If there's anything you want to talk about."

Jeremy sat down. He licked his lips. Then he glanced at me.

"Hey, I'm outta here. You guys need privacy, then I'm cool with—"

"No. If it's true you probably should know, too," he said softly. "But it can't be true. There's just no way..." He lowered his eyes. "Mom...she thinks...well, she says she knows...that Dad was..."

I looked at Mason. *What the hell are we gonna tell him if he flat out asks?* I didn't see any answer in his eyes.

And then Jeremy blurted them out, the words we were both dreading. "The Wraith Killer. She says my father was the Wraith." And then he lifted his head and looked at us both in turn, his eyes welling with tears.

I prayed that the truth wasn't in my own eyes and bit my lips to keep silent, because it was not my place to answer the question implicit in Jeremy's words. It was up to Mason. And I'd back him up, whatever he decided to say.

16

Mason's heart froze solid when he heard his nephew ask the question. And he knew he couldn't hesitate in answering, because if he did, the hesitation would be all the answer Jeremy needed.

So he acted fast, and he chose to lie. For the second time in his life. "Jeremy, you know how sick your mother is. You know that, right?"

Jeremy nodded.

"And you know who the Wraith was. You were there when we caught him. Well, when he caught us."

Rachel said, "Your uncle and I would've been his next victims if it hadn't been for you that day, Jere."

Again, he nodded. "That's what I've been telling myself. The Wraith was still killing people after Dad was gone. So it couldn't have been him."

"There. See?" Mason said.

"But when I walked into the cabin that day, where he had you two, I swore I heard Dad's voice. And when that killer lay there dying after I shot him it sounded like he started to call you his little brother, Uncle Mace."

Mason opened his mouth and closed it again, shot

Rachel a look that was a plea for help. And like always, she read it, and she came up with an answer.

"I knew a guy who called every male he knew brother. 'Nice to see you again, brother.' 'Do you need a ride, brother?' 'Brother, can you spare a dime?'" She shrugged. "It's a thing with some people."

She'd bought Mason enough time to come up with his own input. "The man was dying, Jeremy. Who knows what he was saying, or why? He was a serial killer. He was out of his mind even before he was shot."

Jeremy took a deep breath as he searched Mason's eyes. And Mason forced himself to hold the kid's gaze steadily, without flinching, though he felt like a piece of shit for lying to his nephew.

He'd gone through hell to keep his brother's secret. He'd broken every rule he lived by, gone against everything he believed in, broken the law he was sworn to uphold. He'd concealed evidence. He'd lied. All to protect Jeremy and Josh from the horrible truth of what their father had been. They were too young to have that burden placed on them. It was backbreaking, almost too much for *him* to bear, and he was an adult and a seasoned cop. He'd seen it all. He was tough.

No. The kids might need to know someday. But not yet. Not now.

After studying his uncle's face for a long moment, Jeremy finally released a breath so long and intense it seemed as if he'd been holding it for hours. His shoulders slumped forward, and his eyes fell closed. He believed because he wanted to believe, maybe even needed to believe.

"Thank God," he said softly. Nodding emphatically, he got to his feet. "That's what I thought, but I just…I had to know for sure."

Rachel slapped her hands down on the table and got up, as well. "Well, now that that's over with, we should discuss dinner. I sent Amy on a grocery run today. Mason, you'd have been proud of the boys and the way they pitched in to unload it all from her car. I swear she bought enough for a month."

She was nervous, Mason realized, wanting to push the subject as far away from his dead brother as she possibly could, as fast as she possibly could.

"What do you guys think about a giant pan of lasagna?" she asked. "I make a mean lasagna."

"You're not gonna make a mean anything," Mason said. "The boys and I are making dinner tonight."

"You don't have to do that, Mason."

"We want to. Don't we, Jere?"

Jere looked at Rachel and nodded. "Sure, I'm up for that. I'll go tell Josh."

"Actually, I need to shower and change first," Mason said. "Meet me down here in a half hour?"

"Deal."

Mason watched Jeremy disappear all the way up the stairs, making sure he was well out of earshot before he said, "Was that the right thing to do?"

She would probably never know how much it meant to him when she nodded without reservation. "It's what *I'd* have done."

"But was it *right*?"

"Well," she said, "let's consult my vast body of work, shall we? I wish Amy was here. She quotes my books to me chapter and verse. I'm always writing some version of 'when faced with a choice between two less than ideal options, choose the one that does the most good and the least harm.' Telling him the truth would've been harmful to him, Mason. There's no getting around that. Lying was kinder. Not the perfect solution, but the kinder one. It was an act of love. 'No matter the question, the answer is always love.' That's one of my most retweeted sound bites, according to Amy." She shrugged. "I know it sounds like piles of clichéd regurgitated bullshit, but you know, that's how I make my living, and people seem to find it helpful, so…"

He clasped her shoulders, and kissed her softly and slowly. "Thank you."

"You're welcome."

"You're amazing."

"You too."

"I'm going to take a shower now."

"Okay."

Thundering footsteps came down the stairs, and both boys and both dogs raced into the kitchen, because for some reason, Josh couldn't seem to walk anywhere. Ever. The other three were just trying to keep up.

"Can we take the dogs outside?" Jeremy asked.

"I don't think—" Mason began.

"I'll go with them," Rachel offered. "I've been staring at the computer too long. Fresh air will be great."

Mason eyed her and nodded. "Be careful. Stay inside the fence, okay?"

Josh stomped one foot, tipped his head to the extreme left. "Aww…"

"We'll take Myrtle frog hunting after dinner. Promise," Mason said, because taking Myrtle frog hunting had been Josh's favorite pastime since the ice had melted off the reservoir, and he was super excited that Myrt seemed to be teaching Hugo how to do it.

And that was going to have to be good enough, so he left the room before his younger nephew could launch his customary boatload of arguments. Rachel would keep them in line. He trusted her.

That thought made him stop at the top of the stairs and look back down into the kitchen. Rachel was crouching low, putting a leash onto Myrtle's collar, rubbing her ears and talking to her as if she were human. He trusted her, at a time like this, with the lives of his nephews. That was something, wasn't it?

It was good. We had dinner together, and then we took the dogs across the dirt road and down by the dock to let them splash in the water and traumatize every frog within reach. It was a nice, relaxing, a sort of evening with a whole new feel to it. I mean, we'd had dinner together plenty of times before, the four of us. But it was different now. It was sinking in. They lived with me now. We were…a family.

Jesus, what have I gotten myself into?

I smiled. You're not even convincing yourself, you know that, Inner Bitch?

Yeah. I kinda do.

I shrugged. So it was nice. So I was liking it. Did that have to be a bad thing?

Only if you lose it.

On that, my Inner Bitch and I were in full agreement.

We played in the water until almost eight, then trooped back inside for dessert and TV. The boys opted, of course, to take their bowls of ice cream up to their rooms and their brand-new Xbox. Mason and I hugged them good-night, then sank onto the sofa with our respective bowls. I flipped TV stations, and he pulled a stack of pages off my fax machine and then joined me.

I frowned. "Those weren't there earlier," I said. "Must've come in while we were outside. Or else we were having so much fun I just didn't notice. " I prayed it wasn't a revision letter, then reminded myself it was the weekend. Revision letters never came on weekends.

"I'm glad you were having fun. You have to tell me if this gets to be too—"

"Hey." I put my hands on his shoulders. "This isn't an experiment, Mason. It's not a trial period. It's a commitment." I blinked and sat back hard. "Damn, I can't believe I just said that." And then I looked at him again. "Is that how you feel about it, too?"

He set his ice cream bowl on the coffee table to let it get soft. I loved that he did that. I loved that I knew that he did that. Then he took my chin in his hands, and kissed me, and it was sexy as hell. When he stopped, he said, "*That's* the way I feel about it. Sorry if I left you any room for doubt."

"Well, you know, we're not much for extended discussion of these things."

"True enough."

"In fact, this is probably some kind of record."

"It's also probably enough for one night," Mason said. He tapped the papers into a smoother pile and put them on my lap. "Ah, these are the sealed court documents on Gretchen Young. I asked Vanessa to fax them here as soon as they came through."

I looked down at the papers and right back up at him again. "Let's read quickly, then. I have *The Walking Dead* on the DVR, and I'm ready to watch it."

He nodded, took the report and started leafing through it. "Gretchen's records were sealed because she was legally adopted by her grandmother after her parents were killed. You wanna guess how they died?"

"Gee, let me think. House fire?"

He nodded. "It was determined that flammable materials had collected behind the electrical outlet covers in several spots around the house. Mice, the report suggests. One outlet shorted, and the tinder caught fire."

"Or maybe...?" I asked, because I knew he had more.

"Or maybe someone ignited the tinder first, and the short happened once the coating melted off the wires. And maybe it wasn't mice that put it there at all."

"How old was Gretchen when this happened?"

"Thirteen."

"God, Mason. We've got to get this woman off the streets. She's completely insane."

"Yeah, well, we'd better find her before Marie does, or I'm afraid one of them will have more blood on her hands and the other will be dead."

"Are not!" Joshua yelled.

"Are so!" The two boys came running back down the stairs, dogs following, as always.

"No way, stupid-head!"

"We are so, Joshua."

"Hey, hey, hey." I stood and held up my hands. "Man, you guys weren't this noisy while your uncle was in the hospital."

"Well, you can't throw us out now," Joshua said. "Our house is gone."

"Like I'd ever throw you out," I said, tossing a decorative pillow at his head. He ducked. It hit a vase, which hit the floor and broke into three pieces. The room went dead silent. I looked at the pathetic vase and burst out laughing. And then they all did.

"So what's the argument about?" Mason asked, once we caught our breath again.

"Josh thinks we're canceling my graduation party next weekend," Jeremy said. "Because of everything that happened. I told him there was no way you'd do that to me. Right?"

Mason looked at me, looked at Jere, lifted his hands. "Okay, let's talk about that."

"No way. You're not really—"

"I said let's talk about it. I haven't made a decision. This is the first time things have been quiet for long enough that I've even been able to think about that." He picked up the remote, pushed the pause button and set it down again. "Okay, so…graduation is next weekend."

Josh took the reclining chair. Jeremy sat on the edge of the coffee table, leaning forward, elbows on his knees. "Yes, it's next weekend."

"Most of the work is already done," I said. "The decorations are all at Sandra's. The food and the cakes are ordered."

"However, we'll have lots of people coming and going, and we have two dangerously mentally ill women running around loose, both with a huge inter- est in crashing this event. One of them because she wants to kill us." The boys already knew all this. We'd filled them in so they wouldn't be caught unaware if Gretchen showed up.

"Not all of us," I said. "Not you, Mason. You she wants to…I don't know…*own*, I guess. On a leash or in a cage in the basement for all I know. The rest of us are the ones in her way." I shot a look at Jeremy. "A gradu- ation party is a big deal, but getting killed is a bigger deal. Don't you think?"

"Half the guests will be cops," Jeremy pointed out. "All Uncle Mason's friends are cops. We've got a fence. We can check people at the gate. We couldn't be any safer if we had the party at the police station."

"Now there's a thought," Mason said.

"C'mon, Uncle Mace!" Jeremy was getting whiny, which was particularly unattractive in a seventeen-year-old almost-man.

I looked at Mason and shrugged. "He's got a good point."

"A couple of 'em," Mason said. He sighed. "I'm gonna talk it over with the chief. Your grandmother will be back by then, so we have to take her safety into account, too."

"We can make her wear a bulletproof vest," Josh said. It was his first contribution to the conversation, so I nodded like it was a great suggestion, though privately I thought she would never go for it because it would clash with her pearls. Then I frowned, "When does she get back from her cruise, by the way? She doesn't even know about any of this, does she?"

"I didn't want to ruin her trip," Mason said.

"I can't believe the chief of police gets to decide whether I get to celebrate finishing high school," Jeremy complained.

"Not just her," I put in. "I'm not sure how happy Sandra and Jim will be about having the girls attend a party that requires armed police officers for bouncers. And you wouldn't want to have it without Misty, would you?"

"That's blackmail," Jeremy said softly. "Come on, you guys. I'm *graduating*. It's a big deal."

"It's the biggest," I agreed.

"And don't think we don't know that, Jere," Mason said. "I promise, if there's a way to make it happen, I'll make happen. But I can't risk your life for it. Not after coming so close to losing you."

Jeremy sighed as if we'd just handed him a death sentence and hauled himself back upstairs.

Josh said, "He really wants to have that party." He looked at the stairs and then back again. "With the party barge. He's like…*so* psyched about that."

Mason wiggled his eyebrows to make Josh smile. "You wait till he sees his present."

"What is it?" Josh asked in a loud whisper.

"No way, I'm not telling," Mason said.

"I have to get him something, too, Uncle Mace."

"You need me to take you shopping?" he asked.

"No, I just need your credit card. I'm ordering it online. The newest edition of "Call of Duty," with the rumble pack. It comes out tomorrow, so if I order it tonight—"

Mason pulled the card from his wallet and handed it over. Joshua ran toward my desk, then skidded to a stop. "Is it okay if I use your computer, Aunt Rache?"

Aunt Rache. Well, that was a first. It warmed my cockles, and I wondered if cockles on the body were located anywhere near where hackles resided. *Crying hackles and cockles, alive, alive-o.*

"Sure, kid. Go ahead."

He hit the chair and slid up to the desk, clicking keys like a pro, and pretty soon he had the item placed in his cart.

Jeremy called from upstairs, "Josh, let's finish this level already. We've gotta get up for school in the morning."

Josh looked at Mason, who said, "Go on, we'll finish up the order for you. Leave the plastic."

"Thanks. Night, Uncle Mace. Night, Aunt Rachel."

"Night," we said together as the kid ran up the stairs. Mason went to my iMac, picked up his card and completed the transaction. Then he said, "Normally their phones serve as their computers. If they start pestering you to use yours all the time, let me know and we'll start looking for one."

"Don't be silly. I don't mind if they—"

"No, really, Rache, in this case you have to draw some boundaries. That computer isn't your hobby, it's your work. If they want a computer for play, I'll get one."

"Okay." I crossed the room to where he sat in my desk chair. "However, can I just remind you that I have three? This one, the desktop upstairs, my laptop. And then there's a tablet, too."

"You like your gadgets."

I nodded. "I might be a closet geek."

"You don't play WoW, do you?"

I spun the chair around and grabbed a handful of his T-shirt. "I'll play just as wow as you want me to, mister."

"Damn, woman…"

Before I let myself get too carried away, I said, "What're you gonna do about school tomorrow? You heard Jeremy. He thinks he's going."

"I don't know. Go sit outside the building all day?"

"Sounds like a plan. I'll bring the laptop."

17

The graduation party was on. I didn't think there had ever really been a question. Mason didn't have it in him to deny Jeremy something that meant so much to him. Even if his lunatic mother and Gretchen Young were still on the loose. Half the cops in the state were looking for them. Both of them.

We sat together in the bleachers, Mason and me, with Joshua in between us and Mason's mother, Angela, sitting on his other side. She was dabbing her eyes with tissues even before the first speaker wrapped up. My sister was on my left, with her two girls and Jim nearby. The twins would graduate in a year, and I'm sure Sandra had that on her mind as she watched, because she was weepy, too. Or maybe she'd become as attached to Mason's boys as I had.

Probably a little bit of both.

"I wish your brother could be here to see this," Angela muttered during the applause. "He would have been so proud."

"Dad *is* proud, Grandma," Josh told her. "He's watching, somehow. Mom, too, I bet." He craned his neck to look around the auditorium as Mason and I exchanged a look.

"Have you seen your mother here, Joshua?" Mason asked

"No, not yet. I promise I'll tell you when I do."

"Joshua, you must know your mother isn't going to risk being caught to attend," Angela said.

"She wouldn't miss this, though," Josh replied. He slid a little closer to Mason and took hold of his hand. The poor kid was as afraid of his mom as he was certain she'd show up.

I looked at Mason, wondering if maybe Josh knew his mother better than either of us did. There were cops at both entrances and a unit outside. Still…

"And now, this year's graduates," said the school principal.

I elbowed Mason, who was still scanning the crowd. "Don't miss it. They're alphabetical, and he's a B."

"He's next," Angela whispered, crying even harder now than before. The poor woman had returned from her cruise only yesterday and learned about the house fire, Marie's escape and the boys' abduction all at once. She was probably still reeling. But she hadn't once complained that Mason hadn't phoned her to let her know what was going on. Not once.

And then Jeremy's name was called, and he rose from his seat at the back of the stage, and walked to the front to accept his diploma and shake the principal's hand. He was smiling from ear to ear, and when he found us the smile grew even wider. I snapped pics like a mad paparazzo.

We were applauding madly when I noticed Jeremy's gaze straying over the spectators. He was searching the faces, probably looking for his mother, just like his kid brother was doing. It broke my heart. If she'd tried to show up here, she would have been arrested on the spot. And rightly so, but still…

We sat through the remainder of the ceremony, right up until the entire senior class threw their hats into the air.

I squeezed Mason's hand. "You're so proud your chest is practically swelling."

He smiled. "I am. He's a good kid."

"He's a great young man. He'll make a great cop, too, someday."

"Yeah, unless I can talk him out of it."

I didn't think there was much hope of that. Jeremy hadn't backed down since he'd mentioned it to us a few weeks ago. But maybe college would change his mind.

People were rising, filing out, merging into one flow of traffic toward the graduates, who were now standing in a receiving line. I congratulated every one I came to, and then we made it to Jere and I hugged his neck.

"You did it, Jeremy. You are *awesome*."

"Thanks, Rache. So where's my present?" he asked with a wink.

"I made your uncle let me get some things to go with what he got you. If I give mine to you first, it'll blow the surprise. But rest assured, they're both at the house. You can unwrap them with all the others." I was such a great liar, that he didn't even pick up on it. Mason's present wasn't wrapped. You couldn't wrap a car. But I desperately wanted him to be surprised.

The crowd was starting to dissipate. "Come on, guys. Our party awaits," I said, and I clasped Joshua's hand automatically as we wound our way through the people.

Halfway to the exit a shiver of awareness moved over my spine like an icy finger. I came to a stop and turned my head slowly, by instinct. For the briefest instant I thought I saw Marie in the crowd, but then everyone closed in, and when they parted again there was a woman I didn't know in the spot where I thought she'd been.

Still, that chill didn't leave me, and my feelings were never wrong. I pulled Josh closer and nudged nearer to Jeremy. Mason noticed. What didn't he notice? And he went on alert; I saw it in his eyes. But he did it without alarming anyone else as we continued to make our way out of the auditorium and into the parking lot. He nodded at the cop guarding the door, and he came along with us.

But nothing happened. No long-lost crazy mothers or killer arsonist nurses came springing out from between parked cars. Nothing. We were fine.

And then we were stopping at the closed gate across my driveway. Mason got out to unlock and open it, and Joshua said, "Hey! Someone's already here."

Mason glanced my way as he got behind the wheel again to drive inside, smiling with his eyes but fighting it.

"Nice wheels, whoever it is," Jeremy said.

I shrugged. "It's kind of old."

"Classic. It could use a paint job, but—" Jeremy got out of the car and wandered over to the green Camaro.

We all got out, too, and Mason took the Camaro IROC-Z key ring out of his pocket. He just stood there holding it up, waiting, while Jeremy walked around the car, admiring it, cupping his face to peek through the glass, his back to Mason the whole time.

Joshua got it. His gaze met mine. I gave him a nod, and his eyes went wide. I giggled, and finally Jeremy turned.

Mason remained where he was, holding the key.

Jeremy looked at him. "What are you… Wait a minute. No! Really?"

"It's yours, kid. Happy graduation."

"Oh, my God. Oh, my *God*!" Jere hugged Mason's neck so hard I figured he'd need a massage later, and when he pulled away he came over and hugged me.

My sister's minivan came through the still-open gate with a happy beep-beep, and a second later Jim joined the other males in admiring the car, while Sandra and the twins started unloading covered dishes and boxes of decorations from the back of the van.

Misty paused near Jeremy. "Do you love it?"

"Yeah." He turned to Mason. "Uncle Mace, can I take it for a spin? Just a short one?"

"I wanna go!" Joshua shouted.

"Not without me. Just for now," Mason told him. "The situation—"

I elbowed him. "Go on, Mason. Do a ride-along with your nephew. We can get things under way. We still have an hour."

"An hour?" Sandra asked. "Come on, girls, move it! We only have an hour!"

Misty kissed Jeremy on the cheek and ran to the van to help with the unloading. Mason and Jeremy got into the Camaro. Jeremy started the engine, which actually roared. I smiled as I watched him shift, then give it too little gas. The engine lugged, almost stalled, until he finally caught first gear.

Sandra stood beside me. "You look for all the world like a proud mother today, sis."

"Don't tell anyone, but I feel like one, too. Go figure." I grabbed a box from the back of the van and headed for the house.

It took us every bit of that hour—even with our menfolk back to help us for the second half of it—to get the party set up. We'd rented a huge canopy tent, which the guys took charge of erecting. We set folding picnic tables and chairs under it, and we unboxed the cake I'd picked up from the bakery before the ceremony. It was a full sheet done in maroon and gold with the Whitney Point High School Eagle in the center. Gorgeous cake. Jeremy parked the Camaro where his friends could easily admire it. By the time people started arriving, a lot of them cops who knew they were there as protection as well as guests, the tent was decked in crepe paper. And the pièce de résistance was the rented pontoon boat bobbing serenely by our dock across the dirt road.

I barely sat still for the next hour as food was uncovered and unwrapped, and people, many of whom I didn't even know, mingled. Jeremy's family connections were wide and many. His grandmother seemed to know almost everyone there, and she surprised me by dragging me around to introduce me to most of them as "Mason's significant other." Myrtle and Hugo made the rounds, too, snarfing up every dropped crumb and begging for more. (And mostly, getting it, because no one with a heart can say no to a bulldog, and no one alive can say no to a bulldog puppy.)

Jeremy came over to me, smiling. He'd opened his card from me, which had his insurance ID cards, with a sticky note that said he was paid up till December. "This is the best, Aunt Rachel. And so is the party. Thank you *so* much."

"It was fun, stretching my long-dormant domestic muscles for a change," I told him. "And you know I'm a closet motorhead, right? I expect my own ride-along in that Camaro once things calm down around here."

"You've got it. Anytime you—"

There was a sharp crack that had me frowning and looking around. Then there was another, and one of the guests dropped his knees, a blood stain spreading across his chest. A third crack shattered the punch bowl. People started screaming and stampeding toward the house. Mason hit Jeremy and me from behind, taking us down and flipping a table sideways in front of us. Food flew everywhere. I crouched with his big arms encircling me, realized the sounds had been gunshots and screamed, "Joshua!"

"Right here, Aunt Rache, right here." I should've known Mason had him, too. He was crouching on Mason's far side.

"Mason, your mother—the twins. My sister!"

"Stay put," he said. "I've got this. I'll find them, figure out the safest place and come back for you." Then he got up and raced away.

I heard more shots, then peered around the table to see Myrtle and Hugo snarfing up the spilled food. I clapped my hands. "Myrtle! Myrtle, come!"

She lifted her head.

"Myrtle, come! *Now!*"

She apparently picked up on the urgency in my voice and came trotting toward us, the pup, as always, so close she was almost tripping over him. I pulled them into our little huddle and then dared to peek up over the edge of the table. The cops were heading into the woods to the right of the house, weapons drawn. Vanessa was with them, barefoot, having kicked off the gorgeous pumps I'd complimented her on earlier.

Where was her partner, Sally?

Mason's mom was behind a table nearby. I saw her crouching there, trembling, and she met my eyes across the gulf of space between us. I held up a hand, telling her to stay there. She nodded.

Looking out again, I saw people hurrying in through the front door of the house. Sandra, the girls, Jim.

Do not let them go into the house. Stop them. Now.

The feeling shocked me, but I'd been through too much not to trust it. "Jeremy, there's something wrong in the house. I have to stop them."

He nodded, pulled out his phone and texted at the speed of light, not even questioning me. I saw Misty tense up. She was with her family, crouching between the lilac bush and the front door, which was crowded with people.

She pulled out her phone and stared at it, then looked up and all around the yard.

Jeremy popped up before I could stop him and waved at her. A shot rang out, and the table in front of him splintered. I screamed and yanked him back down so hard I probably dislocated his shoulder.

Misty showed the phone to her parents, and they looked our way, too.

"What did you tell her?" I asked.

"Get away from the house."

His phone chirped and I read over his shoulder.

Where shd we go?

Jere looked at me, and I looked around helplessly and spotted the pontoon boat still moored near the dock, half of it shielded from view by the woods along the shore-line. "All right, here's what we're going to do. Tell Misty to take the family through the woods on left-hand side of the house. Then they need to get to the shore from there, using the woods for cover along the road, then crossing it as fast as possible."

He texted while I talked, then nodded. "Okay, then what?"

"Take Josh and your grandmother, and make a run for the boat."

"She'll pick us off as soon as we're out in the open," he said.

"You leave that to me. As soon as you're on board, get that boat around the trees, out of sight, and head toward the village. But stay close to shore. The trees will hide you. If she's got a rifle, heading out to the middle won't help. She can reach you there."

"You think it's her? Gretchen?" Jeremy asked.

"Has to be."

I watched as Jim, Sandra and Misty darted out of hiding and into the woods on the opposite side of the house from where the shots had come from. I kicked off my shoes.

Another shot rang out, and I saw a puff of dirt explode near their feet. "I have to go. Get to the boat."

"Aunt Rache—"

"Do it." I sprang from behind the table and ran across my front lawn, waving my arms. "Hey, you crazy fucking bitch! Gretchen! I'm talking to you."

She shot at me, but I was moving at a dead run and changing directions at random. "Come out of the trees, you lunatic. Face me, if you're not too scared."

More shots, one after another. I zigged and zagged, and looked back in time to see Jeremy getting onto the boat. He was carrying Myrtle, for the love of God. Josh was already on board, Hugo in his arms, and so was Angela. I glimpsed them just before they ducked out of sight. Then I yelled some more to keep Gretchen from figuring out what we'd done. "Hey, bitch face, come on. You missed me!"

Something hit me like a ton of bricks then.

Not a bullet. A man. *My* man.

He tackled me like a wrecking ball, then lay on top of me, wrapped both arms around me and rolled until we were at the lilac bush by the front door, where my sister had been. "What the fuck are you doing?" he finally asked.

I nodded toward the lake, and he looked just in time to see what I saw. The tail end of the pontoon boat vanishing around the bend, out of sight beyond the tree-lined shore. "Getting our family out of harm's way," I said.

He frowned.

"What, you don't believe me?"

"No. I just realized there were no more shots while we rolled around the lawn."

"Bitch is probably too jealous to see straight."

He gripped my arm, helped me up. "Let's duck into the house."

"No! There's something wrong in the—" The curtain moved, and I saw Gwen, Rosie's wife, peeking out at us. We couldn't just leave her there. "You're right, let's get inside."

"On three. One, two—"

"Three," I said, and we dashed around the little tree and in through the front door. I slammed it behind me and caught a whiff of something. "Jesus, is that—"

"Gas." Mason said.

I heard something click, like when you hold the ignition button on the grill and it snaps a few times before it emits a spark that ignites...

"Everyone out! *Run!*" I shouted, pointing toward the kitchen.

People stampeded in that direction, but there was a bottleneck at the door into the garage. As people crammed together trying to get through, I heard the whoosh and knew what was coming just before the explosion. Mason hugged me to him, and the next thing I knew we were diving through a window, landing on the lawn in a rain of broken glass as my house, my beautiful house, ignited and began to burn.

18

"No, no, no...my house! My house, Mason, *my house!*"

"I know, I know." He had one arm around my waist, dragging me away from the fire and out toward the cars. Other guests were spilling out of the garage, running back down the driveway, with no idea where the hell else to go. I wondered how many had made it out, and whether others were still trapped inside. I wondered where the kids were, and whether they were safe. I heard sirens. My irritating, pain-in-the-ass alarm system was connected directly to the local FD, which—thank God—was located around the corner from the end of my two-mile dirt road.

Vanessa Cantone came racing toward us. "They found the rifle. The shooter's gone. We don't know if she's still armed."

"Shit, the kids! We have to get the kids," Mason said.

"Go on," she told him. "We'll handle this. Did you see Sally?"

I nodded, my face crumpling. "She was inside. So was Gwen," I told Mason. "I don't know if they made it out or not."

Vanessa's face went two shades paler, and her jaw

clenched. "Go on, we've got this." She waved at the fire truck that was pulling in through the front gate, her officers surrounding it, guns drawn, eyes on the woods.

Mason and I got into Jeremy's Camaro, because it was the closest car to the road. We drove around the truck, onto the dirt road, and headed toward the village, the way I'd told the boys to go. He went slowly. "Stay down," he told me. He was crouching behind the wheel a bit himself. Then he looked at me. "You realize you probably just saved the boys' lives, and you risked your own to do it."

I shook my head. "She couldn't hit me. I move like the wind."

We had to keep pulling over to let fire trucks by. It was a narrow road, lake on one side, woods on the other. I spotted the pontoon boat in the distance, near shore, and pointed.

"I see it," Mason said. He sped up, and we pulled into a small pull off designed for fishermen. Making sure the car was clear of the road, we got out and ran down to the water's edge. Mason cupped his hands and yelled for Jeremy.

Jere saw us, waved and then aimed for us. The little boat moved slowly, but I was relieved as hell to see everyone on board safe and sound. Joshua. Misty and Christy. Sandra and Jim. Myrtle and Hugo. And Angela, Mason's mother, who was the first one to step onto shore. She marched right up to me, clasped my face in her hands and kissed me on the forehead—hard. "I've never seen anything like what you just did for my grandsons. My God, Rachel. You're so much more than I knew."

My eyebrows must've looked like the sign on the local Mickey D's. "Wow. Um. Thanks."

I heard something crashing through the trees. Mason and I both spun, pushing Angela behind us. He had a gun in his hand.

"Get back on the boat, Mom."

She did.

"You too, Rache."

"Fuck you, Mace." I stuck to his side as he crept back toward the road. We got there just in time to see Gretchen Young come stumbling out of the woods on the opposite side. Her hair was all over the place, twigs tangled in it. She had a scratch on her face and a gun in her hand.

"You…" She stumbled into the road, stopped in the middle and raised the gun, aiming it at me.

Mason pushed me behind him, raising his own. "Put it down, Gretchen. It's over. Put it down or I'll drop you where you stand, I swear to—"

I heard the car before I saw it. It shot like a missile along the dirt road and hit Gretchen at full speed. She flew one way, her gun another, and when she landed her body bounced twice, her limbs boneless, then lay still.

The car skidded to a stop in a cloud of dust. The driver's door opened, and Marie got out, walked over to the woman who lay still in the road and said, "I told you to leave my family alone."

Mason joined her there, put a hand on her shoulder. "It's all right, Marie. Stay calm for me, okay?"

She nodded jerkily, tears streaming. He knelt to touch Gretchen's wrist, and then looked back at me and shook his head. Gretchen was dead. And I was glad and didn't feel the least bit guilty about that.

The boys and Angela were off the boat, gathering around us. Jeremy went to his mother and hugged her hard. "You were right, Mom. You were right the whole time."

She nodded, crying softly. As soon as he let go of her, Joshua hugged her, too. Mason and I stood close enough to keep them safe, but I didn't think she would hurt the kids. Not after she'd done all this to save them.

For the first time I thought I understood her. Mother to mother.

She stepped back, one hand on Jeremy's shoulder, the other on Joshua's. "I'm really sick. I need to go back to my hospital. I need my meds. It's hard…it's hard to focus."

"It's okay, Mom. It's okay," Jeremy told her.

"I love you, Mom," Joshua said, sniffling.

A police car came screaming up the road and skidded to a stop, but as Vanessa and Rosie got out, Mason held up a hand to fend them off.

"I saw you graduate, Jeremy. I sneaked in with another family."

"I saw you, Mom," he said.

"I knew she was going to hurt you. I had to stop her." She turned to Mason. "I had to stop her, Mason. I'm sorry about your house. I didn't know she was going to do that."

"I'm sorry I didn't listen to you to begin with, Marie," Mason said. "You did great. You did. And you saved the boys."

She nodded. Met my eyes, smiled shakily. It was silent, maybe a thank-you, maybe something else. I wasn't sure. Then she said to the boys, "Mommy has to go now. But you'll visit me again soon. Promise?"

"Promise." They said it in unison and hugged her again.

Hell, I was crying by this point. And so was Angela.

Nodding, Marie let her boys go and walked right over to the police car, opened the back door and got in. Easy as you please. Vanessa looked at her for a second, then turned to me. "Everyone got out of the house," she told us. "Gwen and Sally and everyone else. They're all fine. One guest was hit by rifle fire, but he's being treated and they expect him to live."

I gave her a nod.

"You gonna be okay, Mace? I should ride with the chief," Rosie said.

"Yeah, we're good now. Go on."

Rosie and Vanessa got back into the car. Rosie drove, inching around the vehicle that Marie had just used to kill Gretchen Young.

Gretchen still lay in the middle of my dirt road, but someone else would take care of her. Mason put his arms around his boys. And I put my arms around *my* boys. His mother squeezed in, too, and my sister and the twins, and Jim. And we all made our way down to the pontoon boat and got back on board. Myrtle and Hugo were still there, waiting for us.

Mason started the motor and guided the boat away from shore and back toward the house, promising to bring Jeremy right back for his car. The sun was just starting to set, coloring the surface of the water in gleaming orange and yellow. I sat down and looked at the three males in my life.

Angela squeezed my hand. "It's going to be all right," she said.

"It already is, Angela. It already is." I met Mason's eyes. He told me he loved me without saying a word.

Epilogue

Jeremy and Misty pulled up in the Camaro, revved the engine a few times, then shut it off and got out, laughing. They had a picnic basket so heavy it took both of them to carry it. Or maybe that was just so their hands could be touching as they grabbed the handle.

We'd rented a great big camper, which was parked on one side of the front lawn, so it wouldn't be in the way of the construction workers who were busily rebuilding our home. Between Mason's insurance check and my own, the place was going to be better than ever. And this time it wouldn't be a reflection of my tastes and preferences alone. It would be for all of us. A family home for the family I'd never thought I'd always wanted.

Myrtle and Josh were frog hunting. Hugo was helping, although the "frogs" he pounced on more often than not turned out to be his own reflection. Mason and I were reclining side by side in the double lawn chair we'd bought for just this purpose. Yes, I was sickeningly cuddly where he was concerned. So shoot me.

The sun was going down slowly, painting the lake in a deep, thick orange that made my eyes water, it was so beautiful.

Jeremy said, "We brought KFC."

"Then you've earned another after-market part for the Camaro," I said.

"You're spoiling him," Mason warned.

"Uh, hello, you're the one who gave him a classic car for graduation."

"I guess you're right." He laid his head back again.

Then Josh said, "Holy moly! She did it!" and we both jumped out of the lawn chair at the sudden excited shout. "She *did it*! She got one!" Josh cried. Hugo was barking nonstop in excitement. "Myrtle, come here. Come here, girl!"

But Myrtle was having none of it. She marched right up to where I was standing, sat down at my feet and tipped her head up at me. She had her mouth closed softly around a poor slick green frog, whose legs were sticking out and wriggling like mad.

"Now look what you've done. You've created a frog-eating monster," Mason said.

"I never thought she'd catch one." I looked at Hugo and Josh. "Not without help, anyway. C'mon, Myrt. Drop the frog." I crouched down and said it again. "Drop it, Myrtle."

She opened her mouth, and the frog plopped out, hit the ground and then sprang away unharmed. Three big hops, and it splashed into the water and was gone.

Josh started laughing, and then so did Jeremy, and finally Mason.

I sank back down in my comfy lawn chair and just looked at them. And I knew, more than I'd ever known it before, that everything happened for a reason. I knew that this ragtag band of testosterone was the family I was meant to have, and that they needed me and I needed them. And I knew that everything in my life and theirs had led us to each other.

And one other thing. I knew—for sure now—that the bullshit I wrote had never been bullshit at all.

* * * * *